TEACHER

FIONA COLE

Copyright © 2020 by Fiona Cole

All rights reserved.

Cover Designer: Najla Qamber, Qamber Designs

Interior Design: Indie Girl Promotions

Editing: Kelly Allenby, Readers Together

Proofreading: Janice Owen, JO's Book Addiction Proofreading

No part of this book may be reproduced or transmitted in any form or by any means, electronic or mechanical, including photocopying, recording, or by any information storage and retrieval system without written permission of the author, except for the use of brief quotations in a book review.

This is a work of fiction. Names, characters, businesses, places, events and incidents are either the products of the author's imagination or used in a fictitious manner. Any resemblance to actual persons, living or dead, actual events, or locales is entirely coincidental.

PLAYLIST

Take On the World - You Me At Six
Rescue - Lauren Daigle
Freaking Me Out - Ava Max
Smile - Mikky Ekko
Take Care - Beach House
I Want to Know What Love Is - Foreigner
All Too Well - Taylor Swift
Coming Up For Air - Signals In Smoke
Neptune - Sleeping At Last
I Wanna Get Better - Bleachers
Don't Give Up On Me - Andy Grammar
Someone You Loved - Lewis Capaldi
Angel by the Wings - Sia
I'll Be There - Walk Off the Earth
Remembrance - Tommee Profitt ft. Fleurie
Is There Somewhere - Halsey
Hush Hush Baby - Lxandra
To Die For - Sam Smith

FIONA COLE

Lay Your Head On Me - Major Lazer ft. Marcus Mumford
Better Days - OneRepublic
I Found You - Cash Cash & Any Grammar

To you, the reader.
Thank you for loving this series.

PROLOGUE

HANNA

"When we get out of here, I'm going to take ballet. Fuck everyone saying I'm too old."

"Sofia ... we're not getting out of here."

"Nonsense. What are you going to do when we get out?"

"Sof—"

"Humor me. Please."

The pleading and exhaustion she tried to mask with her usual positivity gutted me. Everything gutted me. I wasn't sure how when I didn't think I had anything left to give.

It'd all been taken. Again, and again, and again.

I wasn't even sure how long we'd been here. If I had to guess, I'd say a few months, but we were kept in windowless rooms, given drugs that made time both speed up and stretch on endlessly. I didn't even know where we were anymore; we'd moved so many times. All I knew was that it was hot, making the flimsy shirt cling to my sweat-soaked skin.

Otherwise, each place was the same. Same dirt-stained mattress. Same smell of piss and hopelessness. Same windowless room.

This time it wasn't a room with a door, but a set of dividers with a curtain. I preferred the room with the closed door. At least then, it masked the sounds of the horrors going on around us.

The grunts, the cries, the disgusting sounds of skin hitting skin.

A tremor wracked my body, cramping my stomach. I hadn't eaten since yesterday, not that I could have kept anything down past the nausea. Part of me craved the drugs they constantly pumped into our bodies. Craved the nothingness. Craved the escape from what was being done to my body. Craved the absence of pain.

The other part of me feared what happened in the darkness when I was unaware.

"Please, Hanna." Sofia's sluggish voice reminded me she asked me a question. What did I want to do when we escaped the men who took us—the men who sold our bodies like cattle?

Stupid tears burned my eyes because I knew what Sofia didn't. We weren't getting out of here unless it was through death —which, as the days stretched on, didn't sound horrible.

But I answered anyway. Because Sofia was my everything, and for her, I'd pretend.

"I don't know what I'd do. I didn't know before all this."

Before we snuck out of our hotel on vacation in Florida and used fake IDs to get in a club. Before I pushed us to make the stupidest mistake of our lives. Before we were broken down to pieces of meat.

"There's lots of things you loved," she argued, her words slurring.

Metal clanked against the headboard as I tried to shift to my side to face her. My arm stretched at an awkward angle from the handcuff, but it wasn't anything I wasn't used to. Sofia laid on her side facing me too, and even though I hadn't seen my reflection in months, I knew what I looked like, looking at her.

My twin.

Her cheeks sunk under sharp cheekbones, and dark circles made her look gaunt. Almost like the zombies we'd dressed up as for last Halloween. Her once vibrant green eyes were lethargic and dull, even under the glassy reflection, letting me know she was still high. The only difference was her stringy, almost black hair falling around her shoulders. Before this, I'd been a rioting teenager, resentful to not have anything of my own, so I'd cut my hair and dyed it bright pink. Otherwise, we were the same, and it hurt to look at her.

Her full lips, dry and cracked, did their best to tip into a smile. "You love math. Do math."

"Math is for nerds," I answered in rote. Maybe saying the same thing I did before this would help make the game a little more real.

"Then be a nerd," she slurred, her eyes drooping. "Let's be who we are supposed to be and fuck everyone else." Her shaking hand brushed my hair back before it fell limply between us. "When we get out of here, we're going to deserve whatever life we want for ourselves. So, take it. Take it with me. Promise. We'll do it together."

As if the passionate demand had sapped the last of her energy, her eyes slid closed.

"Promise," I whispered.

How could I deny her anything? It was my fault we were in this mess, so it was the least I could do to promise her the moon and stars, even if it was just pretending to believe it.

"I'm sorry, Sofia."

"Shut up, Han-Han," she murmured, her eyes still closed. "We'll get out of here. Erik is probably tearing the world down, looking for us."

Maybe. But our captors were like ghosts, moving too quick to be caught, not even real to the outside world.

"He's going to be so mad we snuck out, and I can't wait to see his angry face, his eyebrows pulled so low they'll be right above his lips." Another slow breath rattled in her chest like it hurt to breathe. I almost thought she'd fallen asleep when she spoke again. "But then I'll dance away because I'll be a damn ballerina."

She huffed a laugh, another smile trying to break free.

Just as quick, it slipped away, and she laid still.

"I love you, Sofia," I whispered after a moment.

I waited to hear it back—waited for her words to wash over me with a protective layer, holding in what was left of the old me. I waited and waited, watching my sister sleep. Except...something was off. We were inches apart, and I couldn't feel the huff of her breath on my skin. Her body laid too still. Her chest not rising and falling over heavy breaths like it had before.

"Sofia?"

Too many drugs. It must have slowed everything down. I just needed to wake her up, keep her focused on me. With a trembling hand, I gripped her shoulder and shook her. Her head lolled, and I shook harder.

"Sofia," I whisper-yelled, not wanting to draw attention to us. "Sofia, please."

Nothing.

I shook her harder, my body trembling at the way her arm flopped when she fell to her back.

"No, no, no. Please, no. Please. No. No. No. Please, Sofia. Please, wake up. Please."

Fire squeezed my lungs and burned up the back of my throat. I couldn't breathe. I couldn't focus on my sister, my best friend, with the tears clouding my vision. Stupid, useless tears.

I shook her violently, shouting her name, begging her to wake up, begging her not to leave me. I didn't care who came in. I didn't care about anything but seeing her eyes open and making me promise we had a future together.

Tremors wracked my body, and I clung to her. Pulling her tightly to my chest, I screamed. Screamed until I hoped they'd come in and let me go with her. Screamed until my throat was raw. Screamed until I had nothing left.

The sounds expelled in grief were excruciating, and mine would haunt me forever.

1

HANNA

"Hey, Hanna." My eyes shot up to the woman hanging on my door frame, her red hair swaying like a pendulum. "We're heading to grab drinks after work. Wanna come?"

You should say yes, the voice that sounded a lot like Sofia scolded in my head.

"Ummm..."

I floundered. Part of me wanted to. Part of me knew I should get out and go get drinks with my coworkers like any other normal twenty-six-year-old on a Friday night. Part of me knew I should be like Sofia, who would have had no problem joining everyone else.

The other part of me had a barre class, and a book waiting for me at home.

"Sean's going to be there." Scarlett's smile turned a little devious, and she waggled her brows. "Angela said she noticed the way he looked at you."

Instead of the flutter of butterflies in my stomach having a cute boy crushing on me should create, my chest squeezed too tight, and I fought the need to curl my shoulders in, sinking deeper into my office chair.

Sean was cute. Like, *really cute*. And if I closed my eyes and focused, I could sense the slightest tickle in my stomach, but fear made it hard to feel.

What would I do if I actually talked to Sean outside of work? What if he did like me and wanted to touch me like any couple would want?

Imagining his hand, reaching to brush my hair back, had a shudder working its way up my spine.

I couldn't.

"Oh. Well." I breathed a laugh and smiled, hoping she took it for flattery and not nerves. "I would love to, but I already have plans."

I hated the disappointment dimming her smile.

"Okay. Next time," she said before heading out.

It was nice of her to say because we both knew there wouldn't be a next time. I always turned down drinks or any other outing that wasn't work-related.

Very few people knew what had happened to me, so everyone assumed I was introverted—unapproachable. Maybe even a few assumed I was snotty or entitled because I was the boss's sister.

The truth was, I didn't like putting myself out there with anyone other than the friends and family I already had. Socializing wasn't my top skill, and my words came out jumbled and awkward a lot of the time. That's why I stayed behind the computer crunching numbers, letting other people handle the clients.

Scarlett's words repeated in my head, and the easy smiles Sean gave when passing me in the hallway took on a new meaning. Had he been flirting? Had he wanted me to stop and talk, and I'd totally missed the cues?

"Ugh," I grunted, flopping back in my chair.

I should have said yes.

Then I imagined standing too close. Maybe he'd rest his hand on my back to guide me to the bar. Maybe he'd leave it there and...

And I'd panic.

Intimacy had been the one thing therapy didn't quite mend. Just thinking about it had my shoulders pulling tight and added building pressure on my chest. The one that built and built until I wanted to scream.

I'd done my time in therapy, faced my issues, and conquered my fears. I didn't have nightmares anymore—not many at least. I was able to function in society and make friends, even if it was only on the surface level. My mind didn't fear intimacy—my mind had done the work to heal. But my body? My body quaked at the thought, and I hated it. I hated that it was one thing therapy couldn't seem to fix.

Shaking off the regret, I grabbed the file from my desk and headed upstairs. I pushed open the door to my brother's office and found him and his girlfriend, Alexandra, wrapped like a pretzel on his office chair.

"Gross," I said, announcing my presence.

Alex blushed like she always did, and Erik gave me a mock death glare for interrupting.

"I just came to drop these off," I said a little winded.

"You know, if you let me move your office up here, you wouldn't have to worry about those stairs."

"I'm fine among my people. They're my algebros."

"Oh my god," said a deep voice behind me. Ian, the Bergamo to Bergamo and Brandt, walked up and bumped his shoulder to mine. Or his arm since he was almost a foot taller than me. "Little Brandt, that may be one of your worst puns yet."

Ian always gave me crap about my math puns like any pseudo

big brother would. He'd been part of our family since I could remember, and I'd had a crush on him longer than I wanted to admit. Or, I *used* to have a crush on him. Thankfully, we'd been family long enough to move on from said crush and act like it never happened.

"I thought it was awesome." Alex snickered and moved off Erik's lap to lean against the desk.

I smiled my appreciation at her support as I dropped the files on Erik's desk. "These are the numbers for the London office."

He flipped open the folder and glanced over the first page.

Ian flopped down in the chair next to me and sighed. "When are we celebrating Alex's big twenty-first birthday?"

"You guys don't need to do that," Alex said. She dropped her head and let her dark hair fall, hiding her face. Even after two years of being with Erik, she still hated having things given to her. Which blew my mind since all Erik did was shower her with everything she'd missed growing up. "It's not even for another month."

"For the woman who thawed Erik's heart," Ian said with a wink. "It's got to be epic."

"She's graduating at the end of summer, too," I added.

"Someone's a show-off," Ian joked. "Graduating a whole year and a half early."

Erik smiled at Alexandra, and her cheeks blushed. Just from a look. "I forced her to. She said she wouldn't marry me until she was done with school, so we needed to get this shit on the road."

"You're such a pain," she reprimanded with a huge smile.

"Only for you."

Their love was hard to watch. It hurt. Which made me feel guilty for not wanting to be around it too much. Erik deserved happiness. He'd been too serious for too long, shutting himself off to a future with anyone until he found Alex. I wanted that for him.

I just wanted it for me too, and I knew the chances of having it were slim to none. Watching them together stung like rubbing salt in a wound.

"Speaking of parties," Erik said, turning his attention back to me. "We need to finalize the plans for the gala."

The charity event was fast approaching but coming together smoothly. We were pretty efficient after so many years of hosting it. Each year bigger than the last, bringing in more money to help rehabilitate survivors of sex-trafficking. Almost all the money went to Haven, the all-in-one home to help those rescued through every step of the process, from therapy to drug rehab. Erik took a small portion to help fund his side business of tracking down traffickers and ending their role in the sex trade.

I took the most responsibility for planning the party. I'd never been able to share my past at the event but did my part by making sure the most money as possible was raised each year. I wasn't as brave as the other men and women who stood up each year to tell their story. Sofia would have been a crusader, standing by Erik's side as his partner in picking off the bad guys. She would've stood at the front of the line to share her story so no one would ever have to endure it.

I preferred behind the curtain work.

"Okay. I just can't do it tonight. I have a barre class."

Erik's eyes flicked to mine with an all too knowing look. He knew I took the ballet workout class because Sofia couldn't. It was my way of living for her when she couldn't.

"Well," Alex said, slapping her hands together. "That means now you can take me to dinner."

Erik gripped her hips. "Only if I can have you for dessert."

"Ew." My face screwed up. "That is my cue to leave."

"I'm right behind you," Ian said. "Carina and Audrey are waiting at home."

"Let me know when you're available," Erik said to my retreating back.

I quickly made my way back down to my office and started packing up for the day. My class didn't start for another couple hours, but I could squeeze in some extra chapters before. Maybe it would help ease the pressure from earlier. Usually, the two activities eased any tension that crept up, but sometimes books and sweating it out weren't enough. Hopefully, the extra hour of reading would do the trick.

I'd just slung my bag over my shoulder when my phone vibrated with a message.

Carina: Daniel said he'd give you a pass, but you need to sign an NDA first.
Carina: You in?

Daniel.

Just reading his name had my fingers tingling. It was the oddest thing to me because he was the newest person to my circle of friends, and yet, I didn't have the usual anxiety around him. When I compared the feeling I had to hearing Sean watched me to how I felt just seeing Daniel's name, it wasn't even close.

Sean brought nerves and the unknown.

Daniel made my chest warm, and my heart speed up and slow down at the same time.

I'd only been around him a few times at get-togethers over the past year, but his smile was easy and almost calming. A complete contradiction to his ice-blue eyes, but even those had me heating up from the inside out when they focused on me.

Being honest with myself, I had to admit, I liked him, and it kind of made me giddy.

It made me want to be around him more so I could figure out what it was that made him different than other men. Maybe if I knew, I could recreate it with someone more available than the almost forty-year-old man who owned a sex club.

Or not a sex club, as Carina would reprimand. A club that had sex happen within its walls.

The same club that Carina was asking if I wanted to go to.

She knew my issues with intimacy. She knew my stunted knowledge of liking someone. She'd been on the receiving end of one of my biggest mistakes, and yet she still became my friend. She still wanted to help me.

So, she'd come up with this crazy plan and apparently had talked to Daniel to make it happen.

Fear pressed in hard on my chest, and my fingers tingled with numbness. Every ounce of me wanted to pull back and hide.

Do it. Stop being a baby and do it, Sofia's voice reprimanded.

This is the last thing I needed to conquer. Everything else could be locked tight in a box, but Voyeur could help me get over this one fear.

Before I could back out for me, I answered, living for the both of us when she couldn't.

Me: I'm in.

2

DANIEL

"A little dressed up to meet Carina," Kent commented from where he lounged back on my couch in my office, his feet propped on the table. His comment came off innocuous and innocent, but the smirk I'd known since college let me know he had an ulterior motive for asking.

"I'm not dressed up," I denied from the chair beside him.

"Says the man wearing his favorite shirt with two buttons undone. And is that gel in your hair?"

Kent leaned forward to touch my hair, but I slapped his hand before he could. "Fuck off."

"Hmmm." His lips pursed, and his eyes narrowed, studying me. I tried not to squirm under his scrutiny. "Or is it because Carina is bringing Hanna with her?"

"I'm not dressed up," I growled.

It had nothing to do with Hanna. A man could look nice for a meeting with a new client. That was all this was. Who cared if I picked the blue shirt she'd commented made my eyes brighter the last time we were together.

Kent nodded and winked, holding up his hand in an okay sign. "Of course not."

Glaring at him out of the corner of my eye, I tried to force myself to focus on the spreadsheet in front of me. Kent had been my best friend for almost twenty years, and my business partner for only a few less than that. He knew me better than I knew myself, which made him calling me out hard to deny.

"Besides, she's too young for me."

"Age is just a number. Look at me," he said, gesturing to himself.

"I try not to." I never wanted to look too closely at my almost forty-year-old best friend dating my twenty-three-year-old niece.

"Come on, man. I'm your best friend. I know when you see something you like. Mind you, I've never seen you stumble all over yourself—"

"I don't stumble."

"—and follow a girl with your eyes every time she's in the room, but still," he continued like I hadn't spoken.

"She's hot," I muttered as an excuse.

"She's cute and sweet. Almost demure. Not your usual type." He put his feet on the floor and rested his elbows on his knees, keeping his dark eyes glued to my face for a reaction. "But maybe you're getting to a point where you don't want your usual type."

A knock on the door interrupted any response I could have formed. Not that I had one. I didn't know what to say to that. Kent and I were loners. Or we were until he settled down, with my niece, no less. Being alone didn't bother me.

I'd accepted long ago that I wouldn't find that kind of love with anyone. I wouldn't *let* myself find it. Not again.

"Really, Daniel?" Carina said, pushing through the door. "An escort through the hallway? We could have come in through the front."

She strolled in like she owned the place—with her lacy top,

wide-leg pants, and red-soled shoes. Carina was the embodiment of lady boss, and she walked in everywhere like she belonged.

Hanna strolled in behind her, almost as confident as Carina, but the air around her didn't take up as much space. The nervous glances around the room dimmed her own powerhouse, but not any of her elegance and poise.

Just like Kent accused, I followed Hanna all the way until she stood in front of the seating area. God, she was stunning. She had on black high-waisted jeans that accentuated her tiny waist and a silky green blouse that perfectly matched her eyes.

We almost matched with the way she had the top two buttons undone on her shirt too, her full breasts peeking through the deep vee. She tucked her long dark hair behind her ear, and the gold bangles she always wore sparkled under the dome lights. I'd never seen her without them, no matter where she was.

I shook myself out of her entrancement and leaned back, gesturing for them both to sit. "You know I protect my clients first, and Hanna hasn't signed anything yet."

"Sorry," she said softly, gently perching on the edge of the chair.

"Don't apologize," Carina reprimanded, falling back in the chair, crossing her long legs, and looking like a queen on a throne.

"Hey, Hanna," Kent greeted.

A relaxed smile tilted her pouty lips. "Hey, Kent. How's Olivia?"

"A pain in my ass."

"Hey," I chided.

Kent held his hands up in surrender. "I'm sorry. A pain in the ass, I love." I wanted to be mad at him, but hearing Hanna's laugh, watching her sink back in the chair a bit, made it all worth it. "She's good. Loving life after college and getting ready to start her own business to rival mine. Her words."

"Good for her," Hanna said with a decisive nod.

"Speaking of businesses," Kent said, shifting his attention to me. "I wanted to ask you about New York next week?"

"How long will you be gone?"

Kent rolled his eyes, already knowing I probably wouldn't go if it was more than a weekend. While he loved bouncing from place to place, I tended to like to stick close to home. "Never mind. It will be a couple of weeks."

"Yeah, I'll pass on this one. Maybe next time."

"Fine, Grandpa."

I ignored his dig at my homebody tendencies and slid a paper and pen across the table and started what we came here for.

"Okay, so this is the NDA. It's a typical one that says you won't talk about anything or anyone you see within these walls. I'll need you to sign it before showing you around. Whether you choose to come back or not."

"Okay." She licked her lips before leaning forward to sign the paper. The angle opened up her blouse more, and I caught a slight glimpse of the lacy edge of her bra that barely contained her curves. I was torn between wanting to soothe her nerves and bury my face in her cleavage. But then a foot kicked mine, and I snapped my gaze to a smiling Kent.

Fuck. Heat crept to my cheeks, and it pissed me off that Kent was giving me shit about Hanna at all. So what, I could check out women. It wasn't like she was different than any other woman.

I cleared my throat when she finished. "Any form of judgment will get you removed from the premises immediately, and you will not be welcome back," I said in a harsh tone.

Apparently, too harsh, by the way Carina's eyes widened to saucers and yet still managed to glare.

Tugging at my collar, I cleared my throat again and softened my tone. "Just to protect everyone here. It's a safe place for people to feel comfortable with who they are."

"That's good to know," Hanna said.

"Well, I will leave you three to it." Kent stood, and I joined him. He said his goodbyes and turned to me at the door. "Maybe you can show her the ins and outs yourself. Demonstrate some scenes for her."

"Fuck off," I grumbled.

With a waggle of his brows and a laugh, he left.

"Let's get started, shall we?" When we stood outside the office, I turned to Hanna. "If at any point you want to stop or feel uncomfortable, just let me know, and we can head back here."

I knew a little about Hanna's past. I knew she was what spurred on Erik's charity, but I didn't know the details. While I didn't want to alarm her, I also didn't want to coddle her. I was sure she got enough of that from everyone else who knew.

"This is the bar where everyone can relax," I said, gesturing to the open area in front of us. "It's fully stocked, but there is a two-drink maximum to keep everyone safe."

She looked around the room with wide eyes, and I tried to see what she saw. A dance floor with a DJ booth opposite the bar, backlit with warm lights. High-top tables in between and a seating area toward the back. We designed Voyeur to be a comfortable place to relax and enjoy yourself, no matter what you liked. The colors were warm browns, leathers, and wood.

"Along this back hall we just walked through, you saw a collection of iPads where you can make your selection for what you'd like to view for the night. The options are...abundant. When you check-in, you'll be given a bracelet with a number, and you'll enter that number when you choose, and it will vibrate when the room is ready."

"Okay."

Her eyes were still wide and tinged with nerves, but she'd pulled her shoulders back and stood tall. I admired her strength to push through any fear she may have. A woman with that kind of determination turned me on more than any pair of great tits could.

"It's still early, so the lounge is quiet, but it never gets too rowdy."

I directed her to the bar so she could get a better feel of the layout, and Carina followed like a silent sentinel, watching over Hanna.

"Is there...*activity* out here too?" Hanna asked, stuttering over her words.

"Sex?" I asked to clarify, and also to watch her cheeks flood with color.

An added bonus was to watch her determination show. She swallowed and cleared her throat, but held my eyes, even raising her chin like a regal queen. "Yes. Sex."

My lips twitched along with my dick at hearing such a simple word slip from her lips. When she dropped her gaze, I reprimanded myself. This was a client. This was a young woman who had been through trauma, and here I was, hitting on her like some pervert. Shaking my head, I answered her.

"Things can become graphic out here, but we ask that the patrons keep it subtle. No overt sexual acts in the middle of the room or on tabletops. The allure of the lounge is to tease and excite you about what lays down the halls."

She licked her lips, and her eyes flicked around, stopping when she looked over my shoulder at the seating area. "Like that?" she almost whispered.

"Oh, damn," Carina muttered, fanning herself.

I scanned the leather club chairs and found a section circled around a low table. A woman sat on a man's lap, her back to his chest, her legs on either side of his, with his hand under her skirt as the other gripped her breast over her shirt. Two more men sat —stroking their cocks over their pants—so they could watch the man's fingers move in and out of her pussy. I knew if we sat there long enough, they'd have their dicks in their hands, jerking off to the woman's pleasure.

"The seating area is where most of the public acts happen. It's darker over there and can offer enough illusion of privacy while still exploring exhibitionism."

With a jerky nod, she turned to face the bar, asking for a water. I moved to stand next to her and gave her a moment to collect herself. Her small fists clenched and unclenched atop the bar, and a part of me I thought I'd killed off long ago, ached to soothe her. To ask her if she was okay or if there was anything I could do to make it better. My own fists clenched, holding back the urge to brush her hair back.

She almost emptied the entire glass of water before she glanced my way. "As long as it's consensual."

"Always." When she looked over again, I held her stare so she could feel the sincerity of that promise. "If you ever feel uncomfortable, come to me or any of the staff. Each of the rooms we've walked past has a guard standing outside to make sure everyone is safe."

"Great," she said with a forced smile. "I'm just going to use the restroom."

"Okay. We'll be here."

As soon as she walked away, Carina took her spot. "Thank you. I think she could use this."

"It's nice of you to look out for her after everything."

Hanna had made it very apparent that she'd had a crush on Ian, Carina's baby-daddy. After intense apologies and a girl's night filled with wine and a deeper understanding, they formed a friendship.

"That was the past." Carina waved it away like it was an annoying fly. "Every woman should be comfortable with their sexuality. She deserves this chance."

"Did I miss anything?" Hanna asked, coming up behind me.

"Just a quick BJ on the dance floor. Nothing big," Carina joked.

I expected shock and another blush. Instead, Hanna snorted a laugh and gave Carina a deadpanned stare.

Carina shrugged unapologetically and smile. "Hey, I'm doing dinner at the new house tomorrow night. Wanna come?"

I looked at Hanna to see her response. Not that it mattered. I had to start inventory at Voy, my other regular bar. It'd be a long night, and the earlier I got started, the better. A dinner party would set me back, and I didn't have time for it.

"Sure," she answered.

When Carina looked to me, my mouth opened, and words I hadn't planned tumbled out. "I'll be there."

3

HANNA

I should have put a pin in my top. Maybe I could run back home and change shirts. I almost turned when I stopped myself. I was already late—probably the last person to arrive since the driveway and street were full. Adjusting the wrap sweater to cover more of my chest one last time, I knocked on the door.

I'd just finished taking my forty-seventh deep breath of the night when Carina's smiling face greeted me.

"Yay, you made it. I started to get worried," she said, pulling me in for a hug. "Great top, by the way. Makes your cleavage look top-notch."

Pulling back with a laugh, I muttered a quick thank you and tugged again, trying to cover said cleavage.

"Good choice since a couple of single guys came." She bobbed her brows and turned, missing my eyes trying to bug out of my head.

How many guys? Did I know them? Would they talk to me? I should have stayed home.

Then I saw Daniel talking with Erik and Kent by the fireplace, his hand full with a drink. My anxiety over the possible men settled, just to start back up again. Only, this time, it was different. More fluttery.

God, he was cute.

Cute? Yeah right.

More like hot, sexy, alluring, dangerous in the best way, tempting. Any, and all, of those applied better than cute.

I hovered by the door, taking in the room, cataloging who was there.

Erik and Kent were with Daniel to the left.

Alex and Olivia were in the kitchen with Carina to the right.

Leaning against the couch off to the side were two guys I'd seen around the office. One of those guys was Sean, and my stomach went on a full rollercoaster when he turned to give me his dimpled smile. I awkwardly smiled back but looked away when I could feel the heat spreading across my cheeks.

Ian was the only man unaccounted for, but not for long. "Little Brandt." He strolled out from a hallway, his hand held up as he approached.

I stepped back before he could reach me, my back hitting the door, my finger pointed like an angry school teacher. "Swear to God, Ian, if you give me a noogie, I will punch you."

"I'll allow it," Carina called from the kitchen.

And with that, everyone became aware of my arrival. He pulled me in for a quick hug and muttered, "Party poopers."

I made my way over to Erik first, who stepped back from Daniel and Kent to give me a hug. "You coming to brunch tomorrow?"

"Probably not. I have to go finalize the flowers for the event, and tomorrow was the only time that worked."

"Mom won't be happy."

"I'll meet her for lunch to make up for it."

He leaned a little closer. "How are you doing with all the planning?"

I loved Erik, and I understood his protectiveness. I tried to understand his helicopter brothering, but man, it was hard when all I wanted was to get through a day without being reminded of my past. "I'm fine, Erik."

"When was the last time you talked to Dr. Lane?" he asked, completely missing my exasperation. "I know this time of year can be hard, and I want to make sure you're taking care of yourself."

Casting a glance to Kent and Daniel, I immediately looked away when I caught Daniel's eye, shifting my back to them and growled to Erik, "Can you keep your voice down, please? I hardly think this is the place to ask me about freaking therapy, Erik. It's not like I'm going to crumble at the drop of a hat."

His jaw clenched in irritation, but thankfully, he lowered his voice. "I just noticed you getting a bit tense. I wanted to check in."

Closing my eyes, I took a deep breath, shoving any irritation into the box I keep shoved in the corner of my mind before looking back up. "I'm fine. Really. Just busier with work. I don't need a session with Dr. Lane. I've got barre to help me through any tension I may have."

"Yeah," he said skeptically. "Okay. Just let me know if you need anything."

"I will." One more deep breath. "Okay, I'm heading to the wine and girl talk."

"Have fun. Tell Alex to find me later," he joked.

"Gross."

Before walking away, I turned and offered a small smile to Kent and Daniel.

Daniel merely lifted his glass and nodded. Because what else would he do? It's not like we were friends. He was a nice man doing me a favor. He was only an acquaintance. However, when I met his ice-blue eyes, familiarity hit my core like I knew him more.

"Wine?" Alexandra asked, already handing me a glass.

"Why, thank you. Are you old enough to drink?" I joked.

We all laughed at her glare, her age being a long-running joke we poked about with good nature. She was nineteen when she met my brother, who was in his thirties.

"Age is just a number," Olivia chimed in, as she was dating Kent, who was almost forty.

"What's the opposite of cougars?" Carina asked.

"Call it what you want," Alex started. "But Erik's age doesn't matter because what he does to me in—"

"Nooooooope," I interjected, making them all crack up. "Anyway," I said pointedly, changing the subject to Carina's daughter. "Where's Audrey?"

"Probably watching How to Train Your Dragon for the seven-hundred and eighty-second time. She'll be out for dinner, which I need to finish up."

"I'll help," Olivia offered.

Alex lifted her half-empty glass. "Let me finish my wine, and I'll be right over."

We stepped out of the kitchen, so we didn't get in the way. We'd just made it to the couch when Sean came over.

"Hey, Hanna," he greeted. His voice was deep and soothing if I took the time to break it down. He really was very attractive, almost like a Chris Pine doppelgänger with those lips.

"Hey, Sean. How are you?" I adjusted my position, facing him fully, and placing my hips against the couch. The added bonus was it gave me more space, and no one could stand behind me.

"Better now." It was a cheesy line, but it did the trick to make me laugh.

Alex not so subtly bobbed her brows behind her wine glass.

"Sorry, that was pretty corny."

"A little. I prefer y equals m-x plus b as my favorite one-liner."

"Oh. My. God," Alex groaned.

I groaned internally, cringing at my own words. What was wrong with me, saying a math pun to such a cute guy who potentially also thought I was cute?

Sean's laugh had my eyes snapping open. "That's a good one."

"You understood that?" Alex asked.

"I mean, I'm an accountant. Math is my foundation in life."

Alex shook her head, and I laughed, feeling a little lighter since I walked in.

At least, until he reached out like he was going to push my hair behind my ear, and I jerked back, almost falling over the couch.

His hand froze before dropping. "Sorry," he muttered.

My entire body flamed with embarrassment. I stared down, not wanting him to see my beet red cheeks.

Idiot. Idiot.

Ringing blotted out any sound, and I tried to breathe deep, hoping it all passed. I was sure that by the time I'd decided to look up, Sean would be long gone.

But Alex, my beautiful, soon-to-be, sister-in-law, saved me. She cleared her throat, pulling my attention to her and asked, "How was barre?"

It took me a moment to process her words, and I blinked.

"Barre?" Sean asked.

Jerking my eyes over, I was so surprised that he hadn't run as far as he could get from me, I stuttered over my words. "Oh, um... it's a ballet exercise class."

One side of his mouth tipped up. "That's hot."

"Oh."

Really, oh? That's what you're going to follow that up with? Super smart, Hanna. Sofia reprimanded.

"It totally is," Alex said, saving the conversation again. "And Hanna is amazing. She's so flexible and bendy. *Super* bendy." She leaned over and bumped her shoulder to mine, rambling away. "I mean, how many talents can one girl have. She's gorgeous and a math whiz. Pretty much the whole package."

I stared slack-jawed and shocked at the word vomit; it was like she was trying to get me a job.

"Anyway, Erik looks like he wants me to come talk to him. Nice chat, Sean."

With that, she headed to Erik, who clearly had his back to her and was engrossed in a conversation with Ian.

A high-pitched, slightly manic giggle broke free as I gathered the courage to turn and face Sean. When I did, I found his full lips pinched, trying to hold back a laugh.

"Sorry about that. It was pretty weird."

He let his smile free, showing off dimples and perfect, white teeth. "Not at all. Not that she didn't point out anything I didn't know."

"Oh," I breathed.

I was on a role of eloquence tonight.

"Listen, Hanna. I was wondering if—"

"Dinner's ready," Carina called from the dining room.

Sean's mouth snapped shut and turned into a rueful smile.

"Want to talk after dinner?" he asked.

"Sure."

By the time we made it to the table, the seats had been filled, and he sat next to his friend, Adam, and I took the one next to Daniel.

"Hey, Hanna."

I didn't blush when Daniel said hello. I didn't stumble over my words. No, instead, I relaxed back in my chair and gave an easy smile. "Hi, Daniel."

The meal was delicious, filled with laughter and raunchy jokes. Where Carina death glared at anyone who said anything inappropriate. Apparently, they were at a stage in Audrey's life where she liked to repeat everything.

"I think it's adorable when she says shit," Ian praised. "Ow." He jerked and rubbed his leg where I'm assuming, Carina kicked him. "Fine. It's wrong, and we shouldn't encourage it."

Daniel focused most of his attention on Kent sitting on his other side, and only once turned to ask for me to pass the water carafe. Oddly enough, when our fingers brushed on the handle, I didn't jerk away like I usually would. Instead, a tingling warmth worked its way up my arm and settled in my chest.

"He hasn't stopped looking at you this whole meal," Alex whispered.

I looked past her to find Sean watching me. When our eyes met, he smiled and winked, pulling another blush from me.

What was he going to ask earlier? A date? Would I say no? I wanted to say yes, if for no other reason than to prove I could. But that was the reason behind me going to Voyeur. I wanted to be able to say yes to dates without fearing what it would lead to. I wanted to own my body once and for all.

Go on the dates Sofia surely would have jumped all over. She would have lived a much better life than I currently lived. *She should have lived.*

Shaking that off, I promised myself then and there that if Sean asked me out after dinner, I'd say yes.

Except he never got the chance because Adam got a phone call, and Sean was his DD.

I probably could have stood up and walked him out—given him a chance to ask me then. But I decided a wave goodbye was good enough, rationalizing that it would be too much of a pain to ask Alex or Daniel to move so I could get out.

It had nothing to do with chickening out.

Sean and Adam's departure spurred more until all that was left was me, Daniel, Erik, Alex, Ian, and Carina.

I sat on the couch, holding a very chubby Audrey, playing an intense game of patty-cake, when Daniel plopped down beside me.

"You're good with her."

"She's easy to be good with. And I don't have any other chances to be around babies, so I take what I can get with her."

"You want one of your own?"

A pang stabbed my chest when the reality of my situation wasn't conducive to the children I *did* want. "Someday."

Maybe.

The box I hid in the darkest corners of my mind rattled. It whispered that I didn't deserve to have children when my twin couldn't have any of her own.

"What about you?" I asked, shoving that thought down.

"Nah. I was around when Olivia grew up, and that was enough for me," he said with a laugh. "We're close, and she feels more like my own than my niece."

"Yeah, maybe Erik and Alex will have babies, and I can love them as my own. That sounds good."

"Enjoy the good times and drop them off when it gets rough."

He lifted his knuckles.

Without any hesitation, I bumped my own against his, ignoring the flutter low in my stomach when his mouth kicked up on one side.

"Hanna," Alex called from her perch on Erik's lap.

I jerked my attention her way, begrudgingly pulling my attention from Daniel's smirk.

"Have you decided if you're going to go to Voyeur yet?"

Erik's head fell back with a groan. He knew of the plan and firmly disagreed with it.

"She sure is," Carina answered for me when I remained frozen like a statue. "It's going to be epic."

"I want to go," Alex said.

Erik's head snapped up, and he glared at her. "No. I'm not going to a sex club that my sister is at."

"It's not a sex club," Daniel said, sounding exhausted from having to repeat it over and over to people.

"You know what I mean."

Alex, ignoring Erik's denial, clapped her hands together. "Oooo, let's make it a girls' night."

Having all these women with me, both eased the tension around my heart and tightened it at the same time. Having my friends support me would be amazing, but it would also hold me accountable. They sure as hell wouldn't let me back out.

"I'm definitely in," Ian said with his best valley girl voice.

Carina gave him a *hell no* look and for good measure said, "No."

"Hey," he protested. "I can be one of the girls and gossip. We can look at hot boys and compare. Well, not you. You can look at me."

"Oh, my god, Ian," Carina said, but it was softened by a laugh.

Daniel heaved a sigh beside me. "Well, I'll warn everyone you're coming. It will be interesting if nothing else."

4

HANNA

"I'm just waiting for Daniel to see me and kick me out," Olivia said, stretching her neck to look over the crowd.

I looked too, under the guise of helping her keep an eye out. I hadn't seen him in the entire hour we'd been at Voyeur. Maybe I was so eager to see him because he would be one familiar male face in a sea of unknowns.

Yeah, that was it.

"He can't kick you out. It's girls night," Carina chimed in.

"He's probably hiding in his office," Oaklyn added. "He usually does on Saturday nights." She would know since she'd worked here during a semester of college.

Olivia rolled her eyes, annoyed with the possibility of Daniel ruining her fun. "One of his rules was that Kent didn't bring me here. But Kent isn't here, so as long as Daniel doesn't get weird out here in the lounge with some woman," she gagged for effect, "We should be good."

"I thought my relationship was weird," Alex muttered into her drink.

Olivia hitched her thumb Oaklyn's way. "Can't beat the teacher fucker over here."

Oaklyn slapped her shoulder. "Shut up."

"I think it's safe to say we all push the boundaries with our relationships." Carina held up her glass in a toast. "To kinky relationships."

We clinked glasses, and I sucked the last of my margarita through the straw. I even swished around the ice to get every last drop. I both loved and hated the two-drink maximum. I could easily give in to my nerves and get drunk, but the rule kept me in check and helped me stay sober, making me aware of every increased beat of my heart.

"Come on, let's dance," Carina declared. "Hanna needs to shake her ass in that tiny ass dress."

"It's not that small," I defended, tugging the white fitted material down my legs, only to tug it higher on my chest too. I'd grown to love wearing clothes that made me feel sexy. The first low-cut top I'd worn out had felt like a giant fuck you to the monsters who made me hate my body.

"Nah. But your boobs look great. Also, I'm digging the middle cut out. Very peekaboo."

My arm wrapped around my middle, not feeling as secure as before leaving the house. The dress was a simple white, but it was fitted with one long sleeve and a slim cutout around my stomach. But now, standing in the crowd of swaying bodies under the lights, I felt naked.

I think the girls noticed my nerves rising by the second and banded around me as we danced. I lost count of how many songs we danced to, but by the time we stumbled off the floor, my muscles were more relaxed from the release of energy than what any alcohol could do.

"I think I'm ready," I said, lifting my hair off my damp neck.

Oaklyn tipped her head to the right. "Come on, I'll take you back."

I followed her to the hallway where the iPads were, standing by as she clicked some buttons to get me to the selections.

Trying to calm my nerves, I asked, "So, you worked here?"

Oaklyn's fingers froze, and she tipped her head just enough to look at me from the corner of her eye.

"No judgment," I assured, holding my hands up. "It's more of a fascination."

"I did for a little while to help pay for college. It wasn't too bad, but not exactly my life-long goal."

I nodded, not knowing what else to say. A pinch ached in my chest, and I realized it was jealousy. Oaklyn was a few years younger than me, but she felt so mature in my mind. She had the sexual freedom I dreamed of. I couldn't imagine what it took to work here, to put yourself on display like that, and she had. It made me feel immature and emotionally stunted.

"Okay," she said, stepping back. "It's all yours."

I approached the screen like it was a ticking bomb. Daniel had glossed over the selections during our tour, but nothing could have prepared me for the list of options.

Orgy.
F/F.
M/M.
M/F/M.
M/M/F.
BDSM.
Fisting.

I quickly scrolled past that one and made my selection. Missionary, under sheets, some talking, some nudity, low graphicness. Way, way low. Not thinking too hard about it, I hit enter and stepped back.

"Now what?"

"Now, we wait."

She led me back to the girls at the bar, and I barely focused on anything except the band around my wrist.

"You ready?" Carina asked, almost bouncing in her seat.

"Yes?"

"Oh, come on. This is awesome. You've got this, and it's awesome you're taking your sexuality into your own hands. You're a lady boss, and no one can take that away from you."

A lump built in my throat, and I forced it down. This woman didn't owe me anything, and all this was happening because of her.

"Thank you."

"Anytime," she said with a wink.

My bracelet vibrated, and I almost fell off my seat.

"You've got this," she said one more time.

I walked down the hall until I reached the designated room.

"Miss Brandt?" a large bouncer asked.

Daniel had explained that each room was protected by a guard to make sure everyone was safe and secure both inside and out of the room.

"Yes."

"Head on in. Just flip the switch to let everyone know you're ready to begin. I'm John. Let me know if I can get anything for you."

He opened the door, and I walked into a dimly lit room that looked a lot like a living room. A large white rug stretched across the floor with a dark leather couch and two chairs on each side. There were end tables and lamps to give the room a soft, warm glow.

The only thing not like a typical living room was the lube, handcuffs, towels, condoms, and a slew of other items on a shelf behind the couch. That and the large, floor-to-ceiling, one-way glass window that let me look into the room beyond, which looked like a typical bedroom. Bed, dresser, nightstand, lamp. It was all so normal.

Turning back to the couch, I saw a binder laying on one of the end tables, and I jumped back when I barely lifted the front cover and saw pictures of purple dildos and who knew what else.

Shaking out my arms and stretching my neck, I tried again and even flipped through the selection of sex toys and extras I could request. A high-pitched giggle broke free at the colorful array of penises laid out. Swallowing, I decide to save those for another time. This was more of a test to see if I could even make it through. I'd watched porn on a computer and got turned on, but to see it in real life would push me to my limits of fears.

I turned back to the closed door and saw the switch. With a shaking hand, I took a deep breath and flipped it up. A green light appeared right on the other side of the window, and I guessed that was the cue to begin. On jello-like legs, I stumbled to the couch and barely perched on the edge.

My heart thundered like a stampede of horses, and I sat ramrod straight, unable to relax. Squeezing and relaxing my fists, I tried to get feeling back into my sweaty hands.

I almost bounced off the couch when the door to the left opened, and a couple walked in hand-in-hand. It all started innocuous enough. Light kisses, roaming hands. They stripped down to their underwear, and he took her bra off before they both climbed in bed under the covers.

The first wave of anxiety hit me when he tossed his boxers on the floor. The second was when he sucked on her breast. The third was when I heard their groans and saw the movement of his hips flexing between her thighs.

Tighter and tighter the band around my chest squeezed until I could barely breathe.

Trying to ease the pressure before it became too much, my

eyes flicked from one side of the room to the next, looking for and cataloging five red items.

One, the lamp on the nightstand. Two, her bra lying on the floor. Three, a tab sticking out of the binder.

More moans crept through.

Four, a bottle of lube shining on the shelf.

Five...five...

"Your pussy is so tight," he groaned. "Do you like my fat cock fucking you?"

Snap.

The band snapped, and I crumbled. Everything I'd held together broke free and spun and spun like a hurricane I couldn't escape. Chaos and memories slammed into me and caged me in my worst nightmare.

The room shrunk, and the need to escape became more important than my need to breathe. I stumbled from the couch, fumbled with the handle of the door, and burst free, almost slamming into John. He caught me, his eyes pinched and confused, his hands on my shoulders only adding fuel to the fire.

I jerked back, hitting the wall before running.

Only to hit another wall.

Although, this wall was holding me in place and saying my name over and over.

Trembling, I tried to push back until the wall shook me and barked my name.

"Hanna. Look at me."

With my hands against his chest, I slowly looked up into ice-blue eyes.

Daniel.

5

DANIEL

"Are you okay? Did someone hurt you?"

Adrenaline flooded my veins, preparing me for battle, ready to take down whoever came into *my* club to hurt her after I guaranteed her safety.

She dropped her head, her dark hair falling like a curtain around her face, but it was too late. Her eyes shining like emeralds coated in glass, her full lip pulled brutally under her teeth, the silvery tracks of tears sliding down her pale cheeks was ingrained in my memory.

"Hanna."

Trembling hands swiped at her cheeks, and she stepped back, shaking her head. "Of course, it's you," she muttered. "It couldn't be a stranger I could pretend none of this happened with."

Her body vibrated, and I reached out to console her but stopped when I remembered her stiffening under my touch. Instead, my hands hovered around her shoulders, offering any support I could.

Obviously, she was embarrassed, but calming down. I had two ways of going about this. One, I could keep pushing, demand what happened, and not move until she did. Or two, I could act calm, a feeling that felt light-years away and let her tell me in her own time.

Nothing about Hanna said she did well when pushed, so option two it was.

"I can pretend it didn't happen if you want. Turn around and walk away." God, I hope she didn't want that. Too scared she'd take that option before hearing me out, I spit an alternative. "Or you can come to my office for a drink and calm down without the crowd."

Her shoulders rose slowly before falling with a shaky exhale. Seconds ticked by until she finally tipped her head back and tucked her hair behind her ears. She'd stopped crying but was too pale for my liking.

"Okay."

I stepped aside, extending my arm for her to walk past. I almost rested my hand against her back, but stopped at the last minute, hovering instead.

Her eyes scanned my office when we stepped through the door even though she'd been there before. While I walked to the minibar in the corner, she remained ramrod straight a couple of feet inside the room, looking too scared to come in further.

"What can I get you?"

"Umm…Tequila?"

"Straight?"

She huffed a laugh. "Yeah. I think I need it."

One hand remained clutched at her side as the other took the drink, our fingers briefly brushing.

"Do you want to sit?" I asked, nodding toward the couch.

"Yeah. Sure. Yeah."

She perched herself on the edge of the couch, every muscle ready to bolt, and sipped her tequila. Before she could pull the glass away, she apparently decided a sip wasn't enough and opened her mouth to down half the liquid.

I leaned back into the opposite corner of the couch, stretching my arm along the back, the other resting my drink on my thigh, trying to be relaxed enough for the both of us. "Are you okay?"

Hanna stared down at her glass, swirling the liquid. A humorless laugh slipped from her lips, and I held my breath, hoping it didn't shift to more tears.

"Did something happen?" I asked when she wouldn't look up.

In the moments it took for her to answer, I imagined every scenario possible.

Someone broke into her room and assaulted her.

She never made it to the room, and a patron cornered her.

God forbid, an employee did something to her.

All of these should have been beyond the scope of my imagination. Voyeur had protocols to make every aspect of it foolproof. Absolutely no chance of anyone getting hurt. Yet, here she sat, still shaking from whatever had happened.

Finally, she shook her head, loosening the noose around my neck by a fraction.

"No, and that's what's so freaking ridiculous." She tossed her hand up before letting it slap down on her thigh. "I chose missionary—lame, boring missionary—with some talking, and I lose it."

She choked the last words out and had to swipe under her eyes to catch any tears trying to make a reappearance. The rope threatening to cut off my air supply was gone. Only to be replaced by one around my heart.

This beautiful woman was scared. Not by anything wrong, but by watching basic intimacy and I ached for her loss. I ached to take away some of her pain.

"Sometimes the talking can be intense," I said casually, trying to help her relax and feel comfortable. I was sure she had hordes of people who fell over themselves to make her feel better when she was hurt, and I decided to not be another.

"It probably wasn't. I'm just...Ugh," she grunted in disgust, her fists clenched on her lap. With another shake of her head, she tossed the remaining contents of her glass back.

"It's okay to have a negative reaction, Hanna. This was only a test."

"A test I'll always fail. I'm so tired of it. I'm tired of the fear. Tired of being alone." Her voice rose with each word. "I want to be intimate, but I can't even handle it when someone flirts with me. I can't even handle the word pussy through a glass wall from another room."

I almost choked on the drink I was taking when the word pussy fell from her lips. I'd talked to Hanna a few times, but I couldn't remember if she'd even sworn around me. Gathering myself, I took another drink and watched all the steam from her heated rant seep out of her. She crumbled back on the couch, her shoulders slumped in defeat.

"I wish I could say something to make it better, but I won't waste your time with useless words and platitudes you've probably heard before." Her head rolled along the back of the couch until green eyes met mine. "I couldn't imagine not touching," I said with as much sincerity as I had. "What I can offer you is a quiet room, no judgment, and tequila."

One side of her mouth quirked, and she held up her glass. "I'll take it."

With a smile, I took her glass and refilled it with more tequila. Before heading to the couch, I sent a message to Carina, letting her know that Hanna was in my office, and I'd make sure she made it home okay. When I came back, Hanna had moved more to the middle of the small couch so she could tuck her legs up off to the side.

"To quiet rooms," she said, holding up her glass.

I plopped down next to her and held mine up as well. "To drinks with friends."

Our glasses tapped and chimed like a bell at midnight.

"How did you come up with Voyeur?" she asked after a moment of silence.

I breathed a laugh. "The way most guys come up with ideas. With a friend and a lot of alcohol."

"That friend being Kent?"

"Yup. We met in college and hit it off. We were both business majors and probably watching too much porn. One night we were at a party, and a couple of people were making out and moving on quickly to more. I think they liked that everyone was watching. And everyone *was* watching. I'd never forget sitting on the couch, looking around the room at all the people—boys and girls—frozen, barely even blinking so they didn't miss a second. Kent leaned over and whispered about how live porn would make a killing. And the rest was history."

She giggled softly. "Thankfully, Erik was into video games, so we were saved from any risky ideas. Otherwise, family dinners would've been pretty awkward."

"My parents definitely shook their head at the idea but didn't ask too many questions."

"Did they support you?"

"As much as parents can. They were proud I was a successful business owner and used my college degree they helped pay for."

"What about Kent's?"

"I'm not even sure they know to this day that Kent is the money behind our venture. They are of the ignorance is bliss mindset and don't ask questions. Besides, he's more vocal about his hotel empire than Voyeur."

"Is it like fight club?" she asked with a quirked brow and a smirk.

I couldn't help but smile. There were two sides to Hanna. Everyone saw the reserved, stiff persona she projected. But the more I was around her, the more I saw her sense of humor and that devious smirk that let me know there was more behind the woman than I'd originally thought.

"No, not like fight club. We talk about it. Just don't necessarily advertise it. Word of mouth is usually how we get our business."

"How do you feel about Olivia being out there?"

"Oh, god. I don't even want to think about it."

"That bad?"

"She's like a daughter to me, and it's in my best interest to not think about it too much. She's with Kent, who I know is a good man and she is a smart girl. But yes, I'm still hiding out in my office like a little girl too afraid to face the truth."

A laugh broke free of her lips, light and loud at the same time. It reached across the space and sunk into my chest, moving my muscles of their own volition. Her head tipped forward, and hair fell over her eyes. I couldn't resist reaching out to brush it back.

She tracked the slow movement until she couldn't anymore. The dome lighting almost spotlighted her wide eyes, blinking as if she was in as much shock as me that I was touching her.

She didn't even flinch when I dragged my thumb along her jaw before falling away. I hadn't meant it as sexual, and I wasn't even sure if the emotion expanding in the space between us could be defined as sexual. It felt different. Softer. Bigger. Consuming.

"What is it about you that I'm not scared of?" she whispered.

"I don't know, but I'm glad you're not."

An easy smile spread cheek to cheek, and she fell back against the cushions with a sigh.

"Thanks for helping me out."

"Any time."

Her eyes slid closed, and I couldn't look away. She reminded me of someone from my past, someone I hadn't been able to help. The dark hair and sharp cheekbones were different but all too familiar at the same time.

"*You'll never leave me, right, Daniel?*"

"*No, Sabrina. I'm always here.*"

"*Even when I'm hard.*"

"*Even then. You're my best friend.*"

"*You're my hero—my everything. I love you.*"

"*I...care about you so much.*"

The memory hit me out of left field. It'd been so long since I'd thought of that time of my life. A time I'd wanted to help someone else. Someone I'd failed to help.

But maybe I could help Hanna. Maybe I could even the score in my life.

The idea hit me, and I tossed it around for less than a minute before I opened my mouth.

"I could help you."

Her head snapped my way, eyes open wide and filled with caution. "What?"

"I could help." When her eyebrows slid high into her hairline, I questioned how smart this idea was, but figured I didn't have anything to lose by offering. "I could go into the room with you. It can be a lot on its own, and if you're comfortable around me, maybe I could be there if it gets too intense. It may help to know you're not alone. Or I could be invisible—quiet as a mouse—if you're fine."

"Nothing about you could be invisible," she muttered.

"You know what I mean."

"So, you want to watch live porn with me?" she asked slowly.

I laughed at hearing it put so bluntly. Maybe I should have kept my mouth shut. But no, I didn't want to watch Hanna hurt if I didn't have to. "If it will help you through."

"Wouldn't that be awkward or weird?" She looked down at

her hand, fidgeting with the edge of her dress. "Wouldn't it make you...want things?"

"Hanna." I waited until she looked up so she could read how serious I was. Slowly, her eyes lifted, and I held her stare a moment longer. "I can want all I want, but it doesn't mean it's mine to take." Tears glossed over her eyes, and even the barest hint of what she'd gone through hit me like a freight train, almost knocking the wind out of me. "It doesn't have to be awkward. I'll sit there quietly but be there if you need me."

Her eyes flicked between mine, studying me, and I let her see it all.

"Okay," she whispered, so softly, I almost didn't hear it.

Hanna's trust inflated my chest at the same time as it weighed on me. Her faith that I could help her lifted me while the chance of failure pulled me down.

Hopefully, I could pull through on my promise to help this time.

"So, how do we do this?" she asked.

"First, you go home and get some sleep. Shake the night off, and we start fresh another time."

She looked down at her empty glass like she was confused as to how all the tequila was gone. "Probably a good idea. Between the stress and the alcohol, I'm ready to crash."

"Did you drive?"

"No, I rode with Carina."

"How about I get one of my guys to take you home?"

"It's okay. I can get an Uber."

"Are you sure?"

"Yeah."

"Okay, let me walk you out."

I stood and almost laughed when she held her hands up in front of her. "Help a girl up? I'm a little worried about these heels with a couple of tequilas in me."

I slid my hands in hers and slowly hoisted her up, gripping her hips when she swayed. "You okay?"

She nodded, her hands on my biceps. "Thanks, Daniel. For everything."

"Any time."

She stepped back, and I let my hands drop, but stayed close in case she needed me. My hand hovered behind her back the entire walk to the front, where the driver waited.

"Soooo...should I give you my number?"

Even in the dimness of the night, I saw a flush work its way up her cheeks. "Let me see your phone."

She unlocked it and passed it over. I quickly entered my contact info and messaged myself.

"I'll call soon, and we can set up a date that works."

"Okay. Night, Daniel."

"Goodnight, Hanna."

6

HANNA

Daniel: How are you doing?
Daniel: Still up for my idea now that the tequila has worn off?

My hands froze across my keyboard, and I smiled down at Daniel's name appearing on my phone screen. A flutter of nerves, excitement, and embarrassment filled my stomach. I cringed, remembering how much of a shaking mess I'd been when he found me. But then I remembered how he didn't treat me like a crazy woman running away. He didn't coddle me and handle me like fragile glass like the other men in my life.

All three of them that I was close to: Erik, Ian, and my dad. They did it out of love, but sometimes I wanted to be treated like I hadn't survived trauma—like I hadn't watched my sister die. Maybe if they treated me like that, I would be able to bury it and pretend that it hadn't happened. Maybe it wouldn't be so hard to shove it down when the wave of irritation flooded my system, pulling every muscle too tight.

Taking a deep breath, I hit send on my email before grabbing my phone and leaning back in my office chair.

Me: Are you?
Daniel: Of course.
Me: I wasn't that tipsy.
Daniel: Not at all. *wink, wink*

My laugh echoed around the empty walls of my office. The only guy I'd joked around with like this was Ian. But what I felt around Daniel was a million miles away from what I'd felt for Ian. I never once thought of Daniel like a brother, like I had Ian for most of my life. Even when I'd confused my feelings for Ian for something more, it hadn't resembled the weight of what I felt for Daniel.

Not that I fantasized about Daniel or thought of being with him. It was well known among our circle that Daniel didn't do relationships. Which was fine. He was my...friend.

"What's that smile all about?" Alexandra asked, stepping into my office.

I'd been so engrossed in my messages, I hadn't heard her come in.

"Nothing."

I sat up and laid my phone face down on my desk, trying to give a neutral smile. It didn't work because Alex plopped a bag of food on my desk and slowly cocked a brow. Thankfully, she decided to let me off the hook. I was sure it would come back around again before she left, but I had a reprieve for now.

"Erik's in a meeting, so I thought I'd bring you some lunch. Besides," she said with a slow smirk. "I want the deets on Voyeur. It had to be good if we didn't see you for the rest of the night."

A manic giggle slipped free, and I rubbed my thumb along my brow line, trying to hide my wince.

"Uh, oh. What happened?"

I breathed in as deep as my lungs would allow and expelled the whole story in one single ramble. By the end, my eyes were screwed shut, and my shoulders were by my ears. When Alex stayed silent, I cocked an eye open to find her slack-jawed in a chair.

"This is crazy, right?"

She finally blinked, taking her own deep breath and seemed to process my word vomit. "I mean, if it helps, then it doesn't matter if it's crazy." She held my stare, her blue eyes stark against her pale skin and dark hair. "How much do you want this, Hanna?"

Fire burned up my throat, stinging the backs of my eyes. I had to swallow more than once to get the words past the lump threatening to choke me. The same lump that had been choking me for years. "I don't want to feel like this anymore. I don't want to be alone. I want to feel someone touch me and enjoy it."

Alex got up and rounded the desk, leaning against it and gripping my hand tightly. "You're never alone."

Her hand anchored me from getting lost in my emotions. I held tight until the fire subsided. "Thank you."

She pressed a kiss to the top of my head and rounded back to her seat before pulling container after container out of the bag. Drool almost fell from my lips when I saw the sushi and eggrolls. This girl sure knew the way to my heart.

"Does Erik know?" she asked around a mouthful of white rice and salmon.

"God, no." I pointed my chopsticks and glared. "And he won't find out, right?"

She held up her hands. "Not from me, but I also won't lie."

"Fair enough, I guess."

We both leaned back and propped our feet on my desk, enjoying the food in silence. At least, until Alex had me almost choking on my bite.

"Do you like Daniel?" The question rang of false innocence.

It said, *I'm not asking for any specific reason. I won't have any reaction, no matter how you answer.*

It lied.

Playing it cool, I shrugged, refusing to meet her eyes as I stared at my chopsticks swirling wasabi into my soy sauce. "He's nice."

Her snort had my eyes snapping up. "Nice? Nothing about Daniel is *nice*. Hot, hard, sexy with sharp edges and a smile to melt your panties."

"Do you need privacy?"

"I'm good," she said with a wink.

"Don't let Erik hear you say that. He'd probably kill Daniel on principle."

"Well, he knows I have eyes, and anyone who denies thinking Daniel is hot, is a liar, liar, pants on fire."

"I guess I see it," I muttered.

"You're so full of shit," she laughed.

"Hey," Sean said, popping his head around the door. "Is now a bad time?"

Alex and I dropped our feet and sat upright. I may have brushed my hair back and wiped at my face to make sure nothing was lingering. "No, no. Now's fine."

"We're just having some girl talk," Alex explained, turning to him. "Sean, right?"

"Yeah," he said, fully stepping through the door. "Good to see you again." He returned Alex's nod before placing files on my desk. "I just wanted to drop these off."

Alex bobbed her brows behind him, distracting me. "Yeah. Great. Thank you," I stuttered, heat rising into my cheeks.

One side of his mouth kicked up, revealing a dimple I wanted to press my finger into just to see how deep it went. "I like your shirt today. It matches your eyes perfectly."

"Oh, um..." My hand skimmed over the material as I tried to think of a response. "Thank you."

Alex made sexual hand gestures behind his back, and I thought I'd overheat any moment.

"It was good to see you outside the office at the party. Maybe we can do it again some time."

Alex nodded so aggressively I thought she'd fall out of the chair. I was surprised that Sean hadn't turned around to see what my eyes kept flicking to.

"Yeah." His eyes lit up, and the usual prick of panic forced me to establish an out. "Maybe," I quickly added, dimming his excitement.

"Great. Just let me know when."

Alex made sure the door closed this time after he left, and as soon as the door clicked in place, I sagged back in my chair like I'd just run a marathon.

"Daaaaaaamn. He looks even better in a suit than that polo last week. Not as good as Erik, but not bad."

"Ew." I cringed but laughed.

The truth was that Sean *did* look good in a suit.

The truth was that I *did* want to go out with him. Have a drink. Laugh. Dance...Kiss.

And maybe after working with Daniel, I'd actually be up for talking to him outside of work. Maybe more.

Maybe.

7

HANNA

The third night walking into Voyeur was a million times worse. No matter how much I tried to convince myself my fear was irrational, like the square root of two, it lingered. It more than lingered. It sank into my muscles, making them ache with each step I forced forward.

Jesus, Han-Han. Please, don't make a math pun at a time like this.

"Shut up, Sof," I muttered, looking around the parking lot.

The lights shined bright, leaving barely any dark spots people could hide in, but I still held my keys between my knuckles, holding my breath until I cleared the door into an empty lobby.

Taking advantage, I closed my eyes and inhaled through my nose, counting to ten, and slowly exhaling through my mouth for another ten.

"Better?"

Any calm I gathered through my breathing exercise vanished when my heart jumped so hard it almost leaped out of my throat.

"Daniel," I breathed, slapping a hand to my heaving chest. "I didn't see you."

He casually leaned against the wall beside the door that led inside, arms crossed over his broad chest, his lips quirked up on one side. "I was waiting. I didn't want to give you too much room to run."

"Thanks."

And I meant it. The ten steps between the door to check-in and entering the main lounge might as well have been ten miles. Plenty of time to convince my body it was sick. I didn't want that. I didn't want to chicken out anymore.

"Come on," he nodded toward the door. "Let's get a drink and talk a bit."

He took my coat and passed it to the attendant I hadn't noticed, and I clasped my bracelet around my wrist.

"We can head to my office if you're more comfortable there."

"I think the lounge will be fine."

Maybe I could warm myself up for the big performance if someone performed a small show in a corner I could view.

Voyeur was twice as busy as it had been last week. Daniel must have seen my wide-eyed shock at all the people because he explained, "Valentine's weekend."

"Shit. I didn't even realize."

"I'd probably forget it too if we didn't decorate and host a fifty-percent off for a show."

"Yeah," I laughed. "I guess it's your business to know all the mushy holidays."

"It sure is. Carina usually keeps us in line with our marketing." When we reached the bar, we managed to find two stools. "What can I get you to drink?"

"Tequila. Neat."

A beautiful blonde in hearts lingerie efficiently twirled a bottle and filled two glasses, sliding them our way.

Once I'd finished half my drink, I was finally calm enough to actually talk.

"I hear you just opened another club in New York."

His smile stretched wide. "We did. Kent travels there enough, so it seemed like a good market."

"Do you plan on opening any more?"

"I don't think so. We have this club and the bar, Voy. I'm content with that. I don't need an empire, just a successful business."

I looked around pointedly. "I think you're doing pretty well."

He shrugged but winked before lifting the glass to his lips. I did my best to not stare at the way they curled around the edge of the glass.

"How's work?" he asked

"Good. Busy. We're actually talking about expanding."

"To another city? You guys just set up in London, right?"

"Yeah, but I think we'll stay here. We want to grow our home office. Hopefully, some of the floors below will open up."

He nodded in understanding, gesturing for another round when our glasses were empty. "How is it working with your brother?"

"It's not too bad, actually. We don't work directly together too much. He works more with R&D while I run the behind the scenes. Besides, if he gets too bossy, I'll just tell Mom on him."

Daniel's head tipped back, exposing the thick ridge of his Adam's apple, letting loose a loud, boisterous laugh. It somehow managed to not get lost in the crowd, but instead, wrap around me like a warm hug. It was relaxing—comforting.

"Why don't we go make a selection?" he asked once he'd settled down.

I downed my tequila like a shot and nodded my head, unable to actually agree aloud.

Another couple had just finished with an iPad, leaving Daniel and me alone in the back hall. He tapped the screen, filling out information until finally, we came to the dreaded list of my worst nightmares.

"Anything you want or don't want?"

"No talking," I muttered around my thumbnail.

"Okay." He clicked a few more buttons before stepping back. "How do these look?"

Passionate. Gentle. No talking.

Good. They were good.

Boring.

God, he was going to get so bored. I'd be a ball of nerves, and he'd probably yawn on the couch. What if we never did this again, and it didn't even work because I'd played it too simple? What if I never got a chance to watch again? Would I regret being safe?

No. I needed to be cautious because one thing that would make this beyond awkward would be a panic attack. Bored was fine. This wasn't for him. It was for me.

Yet, before I turned away, I clicked one more box.

Oral sex - female receiving.

"Good choice," he praised.

He finished up on the screen and stood in the middle of my pacing path, forcing me to stop and look at him. He didn't touch me, but he did bend at the knees so he could meet my eyes.

"We can leave at any point. *I* can leave at any point. Just say the word." I nodded like a bobblehead, gnawing the last bit of my nail off. "Even if you need a little alone time to yourself," he said with a wink, his lips slowly lifting.

It took only a moment before his meaning hit me. I knew what he was trying to do, and it worked. I dropped my arms and huffed a laugh. "Oh my god."

His smile grew until he was almost laughing. "I'm just saying."

I slapped his shoulder, and in a dark hallway at a live porn club, with a man I didn't know very well, I relaxed. I bantered and joked. For a second, I almost felt like the old me. The one who used sarcasm like a sword—who always made the dirtiest jokes, who wasn't scared.

Then the bracelet vibrated, bringing any laughter to a screeching halt. I held up my arm to show him it was time.

"Do you want another drink? I know more than two is against the rules, but I know the owner."

Another laugh, but I shook my head. More alcohol may relax me, but it may also lower my guard in a bad way, and I'd flip out. Better to be tense, than panicking.

"I'm okay. Lead the way."

He nodded to the big, hulking man outside the door and let me walk through first. It was a different room but set up the same as the last. The scene beyond the window was the same, but the colors were different. Instead of a blue comforter, there was a white one. The headboard was grey instead of wrought iron.

Turning away from the window, I made my way to the same black leather couch, perching on the edge, but prying myself away from the corner. Daniel flipped the switch and casually sat less than a cushion away from me, bringing his ankle to his knee.

"Is this okay?"

I nodded quickly.

"Do you want to sit back? It may help to relax your muscles a bit if you're not on the edge of running the whole time." Before I could say I wanted to be ready to run, he held up his hands. "I promise to help you if you need to run. I'll slingshot you toward the door faster than you can get up."

Somehow, another laugh slipped free, and I relaxed my spine one vertebrae at a time until my back pressed against the smooth leather.

The door to the other room cracked open, and a man pushed through. He was tall and built under slacks and a white button-up. He looked like Daniel plucked him from a GQ magazine to perform for us. What really caught my attention was the look of adoration he had for the petite woman he towed behind him.

She smiled shyly up through long lashes, letting him walk backward, leading her to the bed. When his legs hit the mattress, he stayed upright and reeled her in, brushing her hair aside and stroking her cheek, her neck. He leaned down, caressed his nose along hers. They breathed the same air for what ran on like an eternity until I felt like I was back on the edge of the couch, begging for them to just do it.

Kiss. Kiss. Kiss.

His hand slid to the back of her neck, and he finally locked his lips with hers. I wasn't sure who whimpered, her or me, but something came out of my throat.

The kiss started slow, her hands on his waist, his cradling her head. But it quickly turned heated, intense, passionate. Their hands roamed each other's bodies, pulling at strings, buttons, snaps, anything to banish their clothes. Her dress fell to the floor, leaving her in nothing but a white lace thong. She reached to remove his boxer briefs, doing nothing to hide his length, when he stopped her, turning them and pushing her to sit on the corner of the bed.

Slowly, he lowered to his knees.

Slowly, his hands dragged up from her ankles to her thighs.

Slowly, his fingers gripped the flimsy lace and slid them down.

Slowly, he pushed her legs apart to make room for himself.

I. Saw. Everything.

He leaned in, holding her folds apart and swiped his tongue along every inch of her. She moaned softly, rolling her head back and then forward again so she could watch his mouth make love to her.

He worked his tongue and fingers expertly inside her, and I

couldn't even blink. My vision blurred, and I realized I wasn't even breathing.

My fingers dug into the leather of the couch as I watched her writhe against his face. Not once did he let up. He held her legs apart when she tensed and cried out, thrusting hard into his eager mouth.

He kissed down her thighs and stood. She held his stare and inched back onto the bed. With the same adoring look he walked in with, he shed his boxers. I watched his thick length bob as he followed her.

Her panting was so loud, it slipped into the room.

Except, it wasn't hers.

It was me.

My quick breaths filled each inch between Daniel and I. Heat flooded my cheeks, but I couldn't stop it. My chest heaved with a tightness I'd never experienced before. I didn't even care that Daniel could hear me. I was too focused on the man sliding between her thighs, kissing her breasts, touching her body.

He built the anticipation until I wanted to slap my hands on the glass and demand he do it. I wanted to beg.

His hand slipped between their bodies, and they both moaned when he thrust forward. My thighs clenched, and I rocked side to side, trying to ease the ache threatening to consume me. The leather creaked, but I refused to acknowledge it.

The man made love to the woman slowly, only picking up his pace after she cried out again with another orgasm. I became so lost in the scene before me, that I almost missed the creaking of the leather beside me. With a quick peek, I found Daniel adjusting his position as well, with his hand clutching the arm of the couch.

Shamefully, my eyes shot to his crotch but were unable to see anything with the way he was sitting. Was he turned on? Was he aching the way I was?

The man thrust harder, deeper, taking his time to swivel his hips and hit every spot. Finally, his forehead dropped to the woman's, and he almost shouted his release, feeding her his pleasure.

I swayed from all the blood rushing to my core, and I had to slap my hand against the cushion to keep from falling, only to collide with long, rough fingers, covered in a light dusting of hair.

My first reaction, surprisingly, wasn't to jerk back. Instead, I clung to Daniel's hand. Almost needing the anchor in the chaos of the man coming on the other side of the glass.

"Fuck," I breathed once he finally stopped.

A few more thrusts and he fell to the side, pulling her into his arms and holding her close, all the love still shining for her.

I slid my eyes closed, needing a reprieve from the intense moment, taking stock of my body. For the first time ever, my panties were damp between my thighs. I no longer leaned back against the couch, but forward, one hand gripping the cushion and the other still holding tight to Daniel's.

"Okay?" his deep voice rumbled between us, sliding up my arm to my chest, leaving goosebumps in its wake.

Was I okay?

I felt like a bomb waiting to go off. I almost laughed when I thought of his earlier words saying he'd offer me privacy if I needed it. Maybe I should take him up on his offer.

Instead, I merely nodded, barely turning my head to look his way.

He'd shifted to lean forward like me and unable to stop myself, I glanced down and quickly jerked my eyes away from the hard length extending down his thigh.

Still holding his hand, I squirmed again.

I needed to get out of this room before I made a fool of myself by rubbing against the leather until I came.

Licking my dry lips, I put on my most calm tone, which wasn't much.

"I'll take that drink now."

"My office or the bar?"

Being alone with him right now sounded like the best worst idea ever. I didn't think I could be held responsible for my actions. "The bar will work."

"Okay."

He flipped the switch and held the door open for me. I walked out on unsteady legs and tried to gather myself now that we were out of the room.

"I'm going to run to the restroom real quick. I'll meet you out there."

"Perfect."

It was exactly what I needed. Time alone to recollect my composure so I could hopefully form coherent sentences that didn't start with *let's do it again*, and ended with, *please never leave my side*.

I forced myself to sip the tequila when all I wanted to do was toss it back and order another. I swirled the amber liquid around the glass, watching the large ice ball roll along the edges. Again, and again, until I could finally breathe easier.

"Okay?" Daniel asked, coming up behind me.

"Yeah. Totally. Why?"

Super smooth, Hanna.

Daniel thanked the bartender for his drink and took his time sipping from his glass before facing me. "I know last time it was a lot, and I just wanted to check in."

His skin looked flushed, and I thought back to the erection I'd noticed tenting his pants. Had he felt what I had? Was that what it was always supposed to feel like? I hoped so.

"I'm good. Thank you for doing this."

"It was my pleasure."

I laughed a little at his word choice and couldn't stop the sarcastic retort if I'd tried. "Was it, though?"

He shook his head and laughed. "You're funny."

I laughed with him, and it was nice to be able to let my sarcasm free without overthinking each word out of my mouth.

But that ease faded quickly. We each faced forward and sipped from our glasses, neither of us speaking. When the silence grew uncomfortable, pressing down on my skin, I finally spoke up.

"This is weird. Isn't it?"

"Not if you don't want it to be." When I only shrugged, he shifted to face me. "Hanna, I own a club where people have sex in the corners so others can watch. I'm not one to judge what someone enjoys."

I closed my eyes and sucked in a deep breath through my nose.

"Did you enjoy it?" he asked softly.

The air left on a puff of laughter. "Yeah. I mean...yeah."

"That's good. That's a first step."

"I just..." I shrugged again, unsure of how to explain it without making everything weirder. But then I reminded myself that Daniel didn't judge. He never made me feel like I needed to justify my feelings or hold back my words. Why start now? "I just feel like a ball of energy. Like a live-wire, and I don't really know what to do with myself."

"What do you usually do when you feel hyped up?"

"Read. Go to a barre class. But sometimes it doesn't feel like enough. I still feel too high-strung afterward."

"Do you still go to therapy?" he asked softly after another bout of silence.

The words poked at my irritation, and I ground my jaw to

hold back my snappy retort that I didn't need another worry-wort hovering over me. Despite my effort, the words still slipped out with an edge. "No. I don't need it. This is all I have left to conquer. I'm not some wilting flower who can't sleep at night. I've conquered all my demons, but this one."

I kept my eyes on the bar, not wanting him to read the lie that I wasn't really one-hundred-percent okay.

"Of course not. Even I can see how strong you are, and I'm not around you as much as everyone else."

His easy response popped the bubble of irritation that had swelled inside me. "I'm sorry. Everyone always gets on my case, and it's a knee-jerk reaction, I guess. Erik means well. Hell, he gets me a new can of mace every Christmas just in case I ever run out. Even though I've never had a reason to use it."

His laugh perked me back up, bringing back my sense of humor.

"I should probably beef up so I can fend anyone off with my own two hands." I hold up my arms and flex my small biceps.

"I don't know, you look pretty intimidating right now. I think I actually see some muscle there…if I squint."

"Oh, fuck you," I said, laughing, shoving his shoulder.

When we'd both settled, he asked, "Another drink?"

"Probably not. It's getting late. I should get home."

"Let me walk you out."

I ordered another Uber and tried to think of how to say goodbye the entire walk to the front. Did I hug him? Wave? Shake his hand? High-five? What was the protocol after watching sex together?

"Message me if you want to do this again sometime."

"Really?"

"Sure."

"Wow. Thank you."

"Anytime."

"Ummm..." I stuttered, standing at the open back door. "Thanks for everything," I said, waving like he wasn't less than five feet from me. "I'll see if this guy wants to do math on the way home. He looks like a good *deriver*. Because derive means to solve problems and sounds like driver."

His lips twitched, but he was kind enough not to smile at my awkwardness. "I like it."

"Night, Daniel."

I didn't wait for his response before diving into the backseat and avoiding opening my mouth again until I got home. I mentally kicked myself for the lame joke as I got ready for bed. But by the time I laid under the covers, my mind strayed to other parts of the night.

I remembered the man's tongue slipping through the woman's legs. I remembered her moans of pleasure. I remembered how I literally sat on the edge of my seat, desperate for him to make love to her.

I remembered Daniel by my side, breathing just as hard as I was.

I remembered the ache that had flooded my core.

Maybe...maybe I could get that feeling back.

Slipping my hand under the covers, I squeezed my eyes closed and imagined being in the room again. I remembered Daniel's bold presence grounding me to the moment. I remembered the moans and touches and how I'd wanted them for myself.

My fingers slipped over my clit, and I jerked at the brief contact, my breath growing faster.

I remembered his cock standing tall before he climbed between her legs. I remembered the desperation I felt for them to do it—just fucking do it.

Swiping to my opening, I collected moisture I'd never been able to get before and slid back up to my bundle of nerves. My chest rose and fell, the tension spreading through my thighs down to my toes. Spreading my legs wider, I pushed my heels in the mattress and pushed up into my hand.

So close. So close.

I'd never been able to orgasm before, and I just wanted this. After tonight, I wanted it so bad I could taste it.

I remembered Daniel's hard length against his thigh. I remembered his hand in mine when the man finally pushed inside the woman. I remembered her moans bleeding together with mine.

Fuck, your pussy is tight. Dry as fuck, but so fucking tight.

My eyes flew open, and I jerked my hand from between my legs, snapping them closed.

Bile rose up my throat, and I sat up, clutching my chest, trying to hold my thundering heartbeat under control. My lungs worked overtime, and I squeezed my eyes shut, but all visions of the club were gone, replaced with dirty rooms and disgusting men.

Snapping my eyes back open, I scanned the room, counting five red items.

Book, lipstick, picture, dress, and pillow.

Slowly, everything calmed down, and I could take a deep breath until another type of tension crept into my muscles.

My jaw clenched, and I gripped my sheets, swallowing back the scream building in my chest. So fucking stupid. It was all so fucking stupid.

Punching the comforter over and over, I released the anger trying to swallow me. I released enough until I could take the rest and shove it down. Back into the box for another time to face it.

Never sounded pretty good.

8

DANIEL

"You did what?" Jackson almost screeched at a pitch I didn't know a man his size could reach.

"Could you repeat that?" Kent asked with a stupid half-smile. He looked like a man on the verge of saying I told you so, but he had nothing to gloat over.

"It wasn't a big deal," I explained, rolling my eyes away from Kent.

Jackson leaned both palms on the wood bar top and narrowed his eyes at me across the counter like some interrogator. "You took Hanna, *Erik's little sister*, into a room at Voyeur and watched live porn, and you're trying to tell me it 'wasn't a big deal.'"

I took a swig of my beer and returned his shrewd look. Jackson was like family to me. He began working at Voyeur when he was in college—one of my best performers. Eventually, with his ridiculous accounting skills, he became a partner of sorts and owned a third of the bar, Voy. He liked to talk a big game, but I knew how to make him back off with my stare. I'd been giving it to him for years. Apparently, his shock prevented him being affected, and he continued looking at me, unblinking.

"Nothing happened."

"Nothing?"

"I mean..." I hesitated, picking the label of the beer off with my thumbnail. Shit, this was going to sound bad. "We held hands."

Jackson's jaw dropped, and he stumbled back like I'd hit him, blinking over and over.

From the corner of my eye, I watched Kent's smirk grow into a full-blown smile.

"Stop smiling before I punch you in your face."

Kent tsked. "Someone's testy. Probably all the built-up tension. Did you at least fuck someone after?"

Stretching my neck, I cleared my throat before answering. Regret over thinking I could talk about this without ridicule washed over me. "No. We had another drink at the bar and talked for a while."

"Talked?" Jackson muttered. "What the fuck."

Kent slapped the bar and barked a loud laugh, drawing eyes our way. "Did you at least go home and jack off to thoughts of her?"

No, because I hadn't even made it home. I'd run to the restroom before meeting her at the bar and came in less than five minutes like some kid with his first boner. I'd refused to think of her as I stroked myself roughly. That wasn't the relationship we were forming. But no matter how hard I tried, a vague petite brunette with full breasts and lips formed behind my closed lids.

"Jesus Christ, Kent. She's a trauma survivor. Not some girl I plan to fuck."

He leaned his elbow on the bar, resting his chin on his palm, giving me his full attention, waiting to catch me in a lie. "Why not?"

"Because she needs a friend, not a hookup."

"It looks like she's trying to prepare for a hookup. So, why not you? Do a little contact therapy."

I scoffed, turning back to finish my beer, but his words had merit. She was trying to get comfortable with touch, and she was already comfortable with me, so why not try with me. I'd heard people use contact therapy when facing their fears. I wasn't sure if anyone used it for sexual abuse, but I made sure to pocket it away to look up later. For now, Kent needed to realize I wasn't trying to get with Hanna in any way outside of helping her.

"Because I'm not that guy. She feels comfortable around me. All the other guys in her life are acquaintances, her brother, or Ian, who's like her brother." I pointed at my chest, fully facing him now. "*I* can be the man who helps her. *I* can be the friend she needs."

Kent's smile slipped for the first time since we started talking, and he sat up. "I'm seeing a bit of the old Daniel coming out. The one that wanted to save all the girls."

His light tone did nothing but poke at old memories.

"*Daniel, she's pulling you down. We're in our sophomore year. You going to keep sacrificing the best years of our lives?*"

"*She's just having a rough week. She's not always like this.*"

Kent pursed his lips, doubt etched on every inch of his face.

"*You've known her for a few months, I've known her for years,*" I defended. "*She's my girlfriend and friends help each other. They don't back off when it's hard.*"

"I know that, but lately, she seems more hard than not. Maybe she should talk to someone about it."

"She talks to me. I'm *all she needs.*"

I reached across the bar for the bourbon and a glass, downing the drink before pouring another. "I'm just trying to help her out."

The loud, laughing patrons enjoying their dinner were nothing compared to all the silent words between Kent and me. I couldn't look at him, knowing what I'd see on his face. Instead, I opted to study the amber liquid filling my glass.

"She's not Sabrina, D," Kent finally said softly.

"I know that," I snapped, jerking my angry gaze his way. I hated when he brought her up. I hated what hearing her name brought up.

"Who's Sabrina?" Jackson asked.

"Fuck," I muttered. I didn't want to talk about this.

"She was Daniel's girlfriend in high school and college. Only girl he ever cared about, even if she was pretty crazy-pants."

I slapped the bar, growling, "Don't say that."

"Sorry." He cleared his throat, and regret clouded his eyes. "Either way, she didn't make it out of college, and Daniel blames himself." He exhaled the explanation like it hadn't defined my future.

"I don't blame myself."

"Okay," he said, his tone condescending.

"Fuck you."

"Uh, let's stop there," Jackson cut in.

He knew Kent and I could go at it like any brothers could, and probably didn't want a brawl in his bar. I didn't want one either.

Kent took a deep breath and sat back. "Seriously, I don't want you to get so entwined in someone else's problems again."

"Kent, you know I don't do serious." Running my hand through my hair, I faced him, letting him see my sincerity. "I'm just being a nice guy with some free time. Why not spend it with a beautiful girl who's pretty funny, too?"

Kent studied me, and I let him see it all. He dug through all my hiding spaces and tried to pull any truth out with only a look.

"I still can't believe you watched porn and only held hands," Jackson muttered, breaking the tension.

Kent's perpetual smirk returned. "Yeah, D's a super freak like that. Really gets off on hand-holding."

"Fuck you," I said again, this time with no heat.

"I would, but your niece wouldn't approve."

My jaw clamped shut, and I glared, doing my best to burn him alive. There were rules to him dating Olivia, my niece, and one of those was not talking about it at all.

"Jeez, it's like *Grumpier Old Men* in here. Do a shot and talk about bowling like the old nerds you are," Jackson joked, making fun of our love of bowling. "Or hand holding if that's what you're into."

I leaped up, trying to take a swipe at him, but he lunged back, laughing.

Laughing I could handle. Prodding into a past I wanted to forget, I'd pass on that every time.

9

HANNA

Daniel: How do you feel about self-defense?
Hanna: Like I'd rather run and scream.

STANDING outside the building Daniel asked me to meet him at, I read over our last few text messages. His question had come out of the blue. It'd been almost a week since I'd heard from him, and in that time, I'd managed to run through every scenario of doom and awkwardness. Out of everything my mind conjured, very few ended with a rational explanation.

So, when his name popped up on my screen just as I was climbing in bed, I'd almost fumbled the phone in my rush to type back. After agreeing to meet him, I'd laid in bed and broke down, the relief flooding every inch of me, that he'd contacted me. Sofia would've laughed if she could've seen me. When we were kids, I was the rebel—the impulsive one, rarely thinking things through.

But life changed me, and after everything that happened, I did my best to never move too fast into anything. I never shrugged off an emotion without analyzing every facet, wondering if it was a feeling that would lead me to irrational action. I prevented old habits by creating new ones.

Unfortunately, these new habits had me awake at two in the morning, wondering how deep my feelings for Daniel went.

Eventually, after turning it every way I could, I understood the feelings I had for him were friendship—at least that was what I was allowing them to be. Maybe a little bit of an obsessive attachment, but what was I supposed to feel when my body and mind allowed me to get close to so few people. Being with Daniel felt like being with an old friend. The closest thing I had to compare it to was how I felt with Ian, but that didn't make sense because even when I thought the way my heart beat for Ian was love, my body never heated for him the way it does for Daniel.

But that was fine. No big deal. As Alex had so eloquently pointed out, Daniel was hot—really hot. But it didn't matter because lots of guys were hot, few had the ability to put me at ease. Even fewer who wanted to help me.

So, curling onto my side last night, I placed Daniel in the friend box. Maybe a clear friend box, so I could continue to appreciate how hot he was.

Even with him firmly placed in a friend box, which included trust, I questioned what I was doing outside of an old building that'd been converted to a gym. I scanned the area residing on the edge of downtown. Despite the run-down look, the location was one of the richest areas in Cincinnati.

When I opened the door, I realized this wasn't a regular gym with treadmills and Stairmasters. The area was open with barbells along one wall, next to stacks and stacks of weights. On the other side stood a large structure creating rows of pull-up bars. A group of men and women lifted weights in the back. Some of the women were even lifting more than the men, and maybe that made me stand a little taller. Woman solidarity and all that.

"Hey, you made it."

Daniel walked out from an office, and like my eyes had a mind of their own, they scanned his body. Some of the men working out were shirtless and glistening with sweat, and it didn't affect me as much as Daniel standing before me in a fitted black T-shirt and gray sweatpants—the lingerie of menswear.

My cheeks flamed when I noticed a bulge, and I quickly shifted my eyes to the people in the back, praying and hoping he hadn't noticed.

"Ye—" My voice cracked, and I cleared my throat, trying again. "Yeah. What is this place? I've never been to a gym like this."

His biceps strained the sleeves of his shirt when he rubbed at the back of his neck. "It's a CrossFit gym. They also do yoga and self-defense classes in the back room. I know the owner and asked if I could borrow it for an afternoon."

"Okaaaay." I dragged the word out slowly, unsure of what to expect. Were we taking a class together?

He huffed a laugh. "I can't believe Erik never had you take self-defense classes."

"He tried to get me to take a few," I said, dropping my gaze to the ground. "I wasn't ready for any kind of contact at that time, and I guess it never came up again afterward."

When I braved a glance, he showed more emotion than I'd seen from him yet. Daniel always treated me normal. He never coddled me or asked if I was okay. He never did anything to remind me I'd been a victim, and I'd appreciated it every time.

Yet, watching his nostrils flare over a clenched jaw at hearing how I couldn't touch anyone after Erik rescued me, warmed a spot in my chest that had been cold for entirely too long.

Just as quickly as it appeared, it left. He nodded his head toward the back. "Come on. I'll show you the room."

Daniel lifted a bag over his shoulder and edged around the

class into an open room with mats covering every inch of the floor.

"I want to teach you how to defend yourself. Just some basics. If for no other reason than to make you feel more comfortable. And, of course, to beef up those biceps you're so proud of."

"You want to teach me?"

He shrugged one shoulder. "I figured a class would be too much. It usually requires you practicing with another student and sometimes the teacher, which wouldn't be anyone you knew, and possibly male."

I couldn't hide the wince that scrunched my face. "Yeah, that's definitely not my jam."

"Figured as much. So, if you're okay with me, I'd like to teach you a few things. If not, we can grab a coffee and head out."

Erik had tried to push me into a private self-defense class, and he still brought it up from time to time, but I brushed it off for the exact reasons Daniel mentioned. The instructor would be someone I didn't know—male or female hadn't mattered at the time, all touch sent me into a panic.

But the thought of adding an extra layer of protection between me and the horrors of the world pushed me to take advantage of what Daniel offered.

"No. I want to do this. Maybe I can regift all those mace cans Erik gets me."

He smiled like he was proud of my answer. "Good. I was going to close the door, but if it makes you more comfortable, we can leave it open."

The music and clanging of weights poured into the room, making it hard to hear. And the bottom line was that I trusted Daniel, even alone in a private room where he may pin me to a mat.

The first ripple of panic washed over me. I breathed hard

through my nose, blocking out the feeling of being pinned, immobile, helpless, and looked to Daniel.

Just like that, the ripple faded, and my heart calmed.

"I trust you."

His shoulders pulled back, and he stood a little taller like my trust filled something in him like it did in me. "We don't have to do this."

"No. I want to. I trust you, and that helps. Besides, you don't always get a chance to run and scream when being attacked. So, this is good."

There was that look again—the clenched jaw and flared nostrils. "That's true," he ground out. He took a deep breath and relaxed his features, becoming the laid-back Daniel, we all knew. "Okay, we'll start with some basic moves, but first, let's stretch."

"Will I have time to stretch before being attacked?" I joked.

He cocked a brow and gave me a deadpanned stare. "Probably not, but I'm an old man and need to stretch before I get my ass kicked by someone almost half my age."

"I am not almost half your age."

"How old are you, exactly?"

"Twenty-six."

He huffed a laugh and bent in half to touch his toes.

"Why, how old are you?"

"Almost forty."

"Oooo," I hissed, wincing. "I don't know how I feel about fighting with a grandpa. I don't want you to throw out your back."

He snapped up and glared, but the twitch in his lips softened the effect. "Someone's got jokes."

"A few."

"Okay, young grasshopper, let's get started."

The room had mirrors lining one wall and four large square mats covering the majority of the floor.

We started small by going over all the pressure points on the body and the ways to reach each one when being attacked from different angles. He utilized the mirrors so I could see him behind me, but I ended up being more distracted by how much I liked looking at him towering over me. Once review time was over, we moved to the mats.

Daniel always kept his space where he could, and slowly worked his way to more contact moves. He started with how to get out of someone grabbing my wrist, and it shocked me how simple the move was. I'd always assumed I was too weak to ever defend myself, but the move wasn't based on strength. He told me the weak spots and how to exploit them.

"Is it okay if I touch you?" he asked.

"You kind of already have."

"Yeah, but this time will have more contact. I'll be coming up behind you."

Everything stopped. My heart, my lungs, my muscles. Everything except my brain. That worked at warp speed, remembering two bands of steel wrapping around me and pulling me back with a hand over my mouth.

My eyes fluttered as I struggled against the images bombarding me.

The past is funny like that. It sneaks up on you when you least expect it. No matter how much work you did to accept and understand and move past it, it creeps back in like you hadn't spent years of therapy working to be okay.

"We don't have to." Daniel's voice penetrated the panic like a needle popping a balloon. Everything rushed back like a wave crashing into me.

All of a sudden, my heart beat too hard, my lungs moved too fast, my muscles wouldn't stop twitching.

You're better than this. You're stronger than this.

I *was* stronger than this. I spent too much time working to be mentally stronger than this. Now, I wanted to be physically stronger, so I never had to have that fear again.

Inhaling as deep as I could, I stretched my lungs, forcing them to slow down. As I exhaled, I found five red things in the room, counting them off.

One, the square mat we were standing on. Two, the zipper on Daniel's bag. Three, the seam of my workout pants. Four, a pile of yoga mats stacked in a corner. Five, the laces on Daniel's shoes.

Another deep breath that came easier this time.

"No, I want to do this. Just go slow."

Daniel collected himself quickly and didn't push me on my near panic attack. He didn't stop everything and ask me if I was okay. He didn't ask if I wanted to talk about it.

He only nodded and talked me through every step of what was happening. When his arms banded around me, they were gentle and almost hovering, rather than gripping too tight. Surprisingly, I wanted to sink into his chest like it was a warm embrace.

There it was again—the comfort I only felt with him. Gratitude had tears burning the backs of my eyes, but I blinked them away. Daniel had already fielded enough emotions from me, so instead, I focused on his words and the way they vibrated against my back.

The last move he taught me was a hip toss if my attacker came at me from the front. That one was harder to maneuver with Daniel's six-three bulky frame and my five-five wimpy body. I made a mental note to join the gym outside. Maybe adding muscle would add to my mental strength as well.

"Okay, let's give it a real try this time," he suggested, picking himself up off the floor.

"I kind of like you falling on purpose for me. Builds my ego."

He laughed as he got into position. "Ego won't get you out of a situation."

"Fair enough," I grumbled, resting my hands on his shoulders.

"Remember, jerk and push as hard as you can."

I jerked him toward me, turning my hips to the left and sticking my leg out behind him. Just as quickly, I shoved him with all my strength. Too much strength because the momentum of the push took me down with him. His arms banded around me when he noticed we were both going down, and he did his best to cushion my fall.

We rolled, and his weight pressed me into the mat. I held my breath and braced myself for the impact of panic, but it never came. Daniel launched up and off me just as fast as we'd fallen.

I laid back on the mat, breathing hard and staring up at the lights, in awe of my body's lack of fear.

"Okay?" he asked, laid out beside me.

"Yeah."

"Good. So next time, let go of my shoulders when you shove."

"That would probably be smart," I laughed.

"Again?"

"Yeah. Definitely, again."

We repeated the move three more times, and I only fell once.

"I'm getting good at this. Maybe I missed my calling as a fighter," I joked, holding two fists up and bouncing from foot to foot.

He shook his head, laughing. "You did good."

I stopped bouncing and watched Daniel pack up his bag. Gratitude flooded me, and I swallowed down the tears threatening to break free. I'd already shown enough emotion in front of Daniel to last a lifetime. I would *not* cry right now.

"Thank you, Daniel," I said softly.

"Any time," he said easily, throwing his bag over his shoulder. "Maybe we can do this again?"

"Yeah. I'd like that." My stomach grumbled embarrassingly

loud, and I pressed my hand to calm it. "Now, it's time to go home and eat."

"Would you want to grab something to eat? Obviously, nothing nice since this is all I have." He gestured down his body, and my eyes were helpless but to follow, scanning over his gray sweatpants again. I somehow managed to not stare the whole time, because Daniel filled out sweats like you wouldn't believe. His thighs pressed against the material, and I wondered, not for the first time, what kind of muscles Daniel hid behind his clothes.

"I think you look great," I almost whispered.

His brows rose a fraction in surprise before his lips followed. "You aren't so bad yourself."

The compliment wasn't even a real compliment. It wasn't like he called me beautiful, gorgeous, or sexy, but heat still bloomed in my cheeks.

I quickly brushed the feeling off. It didn't matter what Daniel thought of me because he was my friend, and friends didn't feel butterflies in their belly when the other offered a simple compliment.

Besides, Daniel was around beautiful women day in and day out. He was probably just being nice.

10

DANIEL

"Do you have any other family besides Olivia?" Hanna asked across the table. "Obviously, a sibling of some sort since you have a niece."

"I have a brother named David. I know, D and D. My parents were super unique."

She dragged her fry through ranch and laughed before popping it into her mouth. "You close?"

"Yes, but I'm closer to Kent than David. Otherwise, it's just my parents. They were both only children, and their parents died when I was little. You?"

Her eyes dimmed, and she looked down at the remnants of her burger before shaking it off and returning her gaze back to mine, the melancholy hidden, but not forgotten. "Erik and I have our parents and a few aunts and uncles who visit. Of course, there was Sofia," she quickly muttered.

I ached, unable to imagine losing a sibling, let alone a twin.

"Then Ian, who's leeched on," she continued.

I laughed at her eye roll and bit back the next question I

wanted to ask, hedging around the rumor of Hanna's previous crush on Ian instead. "How long have you guys been friends?"

"Since he and Erik were kids. I kind of grew up with him as a permanent fixture."

She dropped her eyes back to her plate and let her hair fall around her face. I could peek through enough to see her bottom lip tucked firmly under her teeth.

"You're probably wondering about him. About what happened."

As much as women talked, men talked too, and I'd heard through the grapevine that Hanna had come on to Ian once upon a time—pretty hard too. "You don't have to explain anything."

She brushed her hair behind her ear, and her grass-green eyes shined like emeralds, slipping through the thick fringe of her eyelashes.

"Ian was always the nice one. He didn't have to live with us on a daily basis, so he wasn't so annoyed like Erik used to be. He'd let us tag along. And to be honest, Ian's hot, especially to a teenage girl. Don't tell him that, he already has a big enough ego."

"I won't," I promised, laughing.

"Then, after everything that happened, he was the only male in my life that wasn't truly family. I trusted him and cared about him. Maybe with my naive emotions, I mistook that for more. More than comfort and security." She snorted softly. "Well, there's no maybe about it. I was sure I was in love with him. Which looking back now was stupid."

"It's not stupid. It's good you figured it out."

Her lips tipped in a lopsided grin with more than a little self-deprecation. "It's too bad I couldn't have figured it out sooner."

"There's a lot of things we wish we could figure out sooner. Sometimes it takes a chair to the face to finally make us see what's right in front of us."

"Speaking from experience?" she asked, her brow cocked.

"When you live to be my age, you have your own novel of mistakes."

"Soooo old," she exaggerated. We both laughed until our waitress came by.

"Another round?"

Hanna waved her hand, and I asked for waters.

"So, how does it feel, having your best friend and niece together?"

"Ugh," I groaned, letting my head fall back against the booth. "Don't remind me."

"That bad?"

"Not really. I just like giving them shit. Plus, Kent knows I'll kill him in his sleep if he hurts her, and I won't feel any pity if she hurts him."

"Seems fair," she nodded, her smile wide. "How is it now that your best friend is in a relationship? Carina always talked about how you two were perpetual bachelors."

"Owning a business together helps keep us in touch. And family get-togethers now."

"Does it make you want to settle down?"

"Nah."

"Would it be too forward to ask why?" Her eyes squinted like she was bracing for my rejection.

Any other woman, I'd be questioning the motives behind her seemingly innocent questions. But I knew with Hanna, they really just were out of curiosity. Not because she wanted to get a feel if I was open for a relationship. It was nice to be able to answer without over-analyzing each response.

"It's just not for me," I said with a shrug. "I like taking care of only me and my interests. I have a full life on my own."

"Did you *ever* have a girlfriend, or did you just come out of the womb a loner?"

She asked her question with a smile, not realizing the weight of her words or the effect they'd have. Swallowing down the immediate rejection of the conversation, I choked out my answer. "Once."

I could give her that after all the honesty she'd given me.

Hanna's smile slipped, and she realized the gaffe she'd made. "Oh."

Her wide eyes flicked around the room, looking for a change of topic, but I saw the questions building. Maybe if I gave her an inch, it would be enough to have her let it go.

"We met in high school PE. I kicked her ass in bowling, but she dropped me in soccer. Literally. She kicked the ball so hard, it hit me in the head and knocked me out for a second."

Her hands flew up to cover her gasp, but I saw the laughter in her eyes too.

"We went to college together, and before Kent, she was the best friend I had. She knew me inside and out."

"What happened?" she whispered as if she were bracing herself for the downfall.

But this wasn't about me. Our situation and set up was for Hanna and what she struggled with. We didn't need to shine any more light on a past I'd rather not discuss. We didn't need to shine a light on how I'd failed someone before. I needed her to continue feeling confident in me. Talking about how I'd been unable to help Sabrina would squash that pretty quick.

So instead, I gave the watered-down truth.

"We just didn't work out. Which was fine because, like I said, I'm happy with my life the way it is. I like taking care of only me."

"I understand that," she said softly. Her thumb dragged up and down the condensation on her glass, and she watched, entranced. "While I may want to take control of my body—to be intimate, I'm not sure I want to *be* with anyone." She cleared her throat and looked up with a pain I was all too familiar with. "It feels...wrong without...without my sister."

I didn't have any words for Hanna. Nothing new that probably hadn't been said to her a million times. I was sure she had a routine of thanking people for their condolences, and I didn't need to make her use it. I didn't offer her words about how she deserved her own happiness despite her sister not being there. I didn't tell her that Sofia would want her to be happy. I knew me saying it wouldn't be any different from the other hundred times others had said the same thing.

Instead, I offered her what I could. Comfort. Understanding.

I inched my hand across the table and rested my rough palm over her soft fingers. Her eyes watered, but she didn't cry. She offered her own closed-lip smile and shocked me by turning her hand over under mine, clasping on tight.

She held on to me and something shifted. Each crumb of her trust she offered did something inside my chest I was happier ignoring.

"Thank you," she breathed.

I nodded, becoming desperate to change the topic. "Speaking of intimacy," I started. She blinked, and the moment passed. We unlinked our hands and sat back like the connection had never existed. "I have an idea. If you want to. If you want more help—or if you even need help. Maybe last time worked, and you're perfectly fine without me."

"I actually haven't tried—but any time I'm around a guy, it still feels...not great."

"Okay." All of a sudden, my shirt clung too tightly around my neck, and I tugged at the collar. I'd spent the last few days researching as much as I could find on contact therapy. There wasn't much beyond the basic kinds of contact that anyone would encounter in the world. A pat on the back, a handshake, a friendly hug. It made me question what the hell I was thinking, but this whole situation between us was unconventional, so why not try it. At least I could bring it up to her.

"Hit me," she said, waving her fingers toward herself.

I sucked air as deep as I could, just to exhale it out with two simple words with a world of meaning. "Contact therapy."

"What?"

"Contact therapy."

Her eyes widened like saucers. "Ummmm..."

Her hesitance had me rushing to smooth over any discomfort, trying to affirm that it wasn't an off-hand suggestion. "I'm not trying to be weird. I did research, and exposure therapy is a pretty common treatment. I read a lot about using it to get over fears and anxiety and thought maybe we could use it for your intimacy."

Her eyes narrowed. "You want to sleep with me?"

"No!" I almost shouted, holding up my hands.

Shit.

The slow rise of her brow let me know it came out more forceful than I intended. "I mean...That's not what I mean. Just that next time..." I wave my hands like I'm trying to conjure the least offensive and least alarming explanation. "Just that, next time we touch. Something small. Maybe we hold hands or small touches. Nothing you're not comfortable with."

My god, had I ever stumbled through so many words in a panic in my life? I felt like a teenage boy, trying to convince a girl I liked to go on a date with me. Awkward, embarrassed, and a little terrified.

She sat upright in her booth, her back not touching the cushion behind her, as she studied me. I did my best to remain still and let her see the sincerity in my offer. Hoping she'd see I wasn't being a complete creeper. I also prepared myself for her to possibly smack me and tell me to never contact her again.

I held my breath. One. Two. Three. Four. Fi—

"Okay."

"Okay?"

"Okay," she said with a nod.

"Um, okay, then. Good. Great. Fantastic."

Shut the fuck up, Daniel.

I nodded and ran my hand through my hair, doing my best to relax.

"How far would we go? How much would we touch?"

I held her stare, hiding any nerves rattling around. She needed my confidence. "However far you want to go. We can start little and proceed as your comfort grows."

She looked down at her hands wringing together, chewing on her cheek. Each second that passed, my nerves piled back up.

"Wouldn't that be hard for you?" I opened my mouth to reaffirm I had complete control of my body, but she was already shaking her head. "Not just for you, but for us. Being intimate with someone could lead to...more. Like feelings, and I don't—I'm not ready for that."

Sliding my hands over hers, I stopped their fidgeting and waited for her to look up. "Hanna, I don't do love, so we don't have to worry about either of us falling into that trap. I like you. I like your friendship and talking to you. So, that's all this is—a friend helping a friend."

She looked over my face, searching for any hidden meaning until finally, one side of her mouth tipped, and her shoulders relaxed.

"Friends, eh? Like besties? Can I paint your nails?"

"Dear God," I groaned.

We both laughed, but sobered quickly, knowing there was still so much to discuss.

"How about this?" I started. "We place a no kissing rule. Kissing can make things feel more intimate; having that boundary will help us stay in line."

"That sounds good. Smart." She chewed her lip again. "But everything else?"

"Is fair game." I waited a moment before I continued. "So, how do you want to go about this? Maybe make a list of things you want to try. We can discuss boundaries and any issues you may be worried about."

"What do you think?" she asked around chewing on her thumbnail.

"I think it should be as natural as possible, so it can feel like a normal situation."

She nodded slowly. "Okay. What if I gave you control and speak up if it's too much?"

My heart stuttered over the word control. I loved control in the bedroom, preferred it, but I wasn't sure Hanna knew what she was saying.

"I'm not always a gentle man, Hanna." Her eyes jerked up at that comment, and I smiled softly to ease the anxiety building there. "But I can be gentler for you. You need to have confidence in the comfort you feel with me and know that if at any point you ever want to stop, all you have to do is say it. I can take the lead and follow your cues to keep the situations flowing easily."

"Okay," she breathed. "I'd like that. As much as I don't want to be out of control, I don't want to have to worry about what to do next and if I'm doing it right or wrong. I—I want you to teach me."

"I can do that."

I hope.

"Just one more question, if you don't mind me asking..." I hedged. "How much experience did you have before? Any boyfriends?"

Pink tinged her cheeks, but she swallowed her nerves and lifted her chin. Always so brave. "I had a couple of boyfriends before everything. But we didn't do much beyond touching."

Jesus, she was more innocent than I'd imagined. She'd been

seventeen when she was taken. Plenty of time to do everything under the sun. God knows I had.

"Does that bother you?"

"No, not at all."

"So...we're good. We're going to do this?"

"Looks like it."

She stuck her hand out across the table, her lips stretching into a small smile. "To a friend helping a friend."

I slid my hand in hers, loving her silky soft skin. "To friends helping friends."

She smiled wider, and for a moment, I got lost in her full lips, stretched over perfectly straight teeth, and ignored the way something whispered inside me that this was more than a friend helping a friend.

11

DANIEL

The glass almost slipped from my hand because of my sweaty palms. Looking around the crowd, I sipped my bourbon, looking for Hanna. I decided to let her come to me this time. Maybe because I wanted her to go the extra step tonight. I wanted her to make it through those doors on her own. I wanted her to overthink it all to make sure tonight was what she truly wanted.

I almost laughed at myself, sweating like a virgin on her wedding night. In reality, we may only hold hands again. We may do more—light grazes, more heavy breathing. Anything was possible, and my mind was taking me on a roller coaster ride, waiting to find out. Jesus, last time I barely survived just sitting there.

Running my hand through my hair, I did my best to calm down. As sexual as this was, it wasn't sexual. This wasn't a normal experience. No, she was going to let me touch her body, which might cause her to flip out and make it worse.

I bit back a groan and managed to stop my hand from banging on the bar.

What if I made it worse?

Just because I could hold her hand for less than thirty seconds and teach her to defend herself didn't mean we could watch sex and touch without repercussions.

"Hey," her soft voice greeted.

I snapped upright and turned, forcing a neutral expression to hide all my inner turmoil. "Hey, you made it."

She looked beautiful in a form-fitted, long sleeve dress. The simple burgundy fabric hid her ample cleavage under a square neck and covered her to mid-thigh. It wasn't flashy or low-cut, but on her body, it may as well have been. She was stunning.

Hanna tucked her hair behind her ear and smiled. Unlike me, she looked to have no nerves about this evening. Obviously, I wasn't doing a good enough job at hiding my own because the more she took me in, the more her brows pinched.

"Are you okay?"

"Yeah," I rushed to reassure her. I needed to get it together. My feelings were nothing compared to hers. I waved off her comment and smiled. "Just a long week."

She nodded, looking a little less than convinced, and scanned the room. "It's less busy tonight."

"Yeah. Not being a holiday helps."

One of the bartenders asked Hanna what she wanted to drink, and she surprised me by ordering a shot of tequila rather than the neat drink she usually sipped on.

With the glass firmly clasped between her slim fingers, she peeked my way and offered her excuse. "Just to calm the nerves," she said with a light laugh and shrug.

"No judgment here."

And down it went, quickly followed by a wedge of lime pressed between her luscious lips. I barely held back my groan.

With the shot gone and nervous silence stretching between us, my mind scrambled to fill the gap. Before I could say anything, she turned and asked, "Do you want to dance?"

Not really, was my first reaction. Instead, I said, "Sure."

I lightly rested my fingers at the base of her back and guided her to the edge of the dance floor closest to the wall. I knew she did better when there were less people behind her. The lights swirled around her, different than the direct lights above the bar, making her green eyes flash. The slow, heavy beat of the song surrounded us, and she wasted no time swaying her hips side to side. Every move, simple and alluring. She wasn't trying to garner the attention of every man with the sway of her hips, but she surely had mine.

I did a horrible two-step, which she quickly caught on to and smiled. Pressing up to her toes, she scooted close to talk in my ear.

"You don't dance, do you?"

"I don't know what you're talking about. I'm the best one out here."

She stepped back and smiled, relaxing me more than I'd been all night. One song bled into another, and I made sure she had the space to move. When a slow song came on, I looked to her for direction. Without any hesitation, she stepped into my arms, sliding her hands up and around my neck. I lightly rested my hands on her waist and kept a respectable high school dance distance between us.

"You're much better at slow dancing," she said, smiling.

"A beautiful woman makes it easy."

She scrunched her nose around her smile. "Do women fall for those lines?"

I tipped my head side-to-side. "Sometimes."

Couples around us swayed in each other's arms. Some locked together from hip to lips. One couple had stopped dancing all together and were making out. They'd arranged themselves on the corner of the dance floor, cast in shadow, but enough to still be seen. He kissed down her neck, burying his head in her breasts, and I wondered if I'd be kissing down

Hanna's neck tonight. I wondered what her skin would taste like.

My cock hardened and I shook my head, snapping out of the fantasy. That wasn't what tonight was about. "How was your week?" I asked, keeping a neutral topic.

"Good."

"Any weekend plans?"

Her eyes narrowed, and she hesitated, studying me. "Is this what you do with all the girls you dance with? Keep space and simple conversation?"

"No. Not even a little bit."

Hanna continued to study me, slowly sinking her teeth in her bottom lip, until finally, she stepped closer, pressing her soft breasts to my hard chest. On autopilot, I held her close, my large palms almost spanning across her whole back.

Her fingers dug into my hair, raking her nails along the sensitive skin of my neck. Goosebumps traveled down my spine, shooting straight to my balls, and I fought to keep my cock from hardening against her stomach.

"I used to love to dance," she confessed. "Sofia loved ballet, but I loved hip-hop."

She rolled her hips, and I struggled to bite back my moan. "I can tell."

Her small pink tongue slipped out across her lips, only to be followed by her teeth. I'd begun to realize she did that when she was nervous and considering her words. "How much touching are we doing tonight?" she asked, peeking up from under her lashes.

"This can be it. We don't have to do any more."

"What if I wanted...more?"

My mind conjured every version of more she could want, and probably some that she didn't even know existed.

I breathed a laugh. "Touching you is no hardship. I'm offering anything. My body is yours to do any-fucking-thing you want to it," I said with a bow of my head. "Just ask for what you want. Claim your power to want it."

We'd stopped moving, and I gave her all the time she needed to say what she wanted. "Will you...will you touch me?"

"I am."

"No." She shook her head before nodding to the side. "Like that."

I focused my attention to where she gestured and found two women swaying side to side, their foreheads pressed together. They looked like two lovers lost in a simple moment, except for how one of them had their leg lifted high on the other's hip as the other buried her hand between her thighs. The woman's hips moved, almost like she was fucking her lover's hand.

"Will you make me orgasm?"

The words rippled through me like an explosion. A whisper louder than a roar. I couldn't imagine what it had cost her to be so bold; pride surged through me mixing with the heady arousal of being the man to make her come.

My hands flexed against her back, and unintentionally pulled her closer to my chest. Her breasts pressed up until her full cleavage peeked out of her dress. Her own hands tightened around my neck, bringing my eyes to hers. For just a moment, I got lost in the emerald orbs—large against her gentle features. They stared up like a poor kid begging for more—desperate.

"I've just...never. I mean—after everything. I mean before, I did, I think. And I just wanted to know what it felt like now, and I can't, and I want to," she rambled.

"Hanna." I moved my hand from her back to her shoulder, skimming up her neck until I clasped her chin in my fingers, not allowing her to look away. "Fingering you until you come would be a gift."

"Okay," she breathed, nodding as much as she could within my grasp.

"Come on. Let's go make a selection."

I held her hand and led her to the back. She left the selection up to me, only requesting that there be no dirty talking, but quickly conceded to a little.

Her fear of a filthy mouth had me more nervous than how she would react with my hand buried under her dress.

We walked into a different room than last time. Almost every viewing room was the same with a few variations. This one held a couch with a chaise lounge. It offered more room for what I had in mind to give Hanna what she'd asked for.

On the other side of the glass sat a living room set up. A TV, coffee table, couch, chair, end table, it gave the illusion of normal.

"Hanna," I said, pulling her attention away from the room beyond. "Before we get started, I want you to know I can one-thousand percent control my body. Any time you want to stop, just say the words, and we stop. No questions asked."

She swallowed and nodded. "Okay."

Wincing, I prepared myself for her to storm out at my next speech. "While I can control my body, my mouth can get away from me. So, if I ever say anything that makes you uncomfortable, tell me to shut up. Hit me in the balls. Anything you need to make yourself feel in control."

This time, she laughed and nodded. "Hopefully, it won't come to that."

"Hopefully."

"How do we do this?" she asked, her hands wringing in front of her.

"Come sit between my legs. Your back to my chest."

For a moment, she froze. Not blinking, not swallowing, no more hands wringing. Nothing. "Okay," she breathed.

I flipped the switch to let them know we were ready, and situated myself into the corner of the chaise, spreading my legs wide to make room for her. She gingerly perched on the edge and inched her way back until she stiffly pressed her ass between my thighs.

Fuck, even that uncomfortable shift had me aching. I may die doing this, but if it helped, it would all be worth it.

"Lean back, baby."

She nodded but stayed mostly upright, and I kept my hands off to the side until she gave me a cue that she wanted to begin.

The door opened to a couple looking like they came home from a date. She tossed her purse to the floor and flopped back on the couch, turning the TV on. The man sat next to her and pulled her into his arms. They watched the flashing screen for less than two minutes, but the casual portrayal of normalcy was all Hanna needed. She slowly relaxed one inch at a time until she was fully pressed against my chest, her head tucked back against my shoulder.

The couple in the scene made out, their hands roaming, the moment growing more intense. His hands cupped her breasts, pinched her nipples, pulling a hard gasp from her.

Hanna squirmed against my lap, almost pulling my own groan from me. I took that as my cue to move my hands. I rested them on my thighs outside of hers, stretching my thumb to brush against the soft material of her dress.

As she watched the man kiss down the woman's neck, tugging her shirt out of the way to suck at her nipple, I moved my hands to Hanna's thighs. Other than a quick clench of her muscles under my fingertips, she relaxed, unintentionally rocking her hips back into me. I didn't even think she realized she was doing it.

Each move I made, I held my breath, waiting for this touch to be the one that would have her turn and slap me.

I worked my hand down to the edge of her dress, biting back

a groan at the buttery soft skin that greeted me. One hand rested softly against her hip as the other fingered just under the edge of her dress, moving inward between her thighs.

"Feel good?"

"Yes," she hissed without hesitation.

Dragging my hand up her thigh, I leaned down and pressed my lips against the thudding pulse in her neck. We said no kissing, but it didn't mean I couldn't kiss the rest of her body and taste her skin. She tipped her head to the side, giving me more access, and I took that as my cue for more.

I dragged my tongue along the length of her neck, making love to every exposed inch. I got drunk on the sweet flavor of her skin. Each kiss and suck had her relaxing more and more, her thighs slowly falling apart, making room for my searching hand.

The woman beyond the glass hiked her skirt up and climbed over the man. She wasn't wearing any panties and shamelessly rocked against the hard ridge in his pants.

By the time I could feel the heat of Hanna's pussy, the man had pulled his cock free, and the woman stroked her wet cunt up and down his length.

"Daniel," Hanna breathed. "Now. Please."

Until the day I died, I would never in my life forget the sound of Hanna asking me to touch her—no, *demanding* I touch her.

Still moving slowly, I stroked my finger along the wet fabric of her panties. She stiffened, and I stopped but didn't pull away.

"More."

And that was how we worked. If she would hesitate, I would stop until she whispered for more, and I gave it to her.

I tugged her panties to the side, finding smooth, damp skin. Her dress had ridden up to make room for me, and looking down the expanse of her body, over the beautiful crest of her breasts, I watched my hand move between her spread thighs.

When I slid my finger through her folds, she didn't hesitate or freeze. She flexed her hips and thrust up, her body now begging for more when her mouth was too busy moaning.

The woman gripped her lover's length and slowly slid down, taking all of him in one slow glide.

One of Hanna's hands gripped my wrist, ensuring I didn't move away from where I slowly circled her clit. The other had moved to cup her own breast, where my hand ached to be.

With each pass across her clit, she grew wetter and wetter. She thrust a little more. Holding my breath, trying not to grind against her soft ass to ease my own ache, I moved my fingers lower to her opening, slipping inside a fraction.

On my second pass, she lifted up, pushing me inside more.

"Daniel, please."

The woman panted on the other side of the glass as she rode the man's cock. Hanna watched enraptured by the control the woman was taking over her lover, and I let her have the same control to fuck my fingers.

"You're so tight, Hanna," I groaned against her skin. "So wet."

The words flew out of my mouth, and I waited, but Hanna was too lost to herself to care. She rode my fingers harder, and I used my thumb to rub at her hard, slick bundle of nerves. Her whimpers grew into moans that sank into my soul. Her pussy tightened, getting ready to come, and I feared I'd come in my pants right along with her.

When the man gripped the woman's ass and pulled her cheeks apart, exposing every inch of him entering her, Hanna came.

"That's right, baby. Come for me. Squeeze my fingers with this pretty little pussy."

She gripped her breast tight, dug her nails into my wrist, and came. Her pussy squeezing my fingers tighter than I'd ever felt.

The couple on the other side of the mirror fucked harder as Hanna came down. I softly brushed my finger back and forth across her core, easing her back to earth. I kissed up and down her neck, telling her how beautiful she was and how proud I was of her for being so strong—so brave.

Through it all, I held myself still, waiting for her to jerk away. But it never happened. She relaxed and completely ignored the couple finishing their scene as she shifted and looked to me with flushed cheeks and bright eyes.

"Thank you, Daniel."

Our mouths were inches apart. So close, I could taste the tequila on her breath. Her tongue slicked out across her full lips, and I almost said fuck it and took her mouth. Every part of me ached to flip her over, to bury myself in her heat, but I reminded myself of the one hard rule we'd made. *No kissing*. I reminded myself that this was Hanna. The friend I was helping out. Not some woman I'd picked up for the night.

She squirmed again, brushing against my hard length, pulling a groan from me.

"You're hard," she said in wonder.

I couldn't help the chuckle that broke free. "Yeah. You're pretty fucking beautiful when you come."

"Oh." She looked away and smiled, a blush staining her already pink cheeks. "Can I—" She licked her lips before shaking her head. "Never mind. Stupid question."

I tipped her chin to face me. "Hanna. My body is yours. Ask for what you want?"

Holding my stare to gauge my sincerity, she took a deep breath and asked, "Can I watch you get off?"

I almost laughed in shock but managed to stop my initial reaction. Swallowing it all down, I choked out, "Yeah. Are you sure?"

"Yes. Are *you* sure?" she asked, sitting up to face me, her dress still hiked up around her waist. Her panties still tugged to the side, exposing her swollen, wet lips. "I don't want to make you uncomfortable."

I *did* laugh at that. "Hanna, this is about as uncomfortable as I get," I said, gesturing to my cock straining my pants.

She looked down, her eyes widening more. "Oh."

"Are you sure?" I asked again.

Without looking away from my crotch, she nodded. She looked like a kid in a candy store, and there was no way I'd be able to deny her.

Taking a deep breath, I adjusted and unfastened my pants. There were no more noises coming from the other room, just our heavy breathing mixing with the slow slide of my zipper.

"Oh, wow," she breathed when I pulled myself free.

"You're good for my ego."

She barely glanced up before looking back to my length. I reached to the side table and grabbed the lube. I wanted to ask if I could use hers—to see if she'd let me drag my palm through her wet folds and use her cum to get myself off, but this was about her. Not me trying to fulfill every fantasy crossing my mind.

I'd never felt more like a piece of meat than I did right then, rubbing my cock in slow, tight strokes. And I loved it. I took in her full heaving breasts down to her wet pussy. I watched her fists clench, and her cheeks flush. I remembered how tight her cunt spasmed around me, and I came.

Pleasure ripped from deep in my chest, surged down my spine, and erupted from my cock in long hard pulses. My head dropped back against the cushions, and I groaned, feeling the wet splatter of my cum on my chest and my neck until it dribbled down my palm.

"Fuck," I breathed, tipping my head forward.

Hanna slowly dragged her wide eyes from my softening cock, up my ruined shirt, until she finally met my gaze. "That was beautiful."

"You're beautiful," I said. "And so unbelievably brave."

Her lips slowly tipped up, and something entered her eyes that had an invisible band tightening around my chest. One that had my nerves prickling.

Nervous because she looked at me like I was the answer to all her fears—to her future.

Nervous because I liked it.

Hanna

After leaving the room, we grabbed another drink and talked about work, which was insane after what we'd done. But somehow, it didn't feel weird at all.

We laughed like the friends we were. We laughed like we hadn't just gotten off in front of each other, like he hadn't just had his fingers buried in my pussy. Like he hadn't just given me my first real orgasm.

Lying in bed later, my body still ached. Heat still simmered along my flesh like it never had before. I rubbed my thighs together and giggled at the pure joy that flooded me when the ache grew, spreading up my chest and pebbling my nipples.

Hesitating in fear of having another failure, I said fuck it and slid my hand under the covers. The other grazed my breast over my shirt, and I sucked in a harsh breath at the electric current it sent to my core.

Slowly, I slipped my fingers beneath my underwear and between my folds, gasping as they grazed across my sensitive clit.

I couldn't remember ever being so wet. Was this what Daniel had felt when he'd touched me earlier?

That thought had a whole new wave of heat washing over me. Sweat gathered at my brow, and I pushed against my opening before moving back up and circling. I already stood on the edge of the cliff, ready to fall. I'd never been this close on my own.

Desperate to hold tight and determined to make it happen, I pinched my eyes closed and tried to picture the couple performing. Instead, all I saw was Daniel's long fingers, roughly gripping his thick length and stroking up and down. I saw his thumb swiping across the swollen head of his cock on each pass. I saw his jaw clench, and his grip grow tighter, his arm moving faster. God, he'd been beautiful. I never thought I'd ever consider a penis anything but a weapon, but I'd watched Daniel, enraptured and captivated, my muscles aching from holding back to touch him myself.

My fingers moved faster and faster. I dug my heels into the mattress and swallowed, trying to get moisture back in my mouth.

Guilt poked at my pleasure that I was fantasizing about Daniel as I played with myself, but then I remembered his deep groan that had rumbled from his chest. I remembered the way his eyes watched between my legs, only sliding closed at the last minute before his cum shot out. He hadn't even cared that it landed on his shirt and neck, he'd been so lost in his pleasure.

And just like that, I fell. Waves of ecstasy spread from my core over my body, bringing my skin to life. My lips fell open, freeing moans of pleasure I hadn't even known I was capable of.

My chest heaved as I slowly pulled my fingers from between my legs. My moans changed to giddy laughter that bubbled out.

I'd come.

I'd made myself come.

I orgasmed and hadn't got lost in a nightmare.

More laughter of joy that had tears slipping down my temples.

Guilt lingered that I'd thought of Daniel, but I was too happy to give it any merit.

Besides, we were friends. This was what we wanted. I couldn't help but think he wouldn't care. He'd probably be happy for me.

12

HANNA

Walking into the lunchroom, my steps faltered when I came face-to-face with Sean's broad back. Before I could backtrack, he turned, catching me frozen in the doorway. "Hey, Hanna."

"Hey, Sean," I said lamely, forcing my feet to move deeper into the room.

"Grabbing a late lunch?"

"Yeah. A meeting ran long." I rolled my eyes and grabbed my yogurt out of the fridge.

"Hate when that happens."

He leaned his back against the counter and crossed his feet at the ankles, cradling a container of watermelon. An awkward silence filled the room and pressed on me, urging me to say anything.

"Oh, watermelon. I love watermelon." I think I smiled. I couldn't tell when my inner self was cringing hard. To make matters worse, I continued. "You know, the great thing about math if you love watermelons is that it's the only place you can buy forty-nine watermelons, and no one wonders why."

Sean's eyes warmed, and his lips stretched into a smile, but the more I talked about watermelons, the more the crease between his brows grew. His confusion, rather than making me stop, only pushed me to explain.

"You know because math problems in school...they always had truckloads of watermelons."

"Yeah." He nodded, smiling harder. "I get it."

At no point did he ever look like he was laughing at me. I hoped he found my awkward math jokes charming and endearing. He definitely didn't appear to be judging me, but maybe he was just really good at hiding his reactions because despite having got the joke, he still didn't respond, and the silence stretched on again.

"Sorry," I apologized. "Not all math puns are bad. Just sum. Like s-u-m."

This time, he laughed, and it was nice—deep, a little gruff, maybe sexy? Thankfully, I was saved from analyzing anymore when his friend from the party walked in.

"It's freaking freezing down here. So much warmer upstairs with R and D."

"You should try standing in a corner." Adam turned to me like he hadn't even noticed I was there, confusion marring his face. "Because it's always ninety degrees," I explained.

"What?" he asked, thoroughly confused.

This time I did cringe outwardly. He looked to Sean for help in explaining the crazy girl before him, and I turned, not wanting to see his reaction. I didn't want to hear it either.

"Nothing," I rushed out. "I got to go."

I didn't look back and did my best not to run to hide behind my office door. But I definitely did a thorough speed walk. I shut my door and fell into my seat, letting my head fall forward on my desk. I repeated the head bang a few more times for good measure.

"Idiot," I muttered.

Seeing my phone from the corner of my eye, an idea came to mind. Not overthinking it, I quickly pulled up Daniel's name.

Me: Can you teach me how to flirt?

The three dots popped up immediately, and I held my breath waiting for his response.

Daniel: What?
Me: Flirting. I want to learn.
Daniel: Why?
Me: Because I'm awkward and what's the point of learning to accept sex if I scare guys away with math puns.
Daniel: Math puns?
Me: Shut up.
Daniel: I like your math puns.
Daniel: SUM of them are funny ... ;)
Me: You can't see, but I'm glaring.
Daniel: Meet me at Voy tonight.

Feeling marginally better, I set my phone aside and spun my chair around, smile firmly locked in place.

I was excited to learn how to flirt.

I was excited to see Daniel again.

But mostly excited about flirting.

I hadn't seen him since last weekend when he'd...when he'd touched me.

Flashes of the night, the heat, the feel, the images, his penis bombarded me like they had every day this week.

Embarrassment about the sounds I'd made, of the things I requested lingered, but it wasn't enough to wash out the happiness. My cheeks cramped from smiling so hard when I recalled my orgasm.

I'd *orgasmed*.

And then I'd orgasmed again on my own.

Did someone get to feel pride in that? Because I sure as hell did.

And I didn't regret it. I felt pride in that too.

All because of Daniel.

When he'd first suggested the contact therapy, my immediate reaction had been to say no. But I trusted Daniel, and I heard him out, and in the end, what was the harm in trying. The more years that passed, the more desperate I became to not be broken anymore.

Licking my dry lips, I remembered his rough fingers between my thighs, not too obtrusive, but there. I remembered his lips sucking at my neck and the chills it'd sent down my spine, straight to my core. Probably most surprising of all was remembering the deep rumble of his voice against my back—remembering it being the final straw that broke the camel's back.

Then to watch him come.

I rubbed my thighs together in my seat, trying to ease the building ache, remembering how much I'd wanted to touch myself as I watched him. A feeling completely foreign to me.

Until Daniel.

Now, I had to stop myself from reaching between my thighs every chance I got. Not that I'd been able to actually make myself come again after the first night.

Maybe because I refused to think about Daniel again when I got off. I'd not let my guilt get to me after the first time. Being with him at Voyeur was one thing, but to pleasure myself to thoughts of him jacking off felt wrong. Next time I went, I'd pay closer attention to the performers and add that to my spank bank. I laughed at the word, having heard Ian use it more than a hundred times over the years. I was giddy that I got to use it myself.

It'd been one of the best nights I could remember. I didn't want to ruin that by thinking of him as anything more than a friend. At least, I needed to fight when those thoughts crept in.

By the time the end of the workday rolled around, I was ready for my lesson. I was just about to get on the elevator when Erik stepped out.

"Where are you off to in a hurry?"

"I'm heading home real quick to change before heading to Voy."

Erik stopped and gave me his full attention, and I braced myself for the over-protective brother. "Alex and I can meet you there."

Irritation prickled along the back of my neck. I did nothing to hold back my hard sigh and eye roll. "I'm a big girl, Erik. I can go to a bar without you. Besides, Daniel will be there."

Knowing Daniel would be there did nothing to soften the furrowed brows and pinched lips. "You've been hanging out with him a lot," he said with more than a little suspicion.

"Relax. We're just friends." I gave Erik my best smile. "He's actually going to teach me to flirt tonight."

"He's what?"

I almost laughed at the way Erik's voice rose at least three octaves. But my shoulders grew tight in the apparent way he still thought of me as the damaged girl who couldn't move on. I *had* moved on. Why couldn't he see that?

"Don't act so shocked. I'm a grown woman. I get to flirt."

"Jesus," he groaned, running a hand down his face. "Just...just be careful. Do you have the mace I got you?"

"Ugh. I'm leaving." I brushed past him into the elevator, standing tall.

"Call me when you get home safely," Erik demanded.

"Yes, Dad."

I just caught his own eye roll before the doors slid shut.

I ran home and tried not to overthink my outfit. Otherwise, I'd never make it to the bar. I settled on jeans and a cute top.

As soon as I cleared the doors at Voy, I stopped. Standing at the bar were Ian and Carina. I looked around, expecting Erik to pop out despite me telling him I didn't need him.

With heavy feet, I approached the group with a glare. "Seriously?"

"Well, hello to you too," Carina said with an arched brow. I gave an apologetic stare, she returned with a wink.

"What a coincidence, Little Brandt," Ian said with wide eyes.

Carina slapped his chest and rolled her eyes.

"Erik sent you, didn't he?" I asked.

Ian's face scrunched up, and he looked around like he was shocked I'd asked. "What? No. I've not spoken to Erik since work. Nope. This is all a coincidence."

"Shut up, Ian," Carina said without any heat.

He leaned down into her space, and the look he gave her was almost indecent to watch. "Make me."

I turned away when she shifted to press into his chest. It was their moment.

"Hey, there," Daniel greeted, sliding up beside me. "Can I get you a drink?"

"Sure."

"Jackson, get the girl a drink."

Jackson gave Daniel a deadpanned stare. "I'm spitting in yours."

"Just the way I like it."

Jackson slid my tequila in front of me. "Hey, Hanna."

"Hey. How are you?"

"Good, about to get off work and head home to my man."

"Tell Jake we all said hi," Daniel said. Jackson winked in

return before helping another customer. "Tell me about your day. What happened?"

Remembering the lunchroom, I cringed all over again and refused to meet his eyes as I repeated the incident.

By the end, Daniel's cheeks were red and his mouth white from trying to pinch his lips and hold back the laugh I knew he wanted to let free.

"Go ahead," I said, waving my hand. "Laugh it up."

"It probably wasn't that bad," he soothed, letting a smile finally break free.

"It was horrible."

"Well, let's see what we can do."

"What you need to do," Carina said, hopping in. "Is give them all your attention. Or at least the illusion of it."

Carina faced Ian and stroked her nail down the lapel of his jacket. "Make eye contact," she explained. "Face him directly. None of the hard to get stuff. We're too old for that shit."

"Hey, Ian," Carina breathed in the most sultry voice. My jaw almost hit the floor at the way she made it sound normal and not at all forced.

"Damn, Hell-cat," Ian muttered.

She gave him an exaggerated wink before curling back into his arms. "The trick is to take a deep breath to try and calm down and always, always think before you speak."

"Easier said than done," I grumbled.

"Most things are."

"Another trick," she continued. "Is to make the touches casual. Like they're an old friend. It forms that tiny connection and makes them wonder what it would feel like to be touched anywhere else."

"Jesus," Daniel grumbled.

"Listen," Ian said. "The real trick is to not do those things. You want to hide your assets. Keep them guessing. Bonus is that they look you in the eye and not anywhere else." He awkwardly gestured to my chest before continuing. "This way, you know they're really listening to you. And talk about what you love. If it's math, then go to town with those math puns. Tell him your favorite equations. Guys dig it."

"Oh, my goodness," Carina groaned. "You're an idiot."

"Says the woman who sleeps with me every night."

"Fair point. I can't argue with that."

Ian and Carina went off on a tangent, and I fell back against the bar, exhausted by the overload of information.

"Ignore them," Daniel said. "Just be yourself. Carina was right though, take a deep breath to help keep from word vomiting. Also," he held up a finger. "Always have an out. Feeling trapped in a situation can make it worse."

"A what?"

"An out. A hand signal with a friend to rescue you. A phone call. Anything."

"Okay." I took a fortifying breath, pulling myself upright, stretching my neck side to side.

"How about him?" Daniel nodded to a guy at the end of the bar.

He looked...safe. A button-down with his sleeves rolled up his forearms. Longish, light brown hair that kept falling into his eyes, and a mouth that smiled each time the bartender talked to him.

"He's looked down here more than once."

"He has?"

"Don't look so shocked. You're a knockout, Hanna."

Flashes of Daniel staring between my thighs as he came bombarded my brain, and I shook them off. That probably wasn't what he thought about when he complimented my looks.

"If things get to be too much, just brush your middle finger along your brow. I'll come rescue you."

"My hero." I pretended to swoon.

He laughed and shoved my shoulder. "Go. Remember deep breaths and be yourself."

I edged around the bodies on shaky legs until I was finally able to lean my elbows on the bar next to the stranger. Daniel spoke to Jackson on the opposite end but kept glancing my way, making me feel secure.

"Hi," I said.

He looked to me with the deepest brown eyes I think I'd ever seen. His lips tipped up into an easy smile that was even more devastating less than two feet away. "Hey," he greeted.

His deep voice hit me in the chest, and I took a deep breath before letting words tumble free.

"Can I get you a drink?" I asked.

"Isn't that my line?"

I leaned in conspiratorially. "I know the bartender."

"Ohhh," he nodded in understanding. "Sure. I'm not one to turn down a free drink from a pretty lady."

His compliment hit me, creating a swirl of pride, mixing with the typical fear in my chest. I did my best to shove down all the scenarios where this man kidnapped me, and I was forced to use the one hour of self-defense Daniel taught me to save my life.

Jackson looked over, and I shouted our drinks. When I looked back to the man, he'd shifted on his stool to fully face me, hand held out. "Zane."

I swallowed, looking down at his large hand, mentally preparing to place mine in his. My heart thundered, and just as soon as my hand was in his, I quickly snatched it back. If he noticed my discomfort, he was nice enough to not call me out on it.

"Hanna," I introduced, swallowing the nerves.

"Nice to meet you, Hanna."

With one last look to Daniel and another deep breath, I sat on the stool beside him and tried to flirt.

It ended up being less flirting and more like talking. Two strangers getting to know each other. And the thing I got to know about Zane was that he liked to drink. One drink turned into two and then into three. All within a thirty-minute span. When his attention began to drift more to my chest than my face, red flags started waving. When his hand landed on my thigh, entirely too high for anyone's liking, I knew it was time to get out.

I jerked to the side, pulling away and ramming my knee into the bar.

Glancing over, I thankfully found Daniel's eyes on mine. I rubbed my brow with my middle finger and waited. Less than a minute later, heat pressed to my back, and Daniel's familiar spicy orange scent wrapped around me.

"Baby," he said against my ear. "I know I said we could do a threesome, but I've changed my mind. I want you all to myself tonight."

I could barely focus on Zane's glassy eyes widening. All my senses focused on the way Daniel's arms wrapped around my middle. The quick zap of panic at the first touch quickly faded to a happy buzz.

"Uhhh," Zane mumbled. "What?"

"We like to get a little weird. You don't mind being my bottom, right?"

Zane's hands flew up as he sat back. "Whoa. Sorry, Hanna. Not my thing." His face scrunched up. "You seemed so normal," he muttered.

I could only muster a high-pitched laugh of discomfort.

Warm lips trailed up my neck to my ear. "Come on, baby. I've got plans for you."

Daniel gripped my hand and led me back over to our seat.

Still in shock over the rush of sensations, I could do nothing but sit there, wide-eyed, and waiting for the next move.

He dragged his hand through his hair and leaned his elbows against the bar, smiling. "Still your hero?"

"Yeah," I laughed. "Just a really dirty one."

"You want to try again?"

"I think I'm good for tonight. As not-great as that was, I think it was a step up from earlier."

"I'm proud of you for trying."

His compliment almost had me bouncing in my seat. "I learned from the best."

Daniel slid a water my way, and I took a healthy sip. I'd had enough to drink and watching Zane down his own had me desperate for a water.

"So, can I confess something?" Maybe it was the earlier drinks, or maybe it was just my need to share with him that this process was working, but when he looked my way, eyebrow raised, I found myself admitting what I'd done. "I masturbated."

His eyes widened comically large before he blinked and looked at the bar. His eyes moved back to mine to find me almost bouncing in my seat. Now that I'd said it out loud, I wanted to get it all off my chest and share with someone who knew how awesome this was for me.

"I mean, I'd tried before, and I just couldn't focus my mind enough to make it work, but after what we'd done, I was lying in bed and just...just had to. It was amazing."

His lips slowly quirked up in a smile. I was sure I shocked him with my confession.

"Sorry, I'd usually talk to Alex, but she's been busy, and you're my next best friend. I also figured I'd let you know it's working."

He took a deep breath and finished his drink before setting his glass on the bar and reaching across the space to rest his hand on mine. His smile shifted from a little forced to genuine. "I'm glad for you, Hanna. It's what you're working toward, and I'm proud of you for taking control."

"It was awesome," I sighed dreamily.

"It usually is," he laughed.

"How often do you masturbate?"

He rubbed at his forehead with his thumb and laughed harder. "Honestly?" he asked, wincing.

"I mean, we might as well continue with the honesty."

"Not often. I don't have to."

"Oh." I sat back, the realization of what he meant hitting me. "Well, good for you," I said, forcing a smile I didn't quite feel. Not that it mattered because Daniel and I owed each other nothing.

"I never asked, is there someone specific you're doing this for? I know you mentioned trying to flirt in the office today. A certain someone catching your eye?"

"Umm..." I tucked my hair behind my ear, hesitating. Why was this making me uncomfortable after I just admitted that I pleasured myself? I shook off the nerves. "His name is Sean. He was the guy at the dinner party at Carina's. Someone told me he liked me, which I know sounds very juvenile."

"Not at all," he said, waving away my concern. "Do you like him?"

"I don't know. I have a hard time letting myself get comfortable with him, so we don't get to talk much. And when we do, I start laying down some sweet math puns."

"Well, then how could he resist?" he joked.

"I don't know, honestly. I think I'm kind of focusing all my attention on this and letting the rest fall in place."

"I think that's smart."

"Thank you. For everything," I added softly.

"It's my pleasure. Sometimes literally."

We both laughed until he cleared his throat.

"So, do you mind if I ask if you've tried more than once?"

"Ugh, yeah," I groaned, dropping my head to the bar.

"Well, that sounds less promising."

"I couldn't...I couldn't do it again."

"Is there a reason holding you back?"

Well, I won't let myself imagine you jerking off anymore, and that seemed to be the key to my orgasm. Yeah, that wouldn't go over well. Instead, I avoided answering with a shrug.

"How about we meet at Voyeur again next week?"

I perked up. "Yeah?"

"Of course."

"I can pay for a membership. I don't want to take advantage of your generosity and have you miss out. I know it's a hefty amount."

"Don't worry about it. This isn't about a club membership. This is about me helping a friend."

"Thank you, Daniel."

"Of course. So, what do you want to do next?"

"I don't know. What do you want to do?"

One side of his mouth tipped up, and he turned just enough to look at me from the side of his eye. "A lot of things."

I breathed a laugh, brushing my hair behind my ear. "Okay."

Taking in my nerves, he turned to face me fully. "Hanna, I want to do whatever you're comfortable with. Feel free to use and abuse me."

13

DANIEL

Hanna: Plan something for me...Further than last time, but not by much.

Hanna: I don't know what to do.

Her last message was what won me over.
Now I sat at Voyeur, pounding water, wishing it was vodka. Anything strong enough to calm my nerves, but I wanted to be alert for her. I wanted to do this right.
I *could* do this right.
The last person to ask me to do something was Sabrina, and I had regrets that still clung to me today.
Familiar green eyes flashed in my memory.
"*I want to go to the formal, Daniel. Plan it for me. Surprise me,*" Sabrina pleaded *wistfully.*
"*Sabrina,*" I sighed. "*I just don't want to go. I've got that show I'm going to with Kent. I planned this a month ago, and before I did, I asked about the formal, and you said no. I'm not canceling because you changed your mind.*"

The wistfulness dropped like an anvil, and all that was left was accusation and anger. "You're choosing Kent over me?"

"No. You know I'm not."

"I love you, Daniel. Be with me," *she pleaded almost desperately.*

I ran a tired hand over my face. "Why don't you come with us?"

"Because I don't want to. I want to dress up and feel pretty and dance with my boyfriend. Please. Do this for me."

"Sabrina, I can't."

Anger morphed her features into a snarl, and I braced myself. "Fine," *she shouted.* "Fuck you. I'll go with Kyle. Maybe I'll even fuck him."

Exhaustion wore down my patience. More and more, Sabrina ran scalding hot to freezing cold, and I struggled to keep up. Too often, I found myself putting everything on hold to make her moods less drastic, and right then, I was tired. Too tired to be anything but a selfish asshole.

"You know, what? Fine. Have fun." *I stormed out, not wanting her anger to grow until it crumbled to tears. I didn't want to be there for the long drawn out ordeal.*

"More water?" Charlotte, my bartender, asked.

"Yeah. Thanks."

Scrubbing a hand through my hair, I tugged at the strands as if trying to pull the memory out. Sabrina was always with me, but I tried not to think about her too much. But the more time I spent helping Hanna, the more and more the memories crept in. It was hard when their eyes were so similar.

Remembering how I let Sabrina down that night, just confirmed I was doing the right thing for Hanna. Maybe if I did enough for her, I could make up for all I did wrong before. I could balance my past mistakes with my future.

"Hey."

Hanna's soft voice among the music snapped my attention her way, and I was pretty sure my jaw hit the floor. She wore a long-sleeve, black wrap dress that cut almost all the way down to her belly button. My mouth watered at the curve of her full breasts, wondering how hard I'd have to tug on the fitted material before her nipple popped out. On top of that, it ended about six inches above her over the knee-high black boots.

"Jesus, Hanna."

She stepped from foot to foot, pulling her arms in front of her. "Too much?"

"God, no. Honestly, you're the sexiest woman in the room."

Her nerves slipped away, only to be replaced by a stunning smile she did her best to hide under her teeth.

"Would you like a drink?"

"Actually, I wouldn't mind getting started."

"Eager?" I joked.

"Maybe a little." She shrugged. "You've got me addicted."

"Pleasure isn't a bad thing to be addicted to as long as you're safe about it."

She bumped her shoulder with mine. "That's why I have you."

Her trust hammered away a little more of the distance I kept around my heart, creating a crevice to slide into.

"Well, we're starting out here tonight," I said, gesturing to the bar around us. Her eyes widened like saucers. "*We're* not doing anything out here," I soothed. "Just observing."

She still looked wary but nodded. "I think I'll take that drink."

I got her a tequila and guided her to the lounge in the corner. You could find almost anything for your viewing pleasure back there. Brown, leather club chairs filled the space in little clusters. Close enough to hold a group, but far enough away that if a stranger wanted to come to enjoy the show, they wouldn't intrude.

The club was called Voyeur because people came to watch, but some loved being watched too. Kent and I allowed exhibitionism as long as it remained tasteful and not obscene.

I found what I was looking for in the second grouping of chairs and guided Hanna to quietly sit without disturbing them. She sat stiffly on the edge of her seat, trying to not stare at the couple, but unable to stop from glancing their way over and over.

I leaned across the arms of the chair. "It's okay to watch, Hanna. They want you to."

The woman ground her hips down onto the man's lap as they feasted on each other's mouths. One of his hands gripped her long blonde hair, and the other was under her dress, palming her full breasts.

When the woman shifted to her knees between the man's thighs, Hanna almost finished off her entire glass in one big gulp.

The woman's head mostly blocked the man's cock, but we could watch the man staring down at the woman's mouth. We could watch the way his jaw ground tight, and his eyes rolled back in pleasure.

His groan floated across the space between us when the woman sank down and back up, picking up speed. Eventually, his hand dove into her hair and guided her pace.

Needing Hanna to understand what she was seeing, I leaned over again, brushing her hair aside to whisper in her ear. "She's totally in control."

Hanna's eyes snapped to mine like I was crazy. "He's holding her head down."

"He may be, but she is completely in control. See her hand? He's left it free so she can signal if she wants out. But she won't want out. He's at her mercy. She owns him."

The woman's hand slipped into her lovers and held on tight

as she bobbed faster, pulling a restrained groan from the man as he came.

The woman placed her lover's cock back in his pants before curling up on his lap, where he proceeded to kiss himself from her lips.

Through it all, I watched Hanna more than them. I watched the way she unintentionally squirmed. The way she gripped the glass so tight, her fingers were almost white. The way her chest moved over panting breaths or the way her tongue peeked out to slick across her dry lips.

I especially loved the flush that worked its way down her neck. I couldn't wait to see how far I could make it go tonight.

Sliding my hand along her forearm, I got her attention. "Ready?"

She finished her drink and nodded.

I'd already placed our selection, scheduling it for a certain time—perks of being the owner. So, we were able to head into the room immediately.

Hanna took in the set up on the other side of the glass with wide eyes.

A dark circular stage with a pole extended from floor to ceiling. Low lighting illuminated the single chair faced to watch whoever performed.

"A strip club?"

I couldn't help but smile at her confusion. "Do you trust me?"

"Of course," she answered without any hesitation.

"Then come sit down."

This room had a chaise like the last, and after flipping the switch, I leaned back in the corner, widening my legs for her to slide between again.

This time, she didn't hold her body away from mine. She sank back immediately, making herself comfortable against my chest, her head tucked on my shoulder. The angle gave me a

TEACHER

perfect view down her body. It was impossible to stop my eyes from roaming over the full swells of her breasts, the hard peaks of her nipples pressing against the thin material of her top. I almost became lost in wondering how soft her skin would feel under my tongue or how it would taste.

She gasped when I shifted my hips to get comfortable, unintentionally pressing my hard cock against her back. "You're hard?" she asked with wonder.

"Yeah." I huffed a laugh but rushed to ease any discomfort it may have caused her. "I'm sorry. It doesn't mean anything."

"No, it's okay. It's nice to know I'm not the only one turned on."

"Hardly."

A man came into the room and sat in the chair, not having to wait long before the lights dimmed, and a woman in a silver scrap of lingerie strutted out to a heavy beat.

"Tonight is about finding control in places you wouldn't always look."

She nodded, her hair brushing my chin.

The woman swayed her hips and touched her body, making her way to the pole. The man watched, his hand running along the growing length in his slacks.

Hanna jumped a little when I brushed her hair back and whispered against her ear. "I want you to get yourself off."

She jerked her wide-eyed gaze to mine. "What?"

"I want you to do what I did to you the other night. Take control, Hanna. Find pleasure in your body. It's yours. The more you do this, the easier it will come."

Her gaze bounced between mine as she swallowed before nodding and focusing her attention back on the scene.

"I'm right here."

She nodded again. When the man pulled his dick out and began stroking it, Hanna followed suit and slid her trembling hands up her thighs, tugging the material of her dress with it. She shoved aside the scrap of red lace and ran shaking fingers through her folds.

"Tease yourself, baby. Build up the anticipation."

"I don't know how," she almost growled.

"That's why I'm here. I'll help you." I nodded toward the glass. "See how he's taking his time. Slow, long strokes. Teasing himself—torturing himself by holding back on the pleasure he knows is coming."

Hanna's hand followed my words, moving slowly down and back up.

"Dip your fingers in your pussy, get them wet, and bring them back to your clit, slowly rolling it around. Find the move that brings you the most pleasure. There's no wrong answer."

The woman stripped her top, leaning back against the pole, rubbing her breasts, pinching her nipples before sliding down and tugging her underwear aside to show the man her pussy.

Hanna whimpered in my arms, and I clenched my fists at my side, stopping them from joining her hand.

The man used quick, rough strokes, racing toward his orgasm, his eyes never leaving the woman pleasuring herself. Hanna's hand moved with his, and when he groaned his release, she moaned with him, but she didn't come.

With her lip pinched under her teeth, she continued playing with herself, letting out a grunt of frustration.

"Be patient, Hanna. You don't want a lover to rush with you, so don't rush with yourself. This is your pleasure. Give your body what it deserves."

The man stood from the chair and gripped the woman's ankles, sliding up to her hips to guide her to the edge of the stage. He ripped her panties from her and tossed them aside so he could bury his face between her thighs.

The woman clutched his head and moaned. He moved until

she was perched on the edge of the stage, he was on his knees and feasting on her like he was a starving man at a buffet.

"Daniel," Hanna whispered. "Please. Help me."

That was it. There was no way I'd turn down her plea. My hands lifted, and I looked down her body, unsure of where to start first. Too many places begged for my touch, but her fingers were busy at work between her thighs and her breasts heaved, calling to me like a Siren. I couldn't keep my fucking eyes off them. I was like a man possessed, wanting to dive right in and devour her. She was so ripe for the taking, but I had to do this right.

I hovered on the edges of her dress, letting my thumbs play just a fraction under the material in the valley of her curves, giving her time to tell me to stop.

When she didn't, I pinched the material on the sides, tugging the dress further and further, holding my breath until her pert nipples popped free. I'd seen a lot of breasts—loved a lot of breasts—but *nothing* would ever compare to Hanna's blush rose nipples. The hard buds pulled tight in the cool air, goosebumps prickling along her firm flesh.

I cupped the bottoms, filling my palms completely, and rubbed my thumbs along the tips.

She almost shot out of my arms at the contact, but I loosely held her in place, tugging her back to my chest. The couple beyond the glass ceased to exist as I focused my sole attention on playing with the most perfect tits I'd ever seen.

My large hands barely covered her, massaging every inch, always circling back to her nipples. When her whimpers came fast and hard, matching the woman's, I focused all my attention on the hard tips. Hanna's hips were wild under her fingers, and I knew she was close. Holding the tip between my finger and thumb, I pinched, testing her boundaries. She arched into my hands, and I pinched tighter, twisting and tugging a little harder with each pass. She moaned louder, and pleasure shot down my spine knowing Hanna liked the bite of pain with her pleasure. I leaned in and bit the soft skin of her neck.

Her head pressed back against my shoulder, her thighs held wide, her back arched and she came with a silent scream, her mouth open wide.

"That's it, baby. Come. Feel your pleasure. Look at you, controlling your body. So fucking good."

I slowed my fingers as she slowed hers until she lay panting in my arms. Kissing up her neck, I whispered, "You did so well, Hanna. I'm so proud of you."

She turned her head to me, and I forced myself to not lean in. Again, her full lips were mere inches from mine, damp from her tongue slicking across them, begging for me to have a taste.

"Thank you, Daniel. Thank you," she breathed.

Rules were rules. We had them for a reason, and the ache building in my chest was the perfect reminder to hold back.

"Any time."

"Tonight was perfect." She giggled once her breathing evened out. "I can't believe I made myself come again, and I liked it."

Her words pierced my chest, hating what was taken from her. But then she giggled again, and I was honored to give her something to feel light enough to giggle about.

"I think I'll need a second drink now."

"I can get one for you if you'd like, but we're not done yet."

She looked up, her eyes still glossy from her orgasm, filled with a mixture of shock and excitement.

"How do you feel about third base?"

14

HANNA

Third base?

I quickly scrambled through my high school memories of what the bases were.

First was kissing, second was hands, third was...

"You want me to do oral?" I breathed, feeling my eyes widen. Surprisingly, with Daniel's length still pressed to my back, I didn't hate the idea.

"No. No," Daniel rushed out. "I want you to receive." He licked his lips, and I couldn't help but imagine what his tongue would feel like between my legs. Would it be softer than his fingers? Just as firm? "Tonight is about you accepting your pleasure."

"Ummm." I sat up and considered my options, shifting my clothes back in place. I could give in to the pressure on my chest and say no because I was scared of how I'd react. We could have drinks, and I'd go home wondering what it would have been like. Or I could try. I could trust Daniel to stop if I needed him to—to not judge me if I *did* end up flipping out. I could take a step forward in a safe place with no regrets.

Hell yes, Han-Han. Let the man eat your pussy, Sofia's voice rang in my head.

"Okay."

His smile spread slowly, making me smile too.

"How do you want me?"

"Not here."

Daniel stood and adjusted his length, tucking it out of his way, and there was something so alluring about watching a man touch himself. What would it be like to touch him? Would I feel powerful like the other women did when they pleased their lovers?

Not that Daniel was my lover.

Just a friend, I reminded myself.

With each step down the hall, a new doubt crept in. What would it feel like to have his shoulders between my thighs? Would he think I looked weird? Would he think I tasted weird? A mixture of anxiety and giddiness swirled through my belly like a swarm of butterflies.

But I didn't mind the anxiety because, for the first time in my life, it was based around fears any woman would have with a man for the first time. They weren't about feeling trapped or sent to a flashback, they were average, basic fears.

So focused on my own thoughts, I bumped into Daniel's back when he stopped walking. Standing in front of the door, he turned and lifted my chin with his finger. "We can stop whenever you want. Okay?"

"Okay."

At my confirmation, he moved right, going into the performance room and not the viewing room. I followed, stumbling over numb feet.

"Umm, Daniel?"

Did he want to perform oral while people watched? Holy shit. This was a whole new level of fear I hadn't even considered.

I scrambled with an excuse to get out of that room before my chest caved under the weight of anxiety.

He faced me with a soothing smile. "Don't worry, we're not performing."

He hit a button on the wall, and the black glass faded to clear, showing an empty viewing room beyond. I almost collapsed from relief, breathing for the first time since entering the room. He gripped both my hands and tugged me closer to the bed. When we stood at the edge, he brushed my hair behind my ear, holding me just inches from him.

"I just need more room. I want to taste every inch, and I need space for you to feel it all."

His words rumbled across my skin, flushing every inch with heat like I was catching on fire. I wanted to fall into him and let him do whatever he wanted.

He made me want so much, and for the first time, a new feeling pierced my heart when I looked at Daniel. A warm squeeze I wanted to shove out—crush it before it grew. That feeling had no place between us.

"Do you talk to all your friends this way?" I joked, reminding myself of what we were.

"Kent and Jackson aren't fans of my dirty talk."

"That's a shame. They're missing out."

We both laughed, but then he turned more serious. "Does it bother you?"

I hated dirty talk. I hated what it reminded me of. I'd heard the worst of the worst, and it made me sick knowing it was still in my mind rattling around, just waiting to come out. I hated it.

Except when Daniel spoke, hate was the furthest thing from my mind. I took the words in and let it spread like fire through my veins.

"No," I confessed.

His thumb stroked my cheek. "There's nothing wrong with

that. If it brings you pleasure, is legal, and consensual, then that's all that matters."

That warmth came back, and there wasn't a damn thing I could do about it. Instead, I tried to distract myself. I lifted up on my toes and pressed my lips to his neck. My body tingled each time his lips caressed my neck, and I wanted to return the favor. His arms gently rested around my waist, but as my kisses grew more frantic, so did his hold.

I dragged my tongue along the strong tendons of his neck and nipped softly at the base. The taste of his skin dominated all my thoughts, all my emotions, all the sensations flooding me. I thought of nothing but him. I didn't consider how he spun us and eased me back on the bed. I didn't consider his large body over mine or the way it made room for itself between my thighs. Nothing mattered except it not stopping.

His arms flexed under his shirt as he held himself over me, not letting his full weight crush me. It was his turn to kiss his way down my neck, moving into my cleavage. He gripped the edge of my dress covering my breasts and paused, giving me a chance to tell him to stop without breaking the moment.

"Yes," I almost begged.

He tugged the material aside and growled against my skin, leaving wet, sucking kisses until he reached my breast. I arched, almost coming off the bed completely when his tongue slicked across my nipple that first time. I whimpered a desperate plea for more when he pinched the hardened tip between his teeth.

"You have the most beautiful breasts," he said, moving from one to the other. "I love the way they overflow out of my palms. So perfectly full and—fuck me—they taste like heaven." He lifted, giving me a smirk that shot right to my core. "But I bet you have something that tastes even better."

He worked his way down my abdomen, tugging my dress up my thighs to reach my panties. He gripped each side, sliding the material down my thighs. Each inch the lacy material scraped past had my need rising. They cleared my feet, and I rested my heels on the bed, my thighs pressed together. Daniel's palms rested on my knees but didn't push them apart.

"Hanna," he said, brushing his thumbs against my skin.

I took a deep breath, pinched my eyes closed, and blurted the first thing that came to mind. "I've never done this before, and I'm worried I taste weird or bad or something."

He didn't laugh, and when I inched my eyes open, I only found a small smile, like he thought my fears were cute.

"Hanna, I love pussy. All of it, and I have no doubt yours will be the sweetest pussy I've ever had against my tongue."

"Oh," I breathed, relaxing my thighs.

He slowly slid his rough palms down my sensitive skin until I laid spread before him. He didn't take his eyes off mine when he scooted back and bent over, dragging his tongue down my inner thigh. He kissed up the other, killing me with each pass until I damn near begged him just to do it.

Finally, he hovered over my opening, his breath tickling my wet heat. "Since it's your first time, I better make it memorable."

"No problem the—" The first sweep of his tongue had my eyes rolling toward the back of my head. "Holy shit."

Those were the last intelligible words to leave my mouth as Daniel did as he promised. He licked every single inch of me, inside and out. He sucked on my folds and played with my clit. He pushed me wide and fucked me, his thumb making tortuous circles around my bundle of nerves. I could feel the wetness tricking down, and I didn't care.

My entire focus centered on Daniel's tongue and the need to come. There was no room for anything else.

"Play with your tits, baby."

Without hesitation, I did as told. I had no idea my nipples were so sensitive. I should've been ashamed of how much I liked the rough pinches and hard tugs, but nothing mattered right then. Daniel pushed his fingers into me and latched on to my clit, sucking hard, and that was it. Pleasure crashed over me, flinging me off a cliff, sending me into a free-fall I never wanted to come back from. I wanted to live in this feeling, this pleasure, this oblivion.

Instead of crashing back into my body, soft licks and strokes cradled me back to earth.

"Beautiful."

His praise wrapped me in the comfort I'd come to associate just with him.

He sat back and wiped at the moisture coating his mouth and chin. I should've been ashamed, but my body still vibrated with aftershocks, distracting me too much to feel any embarrassment.

His cock tented his pants, and when he moved, he winced. I wasn't ready for this experience to be over. Sitting up, I reached for him.

"Can I...?"

He held my hand before I could reach him, and brought it to his lips, kissing each knuckle, and groaned, "You're killing me. The thought of those lips around me is enough to make a man insane. But tonight is about you."

"Will you at least...get off again?"

He huffed a laugh. "I guess if I have to," he said, making me laugh with him. "Lay back for me, baby."

He swallowed and unfastened his pants. I liked the idea of him watching me to get off. I left my breasts out, and my thighs spread. I'd never felt sexier than I did in that moment with Daniel kneeling between my legs, gripping his hard length, and watching me to get off.

He dragged his palm across my wet pussy, making me jerk when he grazed my sensitive clit. Then, using my cum, he jerked himself off, barely taking his eyes from mine. His jaw clenched tight, and his arm moved faster.

Tension stretched between us, and without touching, the moment felt more intimate than if he were inside me.

He didn't touch me at all, and I stood on the edge of the cliff again, ready to fall. Too soon, his eyes slid shut, and he cupped his free hand over his shaft and groaned. When he finished, I was squirming on the bed, desperate to fall.

"Fuck, you're sexy," he said. Without any hesitation, he fell between my thighs again and ate me like his last meal. There was no teasing or taking his time. He sucked my clit, flicking it with his tongue, and shoving me until I fell all over again.

By the time we'd both got our breathing back under control, he sprawled next to me on the bed, tugging me into his chest. Like the most natural thing in the world, I rested my head in the crook of his neck and wrapped my leg over his.

"This is nice," he rumbled. "I usually skip the snuggle-sesh."

A laugh broke free, loud in the quiet room. "Did you just say *snuggle-sesh?*"

"Yeah, all the cool kids say it," he explained, smiling down at me.

"Who?" I challenged. "I'm in my twenties, and I've never heard anyone say that."

"You're just not in the loop," he joked. "Geez, get with the program, Han-Han."

And just like that, any heat that lingered froze like a block of ice. All of me froze, stiff and uncomfortable with the memories crashing through my mind like the Hawaiian punch man.

"Hey, are you okay?" Daniel's voice permeated the memories, and I clung to it. "Hanna."

"Sofia was the only person to call me Han-Han," I explained against his chest.

He didn't say anything. He didn't apologize. He didn't push

for more. It was one of the main things I enjoyed about Daniel. He never pushed but was always open if I wanted to talk.

My head rose and fell with his deep breaths, and I sank into the feel of his arm around my back, into the way his palm rested over my smaller hand. His pinky pushed against my sleeve, inching it back enough to stroke the scars that still marred each wrist.

"Sometimes I forget," he admitted quietly.

"I like that you forget." Daniel never treated me like broken glass barely glued together. He treated me like a normal human being—a strong one. "I wish I could forget, too."

"Do you still think about it a lot?"

I hesitated. It was the most direct question he'd ever asked me about being kidnapped and sold, but I found myself wanting to talk about it with him.

"Not usually. I can sometimes go a week or more without it crossing my mind. But I always think of Sofia." He held me tighter, and I took a shuddering breath. "I had a hard time at first—when Erik first rescued us—me. They gave us drugs, and I struggled coming off of it. It left me with a lot of flashbacks. I'd panic, and they'd try to subdue me, but I couldn't stand to be touched. It just made it worse."

"Jesus, Hanna." The words were so soft, they barely vibrated against my cheek, like he didn't mean for them to slip out.

"The worst—the things that haunted me the most—were the moments I was too drugged to know what was happening to my body." Tears burned the backs of my eyes. I'd never told anyone that outside of my therapist. We'd worked on it, but that fear still clung to me harder than any others. "Maybe you going down on me wasn't the first time. Maybe I just don't remember."

Daniel moved then, no longer content to be a passive member of this conversation. He lay on his side, so I had no choice but to meet his gaze, the blue sparkling like ice in the sun. "This is all that matters," he said, his words so intense they crushed through any doubt until I had no choice but believe they were real. "What you choose to give is *all* that matters." His fingers lightly pinched my chin and held me in place. "Do you hear me?"

The tears I'd held at bay slipped, sliding onto the pillow. I managed to hold most of them back and nodded, unable to speak past the lump lodged in my throat. He held my hands and pressed soft lips to my forehead, not speaking again until my tears dried.

In that moment, I almost wanted to beg for him to forget the rules and press his lips to mine. Somehow, I held back.

When I offered a lame smile, awkward and unsure of how to move on from my confessions, he did it for us.

His brow rose high and arrogant, lips tipped with a cocky smile. "Besides, I'm all hyped up and alpha right now at being the first one to eat your pussy. Don't take that from me."

A shocked laugh broke free, knocking away any tears threatening to escape. "Oh, my god, Daniel."

He lifted an arm and flexed, making faces and winking. The sadness washed away with each laugh he made me let loose.

I slapped his chest before gripping my sides. "Stop. I can't take it anymore."

"I'm too alpha, right?"

"Soooo alpha." I poked him in the ribs and loved watching him jerk. "A ticklish alpha."

"Every alpha has a weakness."

"Thank you, Daniel," I whispered.

He pulled me close into his chest and kissed the top of my head again, renewing the ache to feel his lips on mine. "Any time. Anything."

"You mean that? Anything?"

He pulled back, his brows lowered over doubtful eyes. "Yes," he answered slowly.

"How do you feel about being my date to the charity gala?"

"Do I have to buy a corsage?"

I laughed. "Maybe."

"Then I'm definitely in. I love a good flower accessory. How can I say no?"

15

HANNA

Turning this way and that, I examine the blue lace stretched too tight across my chest in the full-length mirror. I'd gone back and forth with how I felt about my cleavage. Boasted about it in high school, loving the attention. Then I hated it and would have done anything to have them gone. Then I'd pretended to be okay with them in the years after. But it wasn't until our last night at Voyeur that I'd truly appreciated them.

I saw them through Daniel's eyes. I saw them through my own. Another part of my body I reclaimed as mine.

"Let's see it," Olivia shouted from the other side of the curtain.

"I'm about to Incredible Hulk out of this dress."

"Well, then you better hurry up. We promised to show everyone."

I stepped out, and everyone oohed and aahed over the dress, but agreed it clung a little too tightly.

"Where's Oaklyn?" I asked.

"Oaklyn, don't make me drag you out," Olivia threatened.

The curtain next to mine flung open, and the light-haired

brunette stomped out, staring daggers at Olivia. I tried to purse my lips together to hold the laugh back, but one slipped out, and it broke everyone else down too. All of us were in a fit of giggles.

"It's not that bad," Olivia defended around her smile.

Oaklyn flung her hands up, the bulky floral fabric rustling around her wrists. "I look like I got my hand stuck in a bush."

I couldn't help it, I laughed again.

Oaklyn grumbled and made her way back behind the curtain.

"I like that one, Carina," I said, watching her twist and turn. The black lace clung to her curvaceous body. "The long sleeves give it a demure look, but the off the shoulder is sexy."

"Also, it clings to my ass like glue." She bobbed her brows before turning to Audrey munching on Puffs in her stroller. "Yes, it does, baby girl. Not that you will have anything that clings to you. Nope. Not with your daddy."

Audrey smiled a four-tooth smile and reach for Carina. "Ma-ma."

Carina pressed a kiss to her fat cheek and went to get undressed.

"Next one," Alex demanded. "This gray is washing me out."

I shed the dress and put on my favorite, an emerald green gown. The sweetheart neckline pushed my breasts up but covered enough to remain decent. The top fitted me until it hit my waist, where the heavy satin flared out.

"You've been busy lately, Hanna," Carina called from outside.

"Yeah. Work," I answered lamely, opening the curtain. She held Audrey in her arms, giving me a deadpanned stare, unimpressed with my answer. "I'm taking a new self-defense class, too."

Alex came out just in time to say, "With Daniel."

Carina's brows rose high.

"Daniel, Daniel? My Uncle Daniel?" Olivia asked, joining the group.

"Yeah. It's nothing."

"He's her date to the charity gala," Alex added, and I glared at her making a bigger deal about it than it was.

"Wow," Oaklyn added. "Daniel doesn't do dates."

"We're friends. It's not a date. It's nothing."

Alex crossed her arms, and I did my best attempt at telepathy to not say anything else. She did one back and said tough shit.

"Why don't you tell them what else he's helping you with," she suggested, smirking.

Olivia waved her hand like she was swatting a bug. "We already know about Voyeur. Duh. Old news."

"Oh, it's way more than that."

I almost stomped my foot. Almost. "It's not. It's nothing." Alex's stare called bullshit. "I hate you."

"No, you don't."

"Spill," Carina demanded, looking way too good for a woman currently bouncing a baby chewing on her hair.

"It's nothing," I tried again. "He's just a friend helping a friend."

"With sex," Alex added.

"I'm out," Olivia said, throwing her hands up and turning back to her room. "He's like my dad, and that's nasty. Ugh. Now I know how he feels about Kent and me."

Alex turned to Oaklyn, who looked stunning in a silver dress. "You know Daniel. Has he ever helped anyone?"

"I mean, yeah. He's not a monster. He helps people, but they're more like acquaintances. He doesn't have many close friends."

"What do you mean, 'sex'?" Carina asked. "Are you sleeping with him?"

"Ew," came from behind the curtain.

"No," I said over Olivia's gagging sounds.

"Not yet," Alex muttered.

I grabbed the closest thing I could find, one of Audrey's stuffed animals, and chucked it at Alex. She easily deflected the rabbit. "What? I said I wouldn't tell Erik. It's good to talk this stuff out with friends."

"Yeah, and now Carina will tell Ian."

"Not my monkeys, not my circus. My lips are sealed."

The attendant snuck up on us all standing in a circle in a standoff. "More champagne, ladies?"

"Hell yes," Carina said, pushing past me and grabbing the bottle the woman offered. Olivia and Oaklyn came out to perch on the couch, back in their jeans, at the sound of more alcohol.

Once the attendant walked away and more champagne was poured, I tried to calm the hoard. "Seriously, it's nothing. The first time I went to a back room, I kind of panicked and bolted. I ran into Daniel and he took me to his office to calm down. We talked and he offered to help. I'm just comfortable around him, and I don't have any men in my life I'm comfortable enough with to...to...try things."

"Things?" Carina asked dryly.

Ignoring her, I continued. "We get along. We're friends and we both understand what we want in our futures. Which isn't a relationship."

"Then why learn how to flirt and be okay with sex if you don't want it," Carina asked.

"I *do* want it. And I want to be able to have it. I want to be okay with my body. I just don't want to commit to anyone."

"Why?"

Carina's pushing and narrowed eyes pricked at my irritation and had me standing taller, crossing my arms, and cocking my hip like an attitude would block her intrusive questions.

"Do you ask Daniel why he wants to be alone, or just me—a

young woman who society thinks should be planning a husband and kids by now?"

Carina's brows tried to merge with her hairline, and I knew I was in for it. She didn't deserve for me to snap at her, but I'd felt cornered.

"First of all, calm down. I'm the queen of women empowerment. Two, yes I ask him, and he's just as big of a pain in the ass about answering as you are." She rolled her eyes. "He says he likes being alone. I think he's full of shit."

"Yeah," Oaklyn chimed in. "I think he holds back. He's not like Kent, who was the wilder one of them. Daniel's a homebody."

"So, why?" Carina asked, turning back to me.

The fight leaked out of me with a heavy sigh, my shoulders slouching in defeat. "I don't want to find a future without Sofia. It's not right that I get to go on and find my happily ever after, and she doesn't. And I just don't want to fall in love to lose someone." Tears burned up my throat, and I dropped my gaze to the ground. "I can't feel that loss again."

My confession brought silence to the circle for the first time all night, and I could feel their stares—their judgment.

"Well, shit," Carina finally said, shocking me. "Now I feel like an asshole."

"Asth-ol," Audrey imitated.

It was enough to break the tension, and we all laughed at the bad word and Carina's resulting shock.

"No, baby. Don't say that."

"Asth-ol."

"Ian's not going to let me live this down."

Conversation broke off into small groups, and Carina passed Audrey off before heading my way. "Just so you know, I think your reasoning is shit—just like his—but I won't talk you out of it."

"Thank you," I said sincerely. I'd had enough pushing and confessing for the rest of the year. I appreciated her calling a truce.

Her full lips tipped into a smile that promised nothing good. "Now, let's pick out a dress that makes your *friend* think you're hot."

I rolled my eyes but couldn't hold back the smile once I closed the curtain.

With no one else around, I had to admit, I liked the sound of that.

16

DANIEL

"Wow, you look...stunning." Hanna knocked me stupid, in her emerald dress, making words hard to think of. Not that stunning did her justice. I'd been waiting in the lobby of her apartment, wondering if going as her date tonight crossed boundaries of our friendship.

Watching her face light up at my compliment, I didn't really care about boundaries.

She shoved her hands into the folds of her dress. "Thank you. It has pockets."

"Well, shit. Best dress ever then."

"You clean up pretty nice, too."

My face didn't light up like hers, but I may have beamed a little when she looked me up and down.

"Stop staring at my sister," Erik growled, walking past me.

I laughed at Hanna's eye roll but *did* stop staring. Hanna was my friend, and while I *may* know what her pussy tasted like—how rosy her nipples got when she came—I didn't want to leer at her.

"Oh, my god, Erik. Shut up. People are allowed to say I'm pretty. It's polite."

Alex snickered, following behind Erik, her hand firmly planted in his. Erik glared at me like I was the reason the women were ganging up on him. I held my hands up in surrender, acting like an innocent man I knew I wasn't.

If Erik knew what I'd done to his sister, he'd probably beat me to a pulp. It wouldn't matter I was doing it to help her.

"Come on, caveman," Alex said. "Our limo is waiting."

Hanna linked her arm through mine, and we headed to our ride. I'd offered to meet them there, or even pick Hanna up myself, but she said they always rode together as tradition and begged me not to leave her alone with the sappy couples.

Sitting in the back, watching the way Erik couldn't keep his hands off Alex, I couldn't blame her. Before heading to the event, we picked up Ian and Carina. Ian didn't even bother to be subtle about touching Carina and letting everyone know how hot he thought she looked.

I looked to Hanna to see how she was handling all the PDAs, but she wasn't even paying attention. She stared out the window, focused on something beyond the sidewalks and city flashing by. Her hands fidgeted, clasped too tightly in her lap, and nerves radiated off her in waves. Every other pass, her thumb would slip under the collection of bracelets and rub at her scars. Not even thinking about it, I rested my palm on hers. Wide green eyes, the same color as her dress, snapped to mine. Her hand relaxed and turned over, linking our fingers.

"Thank you," she mouthed.

I winked and held on tight. Everyone was too busy with their own significant other that no one noticed the connection. At least, almost no one. Carina's curious stare took in our hands before rising to meet my eyes, and I quickly looked away, not lingering on her reaction. Holding Hanna's hand was nothing. Just a friend offering support.

We waited our turn in the line of limos dropping off people ready to spend their money for a good cause. When it was finally our turn, we piled out, quickly making our way inside since none of the girls wore jackets, claiming it would ruin the look.

Hanna held tight to my arm, even after we crossed through the double doors. The vast room hummed with conversation, people mingling around the tall round tables, champagne clutched tight. Some perused the auction items, already placing their bids.

"This looks amazing."

Hanna smiled. "I'd like to think we get better every year. The donations definitely get better as we grow."

"Pretty soon you won't need a simple offering of free food and drinks from a tiny bar," I joked, referring to our donation from Voy.

She slapped my chest softly. "Oh, shut up. You have a lot more to offer than free drinks at a bar. A night at Voyeur would probably be the highest sold item if it was up for sale."

"Probably," I boasted. However, we both knew having a night at Voyeur up for auction at a sex-trafficking event wouldn't be the most appropriate option.

"Thank you for that, by the way," she said, nodding back from where we came.

"What?"

"Just holding my hand. Calming me down."

"It's nothing. I understand why this means so much, and it's a huge undertaking."

"Yeah." She looked around the room, taking in each aspect I was sure she painstakingly chose. "Erik and I do most of it on our own. Mom and Dad help where they can."

"Are they here tonight?"

"No. Charity galas aren't really their thing. My mom's so frugal, she refuses to buy a fancy dress for one evening." She laughed before sobering. "Besides, it's not...how they want to spend their night," she explained delicately. "We host survivors from Haven, current and past ones, and it's hard for them to be here and not see Sofia among them. It's just that time of year. It's hard on all of us."

Hanna sniffed, and I laid my free hand over hers where it clutched my arm.

Forcing a smile, not really making it to her eyes, she continued. "Besides, we do our own thing. We have a big brunch the next morning."

"That sounds good. Brunch is always the best choice."

Soon after that, Hanna was forced to let go of my arm and do her rounds, schmoozing everyone out of more money. I sat back and enjoyed the free drinks and soft jazz playing from the band.

"How's your date?" Kent asked, sneaking up behind me.

"She's not my date," I deadpanned.

He held up his hand in an okay sign and gave an exaggerated nod.

"Leave him alone," Olivia reprimanded.

"Thanks, kiddo."

She beamed but didn't give me the reprieve I was hoping for. "So, I hear you're helping her."

I almost choked on my champagne, the bubbles going down the wrong pipe. I glared at Kent, more than a little pissed he passed on the information to my niece. He held up his hands and pointed to Olivia.

"We all went dress shopping together this week. Girls talk."

"Jesus."

"So, do you like her?"

"Olivia," I growled in warning.

"What? I'm just curious."

"We're friends. That's it."

"Boring. That's what she said too. Some of us were taking bets that it was more. I owe Carina five bucks."

Kent chuckled beside her, and I glared.

"I neither deny nor encourage her. Merely stand by and offer support," he said like he was pleading the fifth amendment.

"I thought we were friends."

"The best, and I will choose you every time. Unless I have to choose her. I'll always choose her." Somehow, Kent made my niece—*the* Olivia Witt—blush. "Thankfully, she'd never make me not choose you."

I groaned. "This is too close to PDA. We had rules to you two dating. Go dance before I get sick."

Olivia laughed and gave me a tight hug. "It's okay to like her, Uncle Daniel," she whispered for only me.

She pulled back with a wink and grabbed Kent's arm, dragging him to the dance floor.

Scanning the room, I found Hanna shaking hands with another person. I laughed as she eyeballed a waiter walking by with champagne, and I could imagine she'd probably been too busy greeting everyone to stop and drink.

Grabbing a glass for her, I walked up just as the conversation ended.

"A drink?"

She turned to me, reaching for the glass with both hands. "Oh my god. Thank you." She drained half the glass in one gulp. "I could kiss you."

I wouldn't stop you.

I shoved that thought down and covered it with a laugh as I offered her my arm, leading her off to one of the high-top tables at the edge of the room. She gripped the table and lifted each leg enough to roll her ankles under the dress.

"These shoes looked so cute in the store, but I can't wait to take them off."

"You could probably take them off and hold them in your pockets. No one would know."

She laughed before taking a deep breath, looking exhausted with only half the night over with.

"How are you holding up?"

"Good," she said but paused and let the mask drop for a moment, her shoulders falling a couple of inches. "I'm okay. It's the ninth year without her this week. It's...hard."

"They say time helps soften the edges of our pain. And it does, but it also doesn't."

She huffed a commiserating laugh. "Speaking from experience?"

She didn't look at me when she asked, and I was grateful she couldn't see the range of emotions washing over me. I avoided talking about Sabrina as much as I could. Kent was the only person who knew of her. Except David, but we didn't talk enough. It'd been a long time since I'd had to look inside and examine my emotions about her. "Yeah. The girlfriend from long ago," I finally answered. I don't' know what made me explain it. Maybe because Hanna was being so open with me, and I wanted to give her some understanding in return. "I miss the chances I had with her. The chances to make things great and follow through on what we'd said we would."

"I get that. Sofia always talked about our future. I think it helped her get through. She made me promise I'd do math, even if it made me a nerd." She laughed softly. "I'd been too cool to be smart before everything. I was only interested in boys."

"Like most teenage girls. And just for the record, men like smart women. Those math puns get me every time," I said, faking an exaggerated shiver.

"Shut up." It had the intended effect, pulling a real laugh

from her. "She wanted to dance," she continued, with a little less sadness clinging to her. "She talked about it all the time, saying that when we escaped, she would be, and I quote, a motherfucking ballerina and fuck everyone who said she was too old. She claimed she'd do pirouettes around them."

"She sounds awesome."

Her smile dimmed but didn't disappear. "She was the best." She finished her champagne before softly asking, "What did you plan on doing with her?"

I took a deep breath. "Travel was the biggest thing. Which is funny since I barely go anywhere outside of Cincinnati."

"Then travel. Just because you aren't together anymore doesn't mean you can't travel on your own."

She said it like it was the easiest thing in the world, and maybe it was. "I should."

"No. I mean it. Travel. Plan it. I'll help you. We can do it together." The words tumbled out like a snowball, gaining momentum in her mind the more she said it.

"What?"

She stood tall and pulled her shoulders back, confidence in her decision radiating off her, doing its best to pull me into her idea. "Yeah. Come on," she coaxed. "Let's go. I'll do it with you."

Humoring her and maybe out of a bit more than curiosity, I asked, "Okay, where to?"

"Hmmm." She tipped her head and tapped her finger against pursed lips. "Italy," she finally said.

I laughed and rubbed my hand along the back of my neck. "I uh, I don't have a passport."

She blinked with a deadpanned stare, one brow creeping high with judgment I deserved. "How do you not have a passport?"

"I got one," I defended. "I just let it expire."

"Daniel," she reprimanded without heat, slapping my chest.

"I know, I know. I'll update it."

"You better."

Her glare changed to an expectant glare, waiting for my answer about traveling together. "Okay, fine. You win. Where would we go?"

"Obviously someplace in the US," she joked. "How about two places? I'll pick one, and you pick one."

"Okay. You pick first."

"Hmmm...Let's do the mountains."

"That sounds good." I thought about where to go and remembered a conversation with Sabrina and how much she'd always wanted to hear the waves. She'd made me promise to take her to the beach one day. She just never gave me the chance. "How about I surprise you?"

"Okay." She nodded, her smile growing. "We're doing this."

We *were* doing this. I was going to travel with Hanna, and the scenarios that flashed through my mind ranged from playing games and laughing to...other things and a lot of moaning. Adrenaline flooded my veins, a heady concoction of excitement tinged in fear of the unknown. But looking down at her wide smile, I didn't question it.

The music finished playing, and Erik stood on the stage with a microphone. "Thank you, everyone. It's that time of night to soak up all the alcohol. Dinner will be served in Corbett Tower, followed by speeches from our wonderful guests, and finally the prizes."

Applause broke out before everyone shuffled to the next room.

"Do you talk?" I asked Hanna.

"God, no. I'm a more behind the scenes kind of girl."

She struggled to hold my eyes, and I knew there was more than just wanting to stay behind the scenes as the reason she didn't share her story at these events. "You should. Maybe it would add to your control you're working on."

"You sound like Erik," she snapped. "Always pushing me to stand up and shout everything from the rooftops. I don't need to talk about it to be fine."

I knew that. A lot of people did fine without discussing too in-depth. But every time her past came into the conversation, her irritation came with it. The more I observed Hanna, the more I saw a pot bubbling a little too high. I had no doubt she dealt with the biggest of her fears and shelved her biggest issues, but just because the biggest monsters were conquered, didn't mean the small ones couldn't do as much damage. The problem was that you sometimes missed them before it was too late.

"Sometimes, talking about it with likeminded people can help."

She ground her jaw but didn't face me. "Sometimes, it's okay to not toss everything out there. Sometimes it's okay to keep it to yourself. Sometimes we get to keep a box just for us, and that's okay. I don't need to tell everyone everything."

By the end, her chest rose and fell over her heated speech. I didn't think she'd meant to admit as much as came out in her rant.

I couldn't blame her for wanting to keep some things to herself. I never really wanted to talk about Sabrina because sometimes the past was easier to pretend to forget. Like it didn't dabble in the decisions we made every day.

It was easier to pretend it didn't happen, and that we're okay if we didn't talk about it.

Yeah, I understood Hanna's reasoning to stay behind the scenes better than anyone.

I liked to pretend the past didn't haunt me either.

I just couldn't help but wonder how full Hanna's box was. I couldn't help but wonder if it was as full as Sabrina's. I couldn't help but wonder if I would have been there to help Sabrina open her box that she would have made it.

Maybe that was all Hanna needed, just someone strong and steady to help her face the remaining monsters.

By the end of the night, I'd already thought of plans to help Hanna like I hadn't helped Sabrina.

17

HANNA

The knock at the door didn't surprise me. What did surprise me was how long he'd waited to come. I took my time, folding a pair of leggings, and placing them in my suitcase.

I let another knock bang against my door before finally opening to a scowling Erik.

"What the hell is this?" Erik held up a paper and pushed past me into my apartment.

"By all means, come in," I muttered, gently closing the door.

"Hanna. Why do you need two weeks off from work? Are you okay? Did something happen?" He fired a new question each time he turned direction in his pacing.

"I'm fine, Erik. I'm just taking a vacation. The first one I've taken in four years."

He stopped and studied me like he could scan my insides like an MRI on the hunt for an issue. I loved Erik, but he took the protective big brother to a whole new level. And he did it with as little tact as possible. "Where are you going?" he barked.

Behind his bite was concern wrapped in misplaced guilt.

He blamed himself a lot for not being on the family vacation we'd taken—the one where Sofia and I snuck out to a bar and never came back. He'd bailed at the last minute because of work, and he never forgave himself. It didn't matter how many times I told him we would have found a way to sneak out even if he was there.

So, now he was here. All. The. Time.

I loved him for it, but I'd hoped time would soften him around the edges. It hadn't, and my irritation grew with each outburst when I was nothing but safe. Trust me, no one prepared for the worst-case scenario more than I did.

"Relax, Erik. The first stop on the trip is to Asheville at a super cute cabin. I'll send you the address if it makes you feel better?"

"A cabin? In the woods? Alone?"

I had to inhale as deep as I could and walk away, not at all surprised when he followed. Knowing the next answer I gave would probably send him on the crazy train, I used my most innocent voice and avoided his eyes by folding another shirt. "No, I'm going with Daniel."

"Daniel?" he roared. "Daniel? The owner of the sex club? Is taking you to a cabin in the woods?"

"It's not a sex club."

"You know what I mean," he growled. "What are you even doing, Hanna?"

"He's my friend. What's the difference between this and going with Alex?"

He huffed a disbelieving laugh and threw his arms wide. "Alex doesn't want to fuck you. Alex doesn't claim friendship when all she wants to do is get in your pants." Grinding his jaw, he dragged his hands over his face. "I'm going to fucking kill him."

Throwing my shirt in the suitcase, I turned with my hands on my hips. "Erik, stop. I'm fine. We're just friends."

"Don't be so stupid, Hanna. Don't be so naive."

I slowly pulled back, my brows joining my hairline, and glared in wide-eyed shock. "Excuse me," I said dangerously low.

"That's not...shit. That's not what I meant."

"No, no. Tell me how you really feel. Don't stop now."

"Dammit, Hanna," he growled again, his palms slapping his thighs. "You know you're smart. But you're putting yourself out there for the first time. It's new, and I don't want someone to take advantage and hurt you." His eyes pleaded with me to hear him, to understand, and I did, but it didn't make it better.

"I know I haven't done this before. I *know* how inexperienced I am. But inexperience doesn't make me stupid." I relaxed my posture and tone. "I know what I'm doing. If you think either one of us is going into this without knowing where the other one stands, then you don't know me at all. I've analyzed every scenario and talked it through."

"I just...I love you, Hanna. I don't want you to get hurt or not be taken care of."

He didn't want someone who didn't know what I'd been through to be careless and put me in a position that could send me into a panic attack.

"He knows."

Erik stopped pacing and turned to me; his jaw dropped. "What?" he whispered.

"He knows. He knows my fears, and he respects them. We both wanted to travel—hell, it was my idea. We're both getting something out of it that has nothing to do with each other. We're just partners in our trip—traveling companions."

"You told him?"

"I mean, he knew enough just being around us. It's not a secret among our circle, but yeah, I've talked to him about it. He's actually been teaching me self-defense classes."

Erik swallowed. "I would've done that. We tried. We can still try. All the resources at Haven are always open to you, Hanna. No questions asked. And I'm always here."

"I know." I swallowed past the lump in my throat. Erik was a giant pain sometimes, but he'd saved me. He'd moved heaven and earth and risked his life to bring both of us home. I loved him more than anyone and knowing he was always on my side, centered me more than anything else. "I know you would have. I wasn't ready then. And, honestly, I didn't realize I was ready now."

"He's not forcing you, is he?"

"No," I laughed. "If anything, he's overly cautious, while also not babying me. It's kind of nice. But he always lets me know we can stop at any moment."

I didn't mention that that was for more than just the self-defense. If Erik knew what else Daniel taught me, nothing would stop him from blowing a gasket, and Alex would be super sad if I made her boyfriend have a heart attack before she could marry him.

"Good. I'm glad. I wish it was with someone else, but I'm happy you're happy. I guess."

"I think that's about as good as it gets from you. Now, go. I have to finish packing."

He scanned the contents strewn across my bed and stopped, his eyes widening like saucers. "What the fuck is that? I thought you said no sex," he accused, pointing his finger toward the pile of lace.

"Those are my panties, Erik. I wear them for me. So, congratulations. Now you know what your sister wears under her clothes."

Erik's face screwed up and he brought his hands to rub at his eyes, turning toward the door. "Fuck, Hanna. I didn't need to know that. Are you trying to traumatize me?"

"Then don't analyze my suitcase," I said, laughing behind him.

I followed him back out to the living room and was just getting ready to open the door when a second knock came. Looking at the clock, I saw he was thirty minutes early.

Well, this should be fun.

I opened the door to a smiling Daniel. When his eyes landed on Erik's dark scowl, the smile slipped a little. I gave him an A for effort to keep it in place.

Erik stepped forward, chest to chest with Daniel, only an inch taller. "If she gets hurt in any way, I'll fucking kill you. Slowly. Painfully."

Daniel nodded once. "Noted."

"Oh, my god, Erik. Just go," I groaned, shoving him out the door.

He walked past and like Robert De Niro in *Meet the Fockers*, held his fingers to his eyes and back to Daniel, glaring the entire time.

I pulled Daniel in and slammed the door behind him.

"Everything okay?"

"Yup. Just a big brother being annoying." I shrugged. "Ready to rock n' roll?"

"Yes, ma'am."

"I just need to finish packing."

"Need help?"

I thought of all the lace bundled on my bed still. "No, I've got it. I'll only be a second."

I'd told a little fib to Erik. Yes, I did wear pretty panties for myself, but maybe I packed the sexiest for this trip. Just in case.

A girl had to be prepared for any impromptu lessons.

18

HANNA

"So, what's on the docket today?" I asked before taking another rejuvenating sip of coffee. We'd gotten into the cabin so late that we'd barely turned on the lights to check it out before collapsing in our beds.

Now, we sat in Adirondack chairs, bundled up in the enclosed porch, watching the fog slowly clear from the mountains. Perfect didn't come close to explaining this moment.

"How do you feel about hiking?"

"I'm open to it."

"Bungee jumping?"

I almost choked on my coffee. "Less open to that."

"But still open?" he asked around his laugh.

"Maybe barely a crack. So small, I'm not even sure paper could slip through."

"Okay. Okay."

"Honestly, I think I could sit here all day and watch the view change with the sun."

"It's beautiful," he agreed.

I glanced his way, stupidly hoping for a romance movie

moment, where he stared at me as he said it was beautiful, but his eyes were firmly planted on the dips and rises of the forest. Not that it mattered. Because we were friends.

"You did a good job picking the place."

"Thank you. It's the least I could do. Literally."

"I wanted to surprise you," he defended.

Daniel had let me pick which mountains we went to and where we stayed, but he planned everything else around it. I wasn't used to letting go of that much control, but I had to admit I liked the excitement of the surprise. I didn't let myself be surprised anymore, always doing my best to stay in control. Somewhere along the way, my trust grew further with Daniel, and I *liked* the idea of him surprising me.

"Speaking of surprises. Where are we going after the mountains? You never told me what location you planned?"

"It's a surprise."

"Ugh." I rolled my eyes. "At least give me a hint."

"There's water."

I glared. "That's a crappy hint, and you know it."

He merely shrugged, completely unapologetic, and maybe gloating a little. "For now, let's finish our coffee and explore. Do you have boots?"

"I sure do. Broken in and everything."

Ian and Erik used to go on local hikes, and I made them take me with them when I could.

"Perfect."

"What kind of hike is it?"

"Nothing too strenuous. Just a few miles."

Nothing too strenuous to Daniel did not mean the same thing to me, I realized almost six hours later.

"You're a savage," I panted. The last half-mile of the hike had been completely uphill, and I was pretty sure my legs would cramp up and fall off at any second.

"Hardly," he said, winking back at me, looking entirely too sexy in a knit cap and flannel shirt. He'd lost his jacket pretty early in our hike.

He hadn't trimmed his facial hair this morning, and it made him look like he was made to be a mountain man. Meanwhile, I was sure I looked like a tomato dipped in water. I could feel the sweat dripping down my temples. How the hell did someone sweat when it was forty degrees?

"Besides, around this bend, and we should be there."

"Where exactly is there?"

"The end. The views are supposed to be phenomenal."

"We've already seen a ton of views. Maybe we should skip this last one. I mean, we still have to hike the whole way back."

"This one is the best."

Part of me wanted to collapse and cry, tell him to just leave me. I was on the edge of slipping into drama queen mode.

We'd been walking along the edge of a mountain, in and out of thick trees, coming along beautiful views. Each one better than the last the higher we climbed. Just when I thought my legs would go full diva and give out without my permission, we broke through another clearing of trees.

"Holy shit," I breathed.

"Told you."

Every ache and pain slipped away at the view laid out in front of me. Daniel grabbed my hand and led me out on the layering of rocks, taking me all the way to the edge. Brown with spots of green stretched out like a thick blanket covering sharp edges and deep valleys. Everywhere I turned, the view greeted, shifting, and changing. Look to the left, the dark patch of sparkling water broke up the blanket. Turn to the right, the highest peak rose in the sky. Look straight out, a valley between the ridges stretching as far as I could see.

It was magnificent, awe-inspiring.

"I figured we'd have lunch here."

"Here?"

"Unless you're ready to turn around and head back now?"

"God, no," I said, dropping my backpack immediately.

Daniel laughed and gently pulled his down, opening up the top to pull out container after container.

"When did you pack all of this?"

"I was up before you this morning. I don't sleep in."

"Damn." I'd been up at six-thirty. I didn't usually sleep late, but that was still early for a day I didn't have to go into work. For some reason, I imagined Daniel sleeping until noon, rolling out of bed and working-slash-partying until three am, just to do it all over again.

I had to admit, seeing this settled part of him broke off a chunk of who I thought he was, to reveal who he really is.

"If you want to open the bottom zipper, I packed a blanket to lay out. Nothing much, just enough to keep the bugs off."

We sat in silence, enjoying our sandwiches, granola, and the most amazing views I'd ever seen.

Finishing off my last bite, I leaned back and sighed.

"Good?"

"Amazing." I tipped my head back and let the sun warm my face, soaking up the vitamin D. "Do you hike a lot?"

"Not as much as I'd like." He wrapped the trash up and stuffed it away before leaning back to mimic my posture. "Like I said, I don't leave Ohio often. I've done a few trails in New York when I can."

"Does Kent go with you?"

"No," he laughed. "Well, he's gone once, but only to bungee jump. He's more city, and I'm more nature."

"I kind of figured you both for city people."

"I love the city. I love Cincinnati, but Kent is more fast-paced, where I like to enjoy these moments. The isolation. The quiet.

But it's good—we mesh. He pushes me to do more, and I calm him down...while sometimes encouraging him," he added with a small smile.

"Did you hike when you were younger?"

"Some. We weren't rich, so vacations were few and far between. Not that we were poor, but we weren't traveling everywhere, and Ohio isn't the best place for hiking. A little flat."

"You could hike the cornfields," I joked.

"Thrilling adventure right there." He looked out over the edge and sucked in a deep breath, his chest stretching the edges of his shirt, before slowly letting it out. "That's why Sabrina and I always said we wanted to travel. She made me promise to take her hiking one day."

Was that his reason for this trip? I knew I'd told Erik we both had our reasons for going that had nothing to do with one another, but who did he see sitting by his side right now. I chose the mountains, but did he choose the hike to create what he missed with the one girl he loved?

The beauty of the view dimmed at the thought, and I reprimanded myself for letting it matter. It didn't matter. We were friends.

"That's the first time you've told me her name."

"Yeah." He laughed and rubbed his hand through his hair. "I don't talk about her much."

"She must have really broken your heart."

When he didn't say anything, I looked over and watched him stare out at the distance and swallow hard.

"She killed herself our Sophomore year."

The words slammed into me like a Mack truck, stealing the air from my lungs. Fire burned up the back of my throat, and I struggled to find words to say.

"Daniel," I breathed.

"I named Voy after her. She always wanted to travel, and we

promised we'd do it together. We'd talk about all the places we'd go and where we wanted to start. She was Puerto Rican, and Voy means I go in Spanish. It fit with Voyeur, so it was kind of perfect."

Unwarranted jealousy hit me, but it faded just as quick. His confession had no place to cause jealousy. This was a man confessing his hardest pain—a man who had helped me through my issues the past few months. I could do the same for him.

All of a sudden, Daniel's ability to handle my trauma almost better than anyone else around me made more sense. He hadn't just loved and lost in a breakup. He'd met death and felt its pain just as I had. He understood.

"What about you?" Daniel asked, clearing his throat and changing the subject back to lighter topics. "Did you travel?"

I had to take a moment to collect myself and flow with the shift back to lighter topics. I wanted to ask a million questions, but I couldn't imagine what it'd cost him to say those words aloud. And for all the times he didn't push me, I wouldn't push him.

"Not really. Both my parents are teachers, and three kids make traveling a little difficult. The trip to Florida was a big deal and mainly happened because Erik fronted a lot of the bill."

"Were you mad he wasn't there?" he asked softly, easing the subject to a more sensitive topic.

"No," I answered easily. I hadn't been mad at Erik at all, but it didn't mean I wasn't mad. Taking a deep breath, I admitted what I'd never admitted before—not even in therapy. Something about Daniel's confession spurred my own. I'd locked it up and shoved it away in my box, unable to deal with it on top of everything else, worried that if I let it out, the anger would swallow me. "I'm mad at myself for pushing her to go out. I'm mad at myself for resenting being her twin for months leading up to being taken." Another deep breath, letting the hardest confession slip out on the exhale. "I'm mad she didn't hold on for a few more hours. Erik showed up the next day, and she was gone." The breeze cooled the wet tracks slipping down my cheeks, and I wiped them away with shaky hands.

After a moment, Daniel's hand slipped over mine before he made his own confession. "I'm mad she killed herself. I'm mad at myself because I didn't see it coming. I'm mad I couldn't stop her."

Shifting, I curled my hand around his and held on tight, letting our confessions linger and hoped they faded away now that they were free.

"I have an idea," Daniel said. He stood and pulled me up with him. He tugged me to the very edge, with layers of rock and steep cliffs stretching below.

I watched him, unsure of his plan. He stood tall, looked out over the vast stretch of the Smokey Mountains, sucked in air, and yelled. I jerked but didn't let go of his hand. His yell vibrated off the cliffs, riling the birds, their wings flapping in the trees. When he was done with that yell, he did it again. Guttural and flooded with the rage he must have felt inside him. The power of it hit me like a thunderstorm, and I ached for all he had been holding inside.

When he'd finally stopped, his chest rose and fell over panting breaths, and he turned to me, looking lighter than when we first stood. "Your turn."

"What? M-my turn?"

"Come on, Hanna. Let it out. I know it's in you like it sat in me. Let it out."

Swallowing, I faced the vast view. Licking my lips, I opened my mouth and yelled—kind of.

"Nice squeak, I think you scared a caterpillar."

I glared and squared my shoulders.

I didn't have to yell. I didn't have to do anything.

I didn't have to open my box for him.

It didn't matter anyway.

Shouting at a bunch of trees wouldn't stop the guilt—the anger. Nothing could absolve me of being pissed at my sister for dying—for leaving me alone when we were supposed to do this forever. Together.

She left me.

She fucking left me, and I hated her for it.

And I hated myself for feeling that.

My chest shuddered, and I realized I was crying—sobbing.

It was too much. Too big. I'd opened the box, and it was swallowing me.

"Let it out," he whispered.

I sucked in as hard as I could, and I screamed. It tore from my lungs, scraped through my throat, ripped from my soul. My body shook, my eyes stung with the force of my rage.

I hunched over, expressing every last inch of it, squeezing it free.

And when I finished, I did it again.

And again.

Until Daniel joined me, and we screamed together.

For the first time, in front of something so big—so vast, my anger looked small—small enough to handle, small enough to set free.

I let nature take it.

We both did.

When I had nothing left to give, I panted, trying to calm the tears that had slipped free with everything else.

A few more moments of silence passed, and I took my first glance at Daniel, his blue eyes sparkling with their own tears.

"Thank you," I whispered, reaching to grab his other hand.

He let go to cradle my face, rubbing my tears away with his thumbs.

"I think I needed it, too. So, thank you. Thank you for pushing me on this trip."

We stood there, washed clean, studying the version of each other left behind.

I wasn't sure who moved first. I wasn't sure it mattered. I pressed up as he dipped down, and our mouths connected softly, afraid to break the fragile moment we'd created.

He drank from my lips, stroked them with his tongue, and I happily opened, needing to taste him. Sliding my arms around his waist, I held on tight, letting the intensity of us kissing wash over me.

We kissed and kissed. Not because we were at Voyeur and this was another lesson to help me accept touch. No, this was because I was Hanna, and he was Daniel, and we wanted to.

What that meant, I didn't know, but I definitely didn't care right then. Rules be damned.

Our kiss slowed to simple pecks and lingering tastes until we stopped, resting our foreheads together. I waited for him to tell me we shouldn't have done that. That kissing was a mistake. That we should forget it happened.

Instead, he whispered. "We should head back before it gets dark."

Unable to help it, I groaned, and he laughed. "Can you carry me?"

"Not a chance in hell."

I glared but smiled too, hoisting my backpack, ready to leave this cliff behind and everything I set free with it.

That night we didn't touch or talk about the kiss or act like anything had changed—and maybe it hadn't. Maybe what happened on the cliff in a moment of extreme emotions, stayed on the cliff. Which didn't sound terrible.

We started a fire and had a quiet dinner before crawling into our beds. But as soon as my head hit the pillow, I got back up and crept to his room. The door creaked as I slid it open, and he rolled over, the light from the hallway revealing his scrunched brows.

"You okay?"

"Yeah," I said, stepping further in the room. "Can I sleep with you tonight? I don't want to be alone."

He paused for only a second before scooting to the left. "Of course. Sure."

I climbed in, and without hesitation, he pulled me into his bare chest. We didn't discuss if this broke any rules or what issue this was helping me with. In that moment, we were two people finding comfort in each other after a long day.

I curled up like I belonged there, and in moments fell asleep, one final thought following me into sleep.

I was falling for Daniel, and I never wanted to let this go.

19

DANIEL

"Are you okay?"

Hanna glanced away from the window and offered a smile that didn't reach her eyes. "Yeah. It's just been a long time since I've been to the beach."

"I'm so sorry. If I would have known..." I'd almost called the whole thing off when she'd told me she hadn't been to the beach since her vacation where she and Sofia were taken. She'd promised me everything was fine, and I'd made some phone calls to ensure she didn't question her safety at all.

"No," she rushed to reassure, fully facing me in the backseat now. "It's okay. I'm with you. I'm okay."

That shouldn't make me feel as good as it did, like superman ready to conquer anything for her.

Something shifted between us in the mountains. I'd kissed her. Not for her or some effort to help her, but for me. Because I wanted to, and despite her crawling in my bed each night, curling into my chest, we hadn't done it again.

I wasn't sure how I felt about that.

Every night I thought about it, and every night I convinced

myself it was a mistake. We were friends. Friends supporting one another. Friends that didn't kiss because it made us feel better than we had in years. Friends who'd specifically made a rule to not kiss to avoid the feelings tickling my chest.

"I hope you like it."

"I have no doubt." She beamed at me, her green eyes shining under the flashes of sunlight pouring in. "I can't believe you expedited a passport."

"It helps when you have certain clients at Voyeur and a bit of luck. A little cancellation and pushing a paper to the top and viola—a passport in less than two weeks." Looking past her shoulder, I saw the large cream archways greeting us. "We're here."

She whirled around and, like a kid in a candy shop, she pressed as close to the glass as possible. "Holy. Shit," she said, her breath fogging the glass. "This hotel is huge."

"We're actually not staying in the hotel."

"What?" She turned back, eyes wide with curiosity and excitement.

"I uh..." I stumbled over my words, running a hand through my hair. "I may have gone a little overboard. I got a cabana on the ocean."

Her jaw dropped and stretched into the biggest smile I'd ever seen. "Holy shit," she screeched so loud even the driver cringed.

"You're okay with boats, right?"

"Yeah."

"Good. We have to take one to the island with the cabanas."

Another squeal. This one accompanied by bouncing in her seat.

After checking in, our driver took us around to a boat that then dropped us off at the dock of our island. Hanna almost squealed again, bouncing from foot-to-foot when the hotel staff greeted us with champagne before taking us to our cabana. Hanna looked around in wonder as our bags were delivered.

"Thomas will be your butler for your stay," the attendant explained. "If you need anything at all, please let him know."

I waved everyone off and turned to Hanna, who looked like a bomb waiting to go off.

"A butler? A BUTLER," she exclaimed when the door shut. She set her champagne down and jumped in my arms. "Thank you, Daniel." She wriggled with excitement, and I had to laugh. Her joy was contagious. "God, my cabin sucks ass. I'm glad we went there first because this would be impossible to top."

I sat her down and handed her a glass. "The cabin was amazing—perfect." She scrunched her face, doubtful but still smiling. "I hope you don't mind the single bed. If so, I can sleep on the love nest or that big net out there." I gestured to the round swing on the deck and the rectangle hammock above the ocean. "So many options."

"It's not like I haven't been sleeping with you these past few days. And I'm not sure that can be classified as a bed. It's its own island."

The cabana was only one large room with a dinette area to the left, the bed in the middle, and the bathroom closed off on the right. The most real estate was outside, past the glass walls, on an oversized patio. Two seating areas, an infinity pool, outdoor shower, a dock that led down to the water, and the large hammock took up all the other space.

"Daniel, look at this." Hanna pulled my attention to where she stood in front of the bed. "We have a glass floor. I can see fish. This is insane."

"How about we order another bottle of champagne and enjoy our room for the rest of the day?"

"Hell yes." She downed her glass and dug into her suitcase for her suit before disappearing into the bathroom.

I lingered on the deck, taking in the clear blue ocean

stretching on for miles, only broken up by dark patches of seaweed.

Sound behind me had me turning around and freezing. "Jesus, Hanna."

She looked down at the scraps of black covering everything important. "What? It's not like you haven't seen it all anyway."

I held my breath, waiting for one wrong move to have her breasts spilling out of her tiny top. My cock grew hard just imagining it, and I realized that maybe we should have stayed in the mountains, where she'd been bundled under layers.

"I know," I choked out. "But barely wrapped up like that is alluring as hell."

She waggled her brow and wiggled her body, pulling a groan from deep in my chest. "Well, go get changed so I can ogle you too. It's only fair."

I walked into the bathroom and wondered if I had time to jerk off before heading back out there. Deciding against it, I quickly pulled on my trunks and went back out. She greeted me with over the top catcalls from the infinity pool, breaking the tension from before.

"You want to head into the ocean?" I asked.

"I want to do it all," she exclaimed, exiting the pool, rivulets of water trailing down her soft skin.

We walked down the steps and jumped into the water, our toes digging into the soft sand. She swam around me in circles, and we talked about nothing and everything. Work, family, games we liked to play, everything.

"We should dry off if we want to have dinner at some point tonight."

"You want to rest on the hammock?" she suggested.

Honestly, I would have done whatever she wanted me to. My feelings were tipping in a dangerous direction, and I wasn't sure there was anything I could do to stop them. The longer they continued, the less I was sure I wanted to stop them.

I climbed on first, and she followed, log rolling into my side, laughing. She rested her head on my shoulder and got comfortable pressed to my side.

"Daniel," she said, tipping her head back to look at me. "I have a confession to make."

Her breath tickled my skin, and I held my breath, scrambling to prepare for whatever came out of her mouth next.

"I'm a little tipsy," she giggled, pressing closer against me. "Maybe we can nap here for just a bit before dinner."

My lungs compressed, exhaling the tension. "Sure. That sounds perfect."

I didn't sleep. And when she rolled to her side, I slid my arm around her shoulders. I held her close, relishing each puff of air brushing against my chest. Unintentionally memorizing the way her curves pressed to my hard edges, doing my damnedest to convince myself that the warmth expanding in my chest was friendship. Just friendship.

"WE DON'T HAVE to go out. They can set up a whole dinner here on the patio if you want."

Hanna popped her head around the corner from the bathroom. "This resort is too nice to not explore."

"I know. I just didn't know if you'd feel more comfortable not roaming."

"It's okay," she said, not concerned at all. "I have you by my side. I'm good."

The warmth from earlier grew until she stepped out from behind the door, and then it all flooded south. "You look...stunning."

"This old thing? I've had it for years."

Pastel flowers decorated the light blue material that stretched all the way to her feet. The slits on each side played peekaboo with her slender legs. The thin spaghetti straps looked tested to their limits containing her breasts.

"You look good, too. I like the buttons undone. Very sexy." She pursed her lips in an exaggerated sexy pout. She was playing with me, and here I was about to come with a strong breeze because of some cleavage.

I was a dick.

Taking a deep breath, I shoved it down and offered my arm, leading her out to where the boat would take us back to the main island.

We chose to immerse ourselves in the location and taste the Caribbean flavors at an upscale restaurant. The breeze from the ocean blew strands of her dark hair across her smiling face the whole meal and she would laugh each time.

This Hanna, the one who'd bounced her way from one thing to the next, hyped up on excitement and pure joy, this was the real Hanna. This was the Hanna who let go of any trauma that clung to her. The one who didn't wear the weight of survivor's guilt.

This was the Hanna I wanted to crack open permanently and not only away on vacation. I didn't want her to bury herself back into work and pull back from every touch when we left here. I wanted this joy for her all the time.

And when she smiled across the candlelit table, I knew I'd do anything to make it happen.

I also knew I needed to remember it wasn't my place to make it happen. She didn't want a relationship just as much as I hadn't—didn't. Still didn't. Nothing had changed in this, and I needed a strong reminder of it.

"How's flirting going?" I asked abruptly.

She blinked, thrown by the subject change. I kicked myself when her smile dimmed, and she dropped her gaze to her glass.

"It's okay," she said, shrugging. "I haven't really tried much."

I shut down the gloating arrogance trying to break free. "What about Sean?"

She bit her lip and smiled. This time it pierced painfully because it wasn't for me. "I think he's tried to ask me out a few times, but I manage to run before I'm forced to answer."

"Do you want to sleep with him?"

Say yes.

Say no.

Say yes.

Please, say no.

God, the thought of her saying yes shouldn't squeeze my lungs like a half-ton of bricks.

"I don't know." Another shrug. "What if I can't?" she whispered.

I swallowed the lump threatening to choke me. "You will. It will come. With comfort and time."

Her wide eyes jumped to mine and held like she was probing for an answer. Her gaze poked and prodded, and I did my best to hold her stare. When I was sure I'd lunge across the table and drag her to a dark corner, she finally looked away.

"Are you seeing anyone?" she asked before downing the last of her wine.

"No. And I don't usually see anyone for longer than a night," I added to reaffirm for the both of us that I don't date. "Even so, I've been busy."

No one had grabbed my interest since her, but I figured that was better left unmentioned.

"Oh." She licked her lips and opened her mouth, only to be cut off by the waiter.

"Any dessert?"

I looked to her and she shook her head. "No. I think we're good."

"Very well. Thank you for dining with us this evening."

When he walked away, I dropped some cash on the table for the tip. "Are you ready to go?"

"Sure."

On the boat, Hanna closed her eyes for the short trip and let the wind blow her hair back. Stunning. It was the only word I could use to describe her. Full lips, sharp cheekbones, bravery embedded in every inch of her. She was just stunning.

I climbed off first and offered my hand, helping her out of the boat. She immediately stripped out of her shoes, and just before we could head to our cabana, she stopped, turning toward the open bar on the other side of the dock.

"Let's go dance."

"What?"

A devious smile in place, she grabbed both hands and tugged me toward the vibrant music and steel drums.

As nice and organized as our dinner was, this place was the opposite, more like a bar, and the dance floor was wherever you wanted it to be.

Hanna decided that the edge of the open area was where she wanted to be. She held my hands and swayed side to side, her thighs peeking out from her slits. Her head rolled on her shoulders, her hair brushing her skin. I barely swayed with her, merely holding tight and getting lost in her moves.

She tugged me forward, licking her lips as she collided with my chest. Sliding her hands around my neck, she smiled up at me, and I held onto her waist, growing harder with each pass of her hips.

I tried to repeat that this was nothing, that this wasn't a lesson I could teach her on. This was two friends dancing on vacation together.

My words were worthless, and my eyes slid closed as her nails dragged over the back of my scalp, sending chills down my spine. She pulled me down until she could whisper in my ear.

"You know," she started and then hesitated.

I tugged back to see her eyes. They dropped away, but I saw the nerves. "Hanna, what is it?"

They flicked back to mine, and I tried to be the comfort she always found within me. "You know, we haven't tried everything yet. Just because we're not at Voyeur doesn't mean we can't do a lesson."

I swallowed, trying for the same aloofness I'd had the first time I'd offered to be hers. "Like I said, my body is yours."

Her eyes darkened and she breathed hard through her nose. "Will you sleep with me? Wi-will you let me go down on you?"

Oh. Holy fuck.

Without thinking it through, my grip tightened on her waist, and I shoved her back, needing the distance.

Hanna's face fell, her eyes immediately brimming with tears. "I-I'm sorry." She looked away, dropping her hands. "I shouldn't have taken advant—"

"No, stop," I pleaded, pulling her hands back to my shoulders, but still keeping a little distance. "Hanna, you are delicious, and in case you couldn't tell, I've been hard this whole time, and here you are, offering to put those luscious lips on me." I closed my eyes and breathed in deep before continuing. "I needed to step back before throwing you over my shoulder and taking you in a dark corner."

"Oh," she breathed.

"Yeah. Oh."

"So, that means you want to?" she asked slowly.

Fuck yes, almost tumbled from my lips without thought, but this wasn't a woman propositioning me at Voyeur. This was

Hanna, and I wanted to handle her offer with care. "You are a gorgeous woman and if this is what you really want—"

"It is. With you," she interjected.

"Are you sure?"

She laughed. "Daniel. You're pretty gorgeous yourself, and I'm comfortable with you. If there's anyone I think I can do this with—*want* to do this with—it's you. I trust you."

The last woman who trusted me, I'd let down spectacularly.

I wouldn't do that to Hanna.

"Okay."

20

HANNA

"Okay?" I asked, just to confirm I didn't imagine what I wanted to hear.

His lips tipped up on one side. "Yes. I'd be honored."

With my lip pinned beneath my teeth, I looked down, unable to meet his sky-blue eyes when nerves kicked in. "Do you want to head back?" I asked softly.

"Not quite yet. Give me one minute and maybe a few more dances."

"Okay," I answered slowly.

He walked toward an employee and talked briefly before returning. "Now, about those dances."

He held his hand out, and I didn't hesitate to let his large palm engulf my smaller one. The slow beat reached across the sand and begged us to get closer. It was like the musician knew we'd made a deal to sleep together tonight and encouraged the mood. Although, I was sure half the people here were couples with plans to sleep together. Not many friends rented out romantic ocean bungalows.

I slid my hands up his chest and over his shoulders, letting my fingers sink into his hair. His fingers wrapped slowly around my waist, resting just above my bottom, pulling me in tight. His hard length reminded me that he'd been that way all night.

How would he feel inside me? Would it hurt? It'd always hurt before, but this was Daniel, and I had faith he would never do anything to hurt me. It was what made him the perfect candidate. That, and the desperate ache that brewed inside me, begging to bubble over and be set free.

His leg slid between mine, and he tugged me tighter. The slit on my dress parted over my thigh and made room for his leg to press right against my core. He swayed back and forth, and the motion grazed my clit, heating my body from the inside out. Somehow, I kept from pressing down and dry-humping his leg. The cool breeze off the ocean brushed my bared thigh, making me imagine what it would feel like to be naked in front of him tonight. He'd seen every inch of me, just never all at once, and the fact that I'd be completely bared felt more intimate than anything else we'd done.

He leaned down and pressed a soft kiss to the corner of my mouth before resting his forehead to mine. "Are you ready?"

"Yes."

He pulled away but never let go of my hand as he led me back to our cabana.

"Everything is as you asked," our butler said, standing stoic by the door.

"Thank you. That will be all tonight."

Chills peppered my skin at the click of the handle, like the hint of electricity and fire we'd created on the other side of the door already flowed through me, ready to burn.

Flickering flames illuminated the space. Rose petals in orange, yellow, and red decorated the floor. Fairy lights hung from the entryway out to our deck, where the ocean played the perfect music for our night.

"Daniel." I brought a trembling hand to my lips. My wide eyes took it all in before turning to him, where he stood looking a little shy.

"Too much?"

It took three swallows before I gave up on talking around the lump in my throat and shook my head.

He walked over and brushed my hair behind my ears, cradling my face. "You deserve for this to be special."

"It's perfect." I slid my tongue across my lips. "For tonight, can we forget our rules? Will you kiss m—"

I didn't even finish before his lips were on mine. The kiss started slow and sensual, but quickly our mouths became as frantic as our hands, trying to hold on to each other every way we could. He walked us backward until his legs hit the mattress.

"What do you want to do?" The words came out like sandpaper and only made my sensitive skin tingle more.

"I want to taste you," I said to his neck.

He tipped my chin and made me meet his eyes. "Whatever you want. It's yours." Never dropping my gaze, he sank to the bed and leaned back. "Take off my pants, baby. Pull me out."

I sank to my knees over the glass floor, the fish swimming beneath, and with trembling fingers undid his belt, his button, and tugged down his zipper. He lifted up so I could tug his pants down. When I hesitated, he reached under his boxer briefs and pulled his thick length free.

Holy shit.

I'd watched him stroke himself twice now, but I'd never come face-to-face with his beautiful length. He held it high, the soft head pulled tight, and flushed red. Without overthinking it, I rested my palms on his knees and shifted to fit the tip in my mouth, sucking like a sucker. He groaned when I went lower, and my tongue played along the ridges.

The rough sound almost had me jerking back, but instead, I

breathed through my nose and slowly shifted back to meet his eyes. It was those ice-blue eyes that would get me through this. The kind, comforting heat would ground me.

"Unbutton your shirt. I want to see you," I ordered. His fingers immediately went to work, and I took over the task of holding his cock in my hand, the skin soft, stretched over steel beneath my fingers. "Do-Don't look away," I stuttered nervously. What if he thought I was weird? Would he jerk back or cringe?

"Fuck me, Hanna. You're going to kill me."

I guessed he liked meeting my eyes.

"Just tell me if I do it wrong."

"You're doing amazing."

"I haven't started," I said with a laugh.

"Still fucking perfect."

I laughed, but it stopped in my throat when his shirt fell open, revealing hard ridges and bumps and valleys I wanted to explore. With one hand around his dick, the other stretched up to rest on his abs, and he did as I asked, holding my gaze as I slowly sank over his length.

I focused on the veins beneath my tongue while keeping my eyes locked on his heavy-lidded ones that looked almost as dark as the shadowed sea beneath me.

He groaned and bit his lip and almost tipped his head back in pleasure. As much as I didn't want him to look away, a flood of desire washed over me when he sat on the edge of losing control.

His hands remained glued to his sides, except for when he reached to brush my hair back so he could watch clearly.

I found a rhythm with my mouth and hand and picked up the pace, listening to his heavy pants match the quick rise and fall of his chest. "Hanna. God. Hanna. I don't want to come in your mouth. Stop, baby. I'm gonna come. Please."

I pulled off with a few more licks, and his head finally sank back on his shoulders.

"Oh, fuck," he groaned. He tipped his head back up, and I was sure I melted on the spot when his tongue slicked across his lips before they tipped on one side. "I'm not as young as I once was and need recovery time between. If I come in that pretty mouth, I may not be able to fulfill my part of the night."

"Oh."

"Yeah." He huffed a laugh and moved his thumb to brush along my lips. "Oh. Now, hop up. It's my turn."

He helped me up, standing with me. His hard length brushed my hip, but his attention was focused on skimming his lips from my shoulder, up my neck, to my ear. "I need to see you."

His fingers played with the straps of my dress, and I knew once it dropped, I'd be in nothing but my scrap of lace panties.

"Wait." He pulled his hands back, and I shoved his shirt from his shoulders. "Okay. Now we're closer to even."

"I can take it all off now if you'd like?" He offered with a smirk, his hands drifting to his already loose pants.

"I'm ready now."

His lips pressed to my neck again, and his fingers deftly flicked the straps off my shoulders, tugging to pull the material past my breasts and over my hips for it to pool at my feet. My body shuddered under his fingertips skimming up my abdomen to cup my breasts.

"You have the most beautiful tits I've ever seen. Full and high. I love the way they spill out of my hands. And these nipples." His thumbs brushed my nipples at the same time he nipped at my neck.

"Daniel."

"Whatever you need, Hanna. Ask for it."

"I—I want to get on the bed now."

He turned me and eased me back against the white fluffy comforter. In the flickering light, with the stars in the open sky behind him, he dropped his pants and stood before me like a

Greek god, all lines and definition. Then it was his turn to drop to his knees. His lips pressed to my knee, and I stared at his blond head as he worked his mouth up my thigh until he spread my legs around his broad shoulders to make room for his full lips to reach my core. He stared up at me when his tongue slid through my slit, stopping to circle my clit.

Fisting the sheets, I struggled to hold still as he did it again and again. Soon he added fingers, dropping his gaze to bury his head against my core and make love to me with his mouth.

In no time at all, my heels dug into the mattress, and I pressed my hips up, desperate for more friction as my orgasm rippled through me.

Daniel worked his mouth up my body, stopping to tongue my breasts, situating his hips between my spread thighs.

"Good, baby?" he asked against my neck.

Was I good? My body still trembled against the sheets, my core still pulsing from the soft orgasm, my mind floating in a fog, trying to ignore the dark corners that reached for me.

"I'm nervous that I'll panic. I'm not nervous about panicking. Just nervous that I will and completely ruin this. Does that make sense?"

"Yeah, and nothing will ruin this. There is no right and wrong, Hanna. Use your words, and we can stop at any point." Even in the dim light of the room, I could still find his eyes and feel the security that I was safe. "Is this okay? Or do you want to be on top to keep the pace?" He held himself above me, not letting any part of him touch me, his arms flexing on either side of my head.

Before he even finished, I shook my head. "No. I don't know what I'm doing. I—" The words caught in my throat, and I looked away, watching my fingers play along the ridges of his ribs. "I know I've done this a lot before. It's not like it's my first t—"

"No," he interrupted so gruffly, my eyes snapped to his. Where there was once tenderness, now lay a fire. Even still, I wasn't scared. "Nothing without your consent counts. This is your choice. This is the first time you are *choosing* to give your body to someone, and that is all that matters. Hanna, this is your first time."

My eyes glossed over, and again I was reduced to nodding. One tear leaked free, and he brushed it away with his lips.

Slowly, he lowered his body, his skin coming into contact with mine one inch at a time, his eyes never leaving mine. He thrust his hips, and we both groaned at the slow glide of his thick length through my folds. My sensitive clit shot electricity through me, and I clung to him, my nails already digging into his skin.

His eyes pinched shut, and he dropped his head. "Fuck, Hanna. Shit."

"What?"

"I don't have a condom," he begrudgingly admitted.

"Oh," I breathed.

"I didn't plan on this happening, so I didn't think I'd need one."

His cock slid through my folds like he couldn't help himself, and I didn't want to lose this moment. I was ready. My body was ready. My mind was ready. "Umm, I'm on the pill," I said softly. "And I'm clean. I got tested, but I underst—"

"Hey," he said, pulling my eyes back to his. "I trust you. If you're sure, I'm clean too. Hell, I've never had sex without one."

"Really?"

"Yeah, I've never been in a relationship to go without one."

"Oh, you don't have to."

"Hanna, I trust you."

I swallowed any rebuttal, trusting him in return. If he had an issue, he'd tell me. "Okay."

"God, baby. I want you."

I expected him to pull back and start working himself inside.

I tensed my thighs and braced for it, but this was Daniel, of course, he didn't rush. He slid his length through my wet pussy, again and again, kissing up and down my neck to my mouth and down to my nipples. When I least expected it, he popped off my breast and pulled back enough to push the head of his cock against my opening, slowly sliding inside.

My eyes rolled back into my head, and my lids slid closed. The darkness for the first time all night, brushed my skin, sending a chill down my spine. I squeezed my eyes shut tighter with every inch he pushed in, and held my breath, holding the memories at bay. I would do this. I could do this.

I could freaking do this.

"Hanna, baby. Look at me." Daniel stopped moving and brushed his thumb along my cheek. "Hanna. Open your eyes. Stay with me."

Clinging to his gruff voice, I relaxed my fists and thighs, and slowly slid my eyes open. The depth of his stare tugged me the rest of the way free. "Daniel," I whimpered.

"It's just me. Stay with me."

His hand slid into my hair, cradling my head, and the other moved to my hip, holding me steady as he worked himself the rest of the way in.

"Talk to me," I pleaded, more because I wanted to hear his voice rather than needed to.

"God, Hanna. I don't know if I trust myself to talk right now," he groaned, grinding his hips to mine.

"I don't care. I want to hear it. I want to hear *you*."

I didn't want this to be some encounter I remembered that got me through to the others. I wanted to remember this as the time Daniel made love to me, and I wanted him to be himself. Dirty words and all.

"What do you feel?"

He slid out and pushed back in. "Hot. Wet. Your pussy is so fucking tight, it's all I feel."

"You're all I feel, too. Stretching me. It fe—it feels good."

As if my dirty words were the scissors that frayed the leash he had on his control, his hips snapped back hard, pulling a cry from my lips.

"Does my cock feel good in your tight pussy?"

Rather than falling back into memories, I clung to him, held his stare, stayed in the present. My nipples pebbled tight and scraped his chest. "Yes. Fuck me, Daniel. Make me come."

He pulled back until just the head rested at my opening. "Hold on, baby."

And with that, his control snapped. He fucked me harder, stopping every once in a while to grind his hips to my clit, to suck my nipples, and whisper filthy things in my ear that did nothing but make me wetter. He made me listen to the slapping sounds of our flesh and admit how good I felt.

My nails dug into his back, and I clung to the reality he created—a reality I never wanted to lose. A reality that had me swirling and drowning in pleasure so deep I couldn't look anywhere but at him. I hoisted my thighs over his hips and squeezed, flexing my feet, tightening every muscle just for them to snap, breaking free, floating away into bliss.

"Hanna. Hanna." He chanted my name, thrusting ruthlessly, groaning his pleasure against my neck. A few more hard pushes until finally, he rested his full length inside me—stretching me to the max—emptying himself deep in my core.

"Fuck. Me." On shaky arms, he lifted himself off but stayed buried deep, leaning down enough to drink from my lips. "You are fucking amazing."

He pulled back, and I brushed his damp hair from his forehead, knowing I could die with the vision of his face above me, and his cock still stretching me.

"Thank you."

Another kiss before resting his head against mine. "For you? Anything."

I wanted to wrap my arms around him and hold him to me so tight he could never break free—so no inch of the real world could come between us. I wanted to live here and now.

But before I could act, he groaned and slid from my core, giving me one last kiss before rolling from the bed and heading to the bathroom. God, how did we go all this time without kissing? Even the small pecks peppered throughout our lovemaking had only added to the intensity of the moment. I wasn't sure I could stop now that we'd started. I wasn't sure I wanted to.

Before I could get under the sheets, he came back with a washcloth, gently wiping his cum from between my thighs. I shuddered when he brushed my clit again, loving the way he groaned at my reaction.

Rather than getting up again, he tossed the rag aside and shifted, so we were both under the covers.

"Are you okay?" he asked, pulling me into his arms.

Staring out at the dark night sky, the waves of the ocean not quite masking the quiet sounds of music, my pussy throbbing in the best way, burrowed in his arms. My answer was obvious.

"I've never been better."

21

DANIEL

A SMALL FIST against my chest brought me out of my sleep. Bright light filtered through the open patio, the crash of the ocean only interrupted by soft whimpers. Another hit and my attention shifted to the petite brunette struggling through a nightmare in my arms. I pulled back as much as I could as to not crowd her and add to her panic. The last thing she needed was to wake up to a man trapping her in.

"Hanna," I whispered, gently shaking her shoulder.

Her brows pinched tight. The same as my chest at seeing her in pain.

"Hanna, wake up." With another harder shake, her eyes jerked open, and her lips parted over a gasp. Her hand slapped to her heaving chest, and she stared at the ceiling as if I wasn't even there. My initial reaction was to curl her into my arms, offering her comfort, but I'd come to realize Hanna liked not being coddled. So, I went with what I would have said if she hadn't woken from a nightmare. "Good morning, gorgeous."

Wide, emerald eyes slowly turned to me, her dark hair bunching up against the white sheets. I kept my face neutral with an easy smile, shoving down any worry I had. After a few blinks, she shakily returned my smile.

"Hey."

I propped my head on my hand and resisted the urge to tug the sheet down over her breasts. Even the outline of her nipples through the thin material was enough to have me hard.

"What do you want to do today?"

I had no idea how to proceed after last night. Did I treat it like all the other nights we'd had at Voyeur—as if nothing had happened? But I didn't know how because every part of me wanted to woo her, to pull her close and make love to her again. The feel of her tight cunt squeezing me would forever be ingrained in my memory, and I'd always want more.

She shrugged her shoulders and fidgeted with her fingers over her stomach. "I don't know. What did you have in mind?"

Taking a chance, I reached over to tuck some loose strands behind her ear. As if on instinct, she turned into my touch. With that cue, I pushed my luck and dragged my fingers down, gripping the sheet on the way and tugging it past her breasts.

She pulled in the sexiest gasp as the edge brushed over the nipples that had been taunting me.

"I have a lot in mind."

When she didn't cover herself, I lowered my mouth to suck at her hardened tip.

"I think I like your ideas," she breathed.

Her hand dug into my hair, holding me to her. I pulled the tip between my teeth and bit, flicking my tongue across the bud.

"Oh, god. Daniel."

Her legs shifted under the sheet, and I moved my hand lower, slowly sliding my fingers between her folds and groaning against her skin when I found her wet and waiting. Without any hesitation, she spread her legs and pushed up, silently asking me for more.

I dipped low to gather her juices before dragging them up to pinch her clit. "Is this what you want, baby? Do you want me to play with your pussy?"

"Yes. Yes." She pressed her head back in the pillow, her eyes closed and lost to the sensation.

"You want me to make you come?"

"Please."

I pinched her clit harder, and she almost screamed. I went back to her nipples and worked my fingers fast and hard between her thighs, alternating between pushing my fingers deep inside her cunt and pulling back to torture her bundle of nerves. I needed to make her come, so I could bury myself inside her again. I needed her.

Her hips went wild, and I popped off her breast to kiss up her neck, sucking at the soft skin to feel the moans against my lips. Seconds later, she broke, crying out as her pussy spasmed. Without waiting for her to finish, I gripped her hips and pulled her over me.

"Fuck me, baby. Take control."

With her skin flushed, her messy hair falling over her breasts, she looked down at me with wide eyes. "I—I don't know what to do."

"Just go with it. Put my cock inside that tight cunt and ride me."

Her lips parted, and the green in her eyes almost disappeared as she lifted up, gripping my dick to position it at her opening. Achingly slow, she slid down my length until I filled her to the hilt.

"Oh, fuck, Hanna. Yes, baby."

Helping her get started, I held on to her hips and shifted her back and forth. That was all she needed.

She fell forward with a moan, resting her palms on my chest and lifted up just to sink down again.

Again, and again, she rode me, finding a rhythm that drove us both fucking insane.

"Fuck, Hanna. Look at you."

She bit her lip and dropped her eyes from mine, not stopping. Reaching up, I brushed her hair back and waited for her to look at me.

"You're a fucking queen. Taking my cock however you want."

Her lush lip popped free, and she smiled, picking up the pace. She leaned back with the most delicious smirk on her mouth. Her back arched, making her bouncing tits all I saw. Needing to taste her, I sat up and latched on, wrapping my arm around her waist to help her ride me harder.

We lost our rhythm, a mass of need and desire twisted together, racing for the finish.

She whimpered and ground on me with each pass, and I needed her to come before I lost my control and came first. I slid my hand between our bodies, pinching her slick clit between my fingers as I bit around her breasts.

"Daniel, Daniel. Yes. Fuck. I'm coming."

"That's it, baby. Feel it. Fuck me."

She wrapped her arms around my head and went wild, screaming her pleasure, ripping my own orgasm from me. I groaned into her skin and dug my hands into her back, needing to hold her to me.

"Wow," she breathed.

I kissed my way up her chest to her lips. I didn't know how long we were keeping the kissing around, but I planned on taking full advantage of tasting her lips every chance I got. She didn't hesitate, sliding her tongue into my mouth, feeding off my own desperation.

"You were amazing," I said against her lips.

"Yeah?"

"Fuck, yeah. Like I said. A queen in control of all she wants."

Her lips spread against mine, and it felt like heaven. Her in my arms, my cock still inside her pussy, filled with my cum. Her soft breasts against my hard chest. Our arms locked tight around each other like we never wanted to let go.

Perfection.

"Okay, so *now* what should we do?" she asked.

"How about a swim?"

"That sounds really good."

"Now."

"Ummm..." she stuttered, her eyes shooting wide when I flipped her over and climbed out of bed in all my naked glory. "What?" she squeaked.

"Come on. We've got the ocean at our fingertips and a private pool even closer. Let's take a swim."

My smile grew when she couldn't stop her eyes from scanning my body, watching each step I made closer to the pool.

"I should get my suit. Someone may see."

"No one will see. But if you want us to wear our suits, we can." I wanted to push her, but just because she let me into her body didn't mean all her fears vanished around me. She always needed to know she had an out.

She sat up, holding the sheet to her chest and nibbled her lips, watching me put both feet in the water, slowly progressing down the steps. Her eyes dropped to my semi-hard cock, and I shrugged. "You make me feel like a teenage boy. You're damn sexy in the morning."

She blushed and dropped her head, but not before I saw her lips twitch into a smile. I'd sunk down into the water, pushing back to the other side when she finally made her decision.

"Ugh, fine," she groaned, rolling her eyes. She whipped the sheet back and held one arm across her breasts, doing nothing to hide their bounce with each step, and one hand over her pussy, as she tiptoed her way over to the pool, looking both ways like someone would pop out at any moment.

"Don't laugh at me," she reprimanded, sinking up to her neck in the water.

"Me? I'd never laugh at you."

She rolled her eyes and splashed me with water before sitting on the bench under the water. She closed her eyes and breathed deep, opening them on an exhale to stare out at the ocean. "This is beautiful."

"It is," I agreed, looking at her, my back to the ocean.

She blushed but cocked a brow and pursed her lips. "Way to be corny," she deadpanned.

I shrugged and made my way to sit beside her. "I'm just telling the truth."

She splashed me again, and I shifted to grip her waist, pulling her out to the middle of the infinity pool.

"Don't you dare."

"What? Don't do what?" I asked innocently, jerking her like I would dunk her.

She squealed and clung tight to my shoulders, wrapping her legs around my waist. We both froze when my dick brushed against her bottom, and her heat pressed to my stomach.

"Sorry," she whispered, looking achingly unsure of herself.

"Me too."

She cocked her head to the side, unsure what I was apologizing about, only getting a second to catch her breath before I dunked us both.

"Dammit, Daniel." She brushed her hair out of her face and slapped my shoulder.

I pretended I would do it again and laughed at more of her high-pitch threats. Anything to keep my focus away from her soft breasts pressed to my chest. I didn't want to scare her with how much I wanted her.

Removing temptation, I sat her back on the bench and went to sit beside her again. We sat in silence, watching the sun glint off the clear ocean, enjoying the peaceful moment.

I didn't know what prompted me to ask, but the nightmare from this morning came back, and curiosity got the best of me. Maybe the progress we'd made on the mountain. Maybe the voice in the back of my head that kept pushing me to make it all better before it was too late. "Why don't you talk at the charity event?"

She stiffened beside me, and the air around us changed. "Because I don't need to. There are plenty of other women who have a story to tell."

"So do you."

"And I've talked to my therapist about it. I don't need to tell everyone."

"Like I said, maybe it'd be good to talk to like-minded people. To own what happened."

Her hair whipped the side of my face with the force she turned to look at me. "I don't want to own it," she snapped.

I should have stopped there, but my stupid misplaced need to get my point across rose above rational thought. "I'm just saying, it's nothing to be ashamed of. Maybe it would help."

"How would telling everyone I was raped almost every day for four fucking months help? Hmm, Daniel?"

Her words landed like a punch to the gut, knocking the wind out of me. It's one thing to know what happened without the details. You can just pin it down to a bad thing and never think too much on it. It can remain a blurred image if you don't look at it too hard. It's entirely different to have the details laid out to where you can't do anything but acknowledge them. And that's what I had to do. I had to acknowledge that Hanna had been raped. Not once or twice, but over and over, and for the first time since meeting her, I wasn't able to hide my shock. I wasn't able to gloss over and pretend nothing happened.

"I just thought it would show how strong you were," I answered lamely.

For as weak as my words were, hers were just as strong—fueled by anger. "I wasn't fucking strong, Daniel. I wanted to die every fucking day. I prayed for it—begged for it to be over, any way possible. Sofia was the one that wanted to survive—who never gave up. But fuck both of us because she died, and I didn't."

More truths bringing me to my knees. It seemed I got Hanna to open her box, but it wasn't going the way I'd imagined. It didn't feel like helping. Was I making it worse? Was this a mistake? Was this what I had done to Sabrina—made it worse? Panic pressed on my chest; the euphoria of the morning gone.

"Hanna," I almost pleaded with her to hear me—to hear what I realized she couldn't see in herself. "You *are* surviving. You're here living your life even when it's hard. Talking to others lets them know it's possible. It gives you something to be proud of."

She was beyond hearing me. She'd scooted back, her shoulders tight, and her jaw clenched. "What about you?" she practically sneered. "Have you let it out?"

Warnings went off in my head, and I squared my own shoulders. I didn't like being cornered, and Hanna was doing her best to get out of the corner I'd put her in, by forcing me into my own. I'd opened myself to her to make her feel safe enough to open to me. I hadn't done it to be psychoanalyzed. I didn't need to talk about Sabrina. I didn't *want* to.

I braced myself, fortifying my walls, knowing how I lashed out when Sabrina was brought up outside of my control and not wanting to do it to her just because she was hurting from the mess *I* put us in. "I don't have anything to let out."

"Really?" she asked, slapping the water. "You don't talk about your precious Sabrina."

"That doesn't hold me back," I ground out—*I lied.*

She rolled her eyes and scoffed. "Says the man who didn't

even mention she *died*. Are you even honest with yourself about her, Daniel? Or do you tell yourself it's fine?" She pushed harder, her anger hitting me in my weakest spots. "Says the man who wants to be alone his whole life to avoid getting hurt. That seems rational and not at all keeping you from living life. You pretend you don't have a box you shove everything into. Like you don't lie to yourself just like everyone else."

Crack.

Just like that, she broke through the flimsy walls. I hadn't had enough time to erect them—my guard down—and she reached the raw anger underneath.

"This isn't about me. All of this is for *you*. *You* needed my help. You *asked* for it. I didn't ask for you and your sad attempt to help me to avoid your own issues. Because that's what you do, Hanna. Avoid. Your. Issues."

Hanna sat back and lifted her chin, looking down her nose at me, as if she could get high enough, I wouldn't be able to see the pain glossing over her eyes. She didn't even lash back. She merely pulled her shoulders back and turned to leave, not bothering to cover herself as she climbed the stairs.

I let her go.

I'd fucked up and ruined the morning but was too mad—too vulnerable—to go after her right now. I knew I'd apologize for being an epic dick, but I just needed to breathe.

The bathroom door slammed, and I cringed, hating myself. Panic gripped me when I thought maybe I'd pushed too far too fast after everything we'd done in the last twenty-four hours. My lungs seized with fear that maybe I'd thrown everything at her when she was at her weakest, and now she was in the bathroom doing God knew what.

I just wanted you to love me. But I wasn't good enough. I loved you so much, Daniel. Why couldn't you have loved me? I wanted to spend forever with you. Be your wife. I could have waited for you to be ready. I know we're young, but no one was ever going to want me like I am. I wanted to wait for you, but I needed to do it as more than your friend. I know I said I was fine, but I'm not. I needed more. You're all I have and if you couldn't love me. No one will. And I can't live with that. I'm never going to be good enough. Never. So, why bother. I can't do it anymore. It's too hard. Life is too hard. My mind is too hard to live with. I just wanted to love you. I wanted you to love me. I can't do this. I'm sorry. Even if you don't love me, I'll always love you.

She'd killed herself that night when I went out with Kent.

Bile rose up my throat, and I almost fell on the deck in my rush to run to the bathroom. I slammed against the door, ready to fling it open, only to find it locked.

"Hanna," I shouted, slapping my palms to the door. "Hanna. Open up, baby. I'm sorry. Please, open up." Sweat beaded on my forehead, and I took in the door, looking for the weak spot to break it open. "Fuck, I'm sorry, Hanna. Talk to me. Please."

I shook the handle, the adrenaline flooding my muscles, making me feel like I could rip it off.

I didn't need to worry about it because, in the next instant, the door flung open. Hanna stood with a towel wrapped around her body, her hair sopping wet, hanging down her back. Her beautiful green eyes wide in shock.

Without any thought at all, I yanked her into my arms, squeezing her too tight, but not caring.

"Daniel? What the hell?" she asked with no heat.

"I'm sorry I pushed. I just wanted to help, and I pushed too hard, and I snapped when I shouldn't have."

She pushed against my chest, but held on to my arms, looking up with furrowed brows. I could only imagine what I looked like. I could only imagine the wild fear marring my features.

"Are you okay?" she asked slowly.

Swallowing, I take deep breath after deep breath to get

myself under control. "Yeah," I breathed. "I'm sorry I snapped. And you stormed off, and I panicked. I just worried when you locked yourself in here—I just..."

I just worried you'd hurt yourself like Sabrina, and it would be all my fault.

I couldn't admit it, but I think she understood because her hands slowly moved up and down to soothe me.

"I'm okay. I think we both just needed to cool down."

"Yeah." I nodded and took another deep breath, leaning down to press a kiss to the top of her head. "I'm sorry. Really fucking sorry. I lashed out, and it was wrong. You know I want to help you. Hell, I offered, and I'm a gigantic asshole for making you question that. I'm sorry."

Her shoulders relaxed, and the Hanna from the past few months shined through a little more than moments ago.

"I shouldn't have pushed you."

She nodded. "You shouldn't have. And I shouldn't have pushed you either. I'm sorry, too."

"I just worry. I like you. And as you pointed out, I'm aware of how shit can break free at the worst time." If I wasn't aware of that before, my near panic from seconds ago made it clear as day. "I don't want that for you."

She stepped out of my arms and crossed her own across her chest but looked more open like she had this morning. "I understand. I guess I can appreciate you looking out for me," she said with a small smile. "Just not today."

"I can agree to that."

I ran my hands through my hair and became very aware of the fact that I was still naked. Especially when her eyes dropped down my body, and she flushed.

"So, what now?" she asked softly.

"How about you finish getting ready, and we check out the island activities?"

"Sounds like a plan."

"I'm sorry again," I said before she could close the door. I could see the doubt still lingering from our argument. Maybe that was why I let another one of my truths free. "I'm sorry for thinking the worst when you stormed off. I guess my past snuck up on me when I least expected it. I just wanted to make sure you were fine."

Her green eyes softened in understanding. "It's okay. I promise you, Daniel. I'm fine."

That's what she said too.

22

HANNA

"You can do this, Hanna. Just go up. Drop the papers off. Act like nothing happened. Ignore the big brother knowing glare."

I stood behind my office door, a stack of papers firmly in my grip, and pep talked myself into heading upstairs.

I got back on Saturday and skipped the family dinner last night because I wasn't sure my week away with Daniel wouldn't be written all over my face. I dreaded the thought of them knowing I slept with him. I dreaded them knowing that I'd begun falling for him.

I dreaded *anyone* knowing that.

Especially Daniel, the man who didn't do relationships.

We'd promised friendship and no feelings, and here I was, trying to calm my racing heart just thinking of him.

I couldn't even blame it on the sex. This feeling, these butterflies and warmth, and tingling awareness had been there for a while. A slow build that consumed me on this trip. The sex had only made it so apparent, not even I could deny it anymore.

And if I couldn't deny it, how the hell was I supposed to hide it?

"Ugh." I barely managed to stop from banging my head on the door. Taking a deep breath, I stood up straight, shoulders back, chin high. "I can do this. I can be a blank face. No one has to know anything. If worse comes to worst, just run away. Totally rational."

Having talked myself up enough, I opened the door and proceeded to walk right into a wall, dropping my stack of papers.

"Oh, shit."

"Fuck, I'm sorry," we said at the same time.

Sean crouched down with me to help me stack the papers.

"It's totally my fault. I was in a zone," I excused.

"No, no. I wasn't looking where I was going."

We stood, and I finally met his blue eyes, so much darker than Daniel's. He gave a soft smile, bringing out the dimple I used to get lost staring at. Now, I found myself looking past him, down the hall to where I needed to go.

"How was your trip?"

"Oh, good," I said, bringing my attention back to him.

"We—*I* missed you around the office."

His words were soft, only for me, and my cheeks flamed at the intimacy. A couple of weeks ago, I was desperate to flirt with this man, to find the courage to go on a date with him, but now all I saw when I looked at him was not Daniel.

Trying to hide my reaction, I dropped my head, looking at the floor. "Yeah, it was a long trip. But my first vacation. So, yeah."

My cheeks flamed hotter with each stuttering word. This time it wasn't because of a rush of adrenaline thinking about flirting with him, but more about how unbelievably awkward I felt. I needed to get going before I made it worse.

"Well, I should—"

"Now that you're back—"

We spoke at the same time, and he gestured for me to talk first.

I held up my stack of papers like a shield. "I should get these dropped off."

He ran a hand through his hair and stepped back enough to be noticeable, but quickly covered it with a smile. "Yeah. Sure. Maybe I'll see you around the lunchroom again. Missed those math puns."

"You know what they say. Math puns are the first *sine* of madness," I said, walking past him, giving an awkward laugh to go with the lame pun.

Still, he smiled, and all I could think was that it didn't affect me like it did before. Not like Daniel's.

I skipped the elevator and took the stairs, waving to Erik's assistant, Laura, as I passed.

"He's not in right now," she said.

I almost sagged in relief at not having to face him.

"But Alex is in there. His meeting is running late, so she's waiting."

Shit. Alex was worse than Erik. She'd see through the best of masks I could create. I considered dropping the papers off with Laura and avoiding the office altogether, but deep down, I didn't hate the idea of talking to Alex. She'd give me shit, but she'd also listen, and maybe that was what I needed.

"Hey," I said, pushing the door open and closing it behind me. I'd need privacy and a sign if Erik was back. God forbid he overhear anything.

"Hey to you," Alex greeted from behind Erik's desk. "Long time, no see. How was your vacation?"

"Good." And just like that, I blushed and smiled. "Great, actually."

When I found the courage to peek up from under my lashes across the room, Alex had both eyebrows pushed high over wide eyes.

"What?" I asked, all innocence.

She blinked unimpressed.

"Come on. I brought Erik lunch, but he's not here to eat it, and I have a feeling fries are going to be needed for this conversation."

She grabbed the bag and gestured for me to follow her to the seating area. "It was just a trip," I said, laughing awkwardly. I didn't know why I continued pretending when we both knew I'd spill eventually.

"Where did you go? You look tan."

"We went to Asheville and the Caribbean."

"The mountains and the ocean. Not bad." She nodded and shoved a handful of fries in her mouth. She considered me as she chewed. "Now, did you start having feelings for him before the trip or during?"

I choked on my drink, unprepared for her directness. I thought we had more time of innocence and beating around the bush. "What?"

"I mean, you've always stared at him with googley eyes, but who wouldn't. He's hot. But now, just mentioning your trip, I thought you'd melt into a puddle right before my eyes, and I didn't even mention him yet."

"Maybe I just enjoyed my trip that much."

"The mountains and ocean aren't that great. Unless there is a sexy man with you. Tell me," she started, one brow cocked high. "Did you continue your lessons while you were there?"

Not even bothering to look away, I took a huge bite of my burger, buying time.

"So, you did," she assumed correctly.

"It doesn't mean anything."

"It obviously does."

"It doesn't to him."

Alex's deviousness softened to concern, and she turned serious. "Are you sure?"

Flashes of Daniel above me, watching me so closely as he moved inside me. The way he held my hand like I was his haven when he fell apart in my arms. The way we made love anywhere and everywhere we could on our trip. The way he always made sure I knew I was safe. The way he kissed me and made me forget this wasn't anything but a way to get me comfortable with touch.

Sometime over the trip, the lines blurred. I just didn't know if they only blurred for me, or maybe they had for him too.

"We said no relationships."

"Things change. Do you feel like they've changed?"

"For me, they have. But I can't tell if it's just for me. Maybe I'm imagining the way he looks at me because I want it to be more."

"I understand. But maybe you're not imagining it." We both stopped to take a bite, thinking over the possibility. "What happened on the trip? What happened that made you realize it was more?"

Biting my cheek, I considered not telling her, pretending nothing happened, but why bother. I needed to tell someone. "We slept together."

Her eyes grew comically wide before her jaw dropped and stretched into a smile. "Noice."

I couldn't help but laugh. "Oh my god. Stop."

"Tell me about it? Good? Big? Long? Hooked to the left? Maybe right?"

"Stop." I laughed harder, my hands covering my face.

"Oh, come on. I'll tell you about Erik."

"Ew. No. Please, don't. I'll tell you what you want to know, just please, not that." She smiled victoriously and gestured for me to spill the beans. "It was great. More than great. It was perfect."

"Was it like fucking? Or did it feel like more?"

I thought back to the moments he never looked away, moving slow and hard. Then I thought back to the moments he nipped at my breasts and held my hips in a bruising grip, and he lost control. "Yes."

"Damn," she breathed. "Both? That's the best."

I took the last bite of my burger to avoid saying anything else.

"Have you thought about telling him how you feel?"

"God, no. I just realized it myself. I need to make sure it's not some rash feeling based on him being the first guy I slept with."

"If it makes you feel better, he seems different with you. I don't know him very well, but the way he looks at you reminds me of the way Erik looks at me."

"Ugh." I dropped my head to my hands. "What would you do?"

"Well, with all of my knowledge from my one relationship ever..."

"I know. It's like the blind leading the blind here."

"We could always ask Carina," she suggested.

"I already know what she would say."

"Go for it," we both said together.

Once we stopped laughing, Alex sobered. "I don't know, Hanna. Maybe just let it ride and see where it goes. The bottom line is you have to consider each outcome. You could tell him, and he could feel the same. Or you could tell him and..."

"And he pulls way back, and I lose my friend."

"Like I said, consider each option and find the best one. Sometimes the best one is the one that still hurts but maybe hurts the least. Sometimes, there's no good answer."

That's what scared me the most. At the end of this, I'd end up just as damaged as when I started.

23

DANIEL

I opened the door, and for a moment, froze just to take Hanna in. Somehow, even dressed down, she managed to steal my breath. Like she was in risqué lingerie, instead of jeans, a black tank, and an oversized cardigan.

"Hey," she said, bringing me out of my stupor.

"Hey. You came."

"Of course, I did," she said, laughing, stepping past me into my apartment. "Besides, why wouldn't I?"

I closed the door and led her to the kitchen, pondering how I wanted to answer her question. I could think of a million reasons that she should stay far away from me, but the one most prevalent was that she didn't need me anymore.

"I figured we covered all the bases, so to speak."

Another laugh. This was with a shy smile and a blush.

Somewhere over our time in the Caribbean, boundaries blurred. Justifying my actions by saying I wanted to help her couldn't mask the way I craved her. I couldn't lie and say I did it all for her. I wanted to be around her for me. I liked her. A lot.

And breaking down those boundaries left me in a limbo I didn't know how to navigate.

Did she want to continue how we were those last few days on the beach, like a couple who had a right to touch and kiss? Or did she want to go back to friends, who only touched at Voyeur?

I guessed tonight would test the last one. I invited her to my apartment because I wanted privacy and time.

"You're still my friend. Whether the benefits end or not."

She perched on the edge of a bar stool as I grabbed a bottle of wine, but I stopped at her words. She said them as a statement, but I heard the question behind them—the same uncertainty that swirled inside me slipped out with one sentence.

I set the wine on the counter and waited for her to meet my eyes. "Like I said, I'm all yours."

Her hand slid over mine to grab the glass and stayed there. The moment stretched as we danced around the real question of what we were doing, or better yet, how much longer we could do it before something imploded.

I wasn't ready yet. I couldn't have the actual conversation our eyes were sharing right now. I cleared my throat and softly extracted my hand.

"It's no hardship. You're a beautiful woman."

"You're not too bad yourself."

"I do the best I can for my age," I joked with a wink.

"Yeah, I mean, how old are you? Sixty? Seventy?" She tried to hide her smile behind her glass, but her eyes glimmered with humor.

"You're a riot."

"Numbers are my jam. What can I say?"

"Speaking of numbers, how was heading back to work today?"

What I really wanted to ask was, *how was it seeing what's his face? Did you flirt? Did you finally accept his date? Is this ending soon because you're good to go now that you know you can have sex?*

"It was fine. I had lunch with Alex and avoided the third degree from Erik by hiding in my office and catching up on work."

"He worries about you."

I worried about her. We'd managed to move past our argument in the Caribbean and enjoyed each other the rest of the trip, but I couldn't shake her denial of the past still bothering her. Every time she snapped about it and then said she was fine, my fears grew. How much longer could she go before she exploded?

"That he does. And I love him for it. But I'm also in the latter half of my twenties. At some point, I have to be able to live my life without explaining everything like I'm twelve. Hell, my mom and dad don't even pester me so much."

"I can't imagine. David and I were wild, but as long as we didn't set anything on fire or get arrested, our parents didn't really care."

"And were you able to do that?"

"I never got arrested. We may have set a few things on fire."

"You hellion," she joked. "So, what do you have planned for tonight?"

Walking around the bar, I studied her, tried to pick up on any nerves she may have. The closer I got, the harder the pulse against her neck got. Her lips parted when I slid my hand against her neck, moving up into her hair. Her eyes dilated, almost swallowing every centimeter of green when I fisted my hand and jerked her head back.

She gasped but quickly looked down, hiding her reaction like she always did when a bite of pain turned her on. Her body and mind were at war, and my goal tonight was to make sure they were in sync.

"Is that okay?" I asked softly.

She still didn't look up but nodded as much as my grip would allow. I scanned down her body, analyzing every inch for signs of distress. Her palms spread on her thighs and gripped tight. She squirmed on the seat, and I swear to god, if I dipped my head, I was sure to smell her desire. My eyes snagged on her full breasts, her perfect fucking nipples poking hard against the thin material of her shirt. Wanting her to be aware of her reaction, I flicked the hard tip with my finger, and her eyes shot to mine, dark and wanting.

"It's okay to like it, Hanna. It's okay to take control of your pleasure and what you like. If a bite of pain turns you on—makes you wet—" I breathed against the skin of her neck, nipping at the tender flesh. "Then that's okay. Your past has no control over that."

When I pulled back, I jerked her hair again, and this time, her eyes stayed glued to mine. This time her tongue peeked out to slick across her lips, almost begging me to taste them.

"What do you want?" she asked breathlessly.

I relaxed my fist in her hair and moved my thumb to brush along her cheek. "I want to test your limits. I want you to accept that they may be further than you think. Can I do that, Hanna?"

Another wipe across her lips, and I couldn't resist. I leaned down and bit the lush bottom one, loving the moan tumbling out.

"Yes," she whispered.

"Good girl," I praised, stepping back. I gripped her hand and tugged her off the stool, pulling her behind me into my bedroom.

She held on tightly and scanned the simple setup. I rarely brought women to my home, and I kept it simple. A dark bedspread over a king-size bed with a headboard with slats. I liked to be able to loop things through if need be. Not that I would tonight.

The scars hidden under Hanna's thick bracelets spoke volumes that being cuffed to anything was a hard limit.

"Strip," I ordered.

She jerked wide eyes to mine. "What?"

"The tease tonight isn't about the slow reveal. It's about everything after. So, strip."

To help get things started, I lost my shirt but kept my jeans on. If I lost too many layers between us, I'd probably give up and fuck her as fast and hard as I could.

Pulling her shoulders back like the warrior she was, she shrugged out of her sweater, letting it pool at her feet. At the same time, she kicked off her shoes before moving on to her jeans. Watching her breasts sway under her top while she worked her jeans over her hips had my cock aching to break free.

She stood in a purple scrap of lace and her flowy black shirt. This woman owned some of the sexiest lingerie I'd ever seen. I loved it.

"All of it."

One more deep breath and she whipped the shirt over her head and flicked down her panties. God, I'd never tire of her naked body. The way she stood there, shoving down any insecurity she may have felt, only made her sexier.

I walked over until I stood right in front of her and skimmed my hands over her breasts, barely stopping to pinch the tips before sliding my hands in hers and leading her to the bed.

"Lie down."

"When will you get naked? I want to see you."

"Hanna, if I get naked now, it will all be over. I'm keeping these pants on for the both of us."

She scooted back on the bed with a sly smile, enjoying the effect she had on me. Just to make sure there was no doubt, I gripped the hard length stretching against my thigh.

"Hold on to the headboard," I said softly, losing any hard edge I may have had before. She needed to know she could say no, no matter what.

"Y-you wo-won't shackle m-me?"

Resting my hand on her calf, I squeezed. "No, Hanna. You are in complete control. I just want you to focus on what I'm doing to your body and not on touching me."

"But I want to touch you."

"You will. Later."

With a nod, she slowly moved her hands to grip the frame.

Kneeling at the edge, I bent low and kissed and bit my way up her legs, avoiding her pussy and reaching her breasts. I held each full globe in my hand and bit, sucked, and licked every inch. When her nipples were rosy and plump, I grabbed the box from my nightstand and showed her the clamps decorated with emerald jewels that perfectly matched her eyes before pulling them out. I didn't ask for permission, but I wanted her to know what would happen. After she gave no denial, I pulled them out and slowly eased the clamp over one tip before doing the same to the other.

She pressed her head back against the pillow, widened her legs to wrap around me, and thrust up for any friction at all. When they were firmly in place, I gently rubbed my thumbs across each tip.

"Beautiful," I whispered. "How does it feel?"

"It hurts," she whimpered. "But it—it feels like they're attached to my clit. Both are throbbing, Daniel."

"I know, baby. Let me make it feel good."

"Please."

Kissing my way back down to her core, I pushed her legs open and made sure my eyes were available to her at any point she may need them. I wanted to be able to anchor her in the moment should any memory try to break into our time.

I slid my tongue through her slit, and her head fell back, her mouth opening over a loud moan. I teased and bit at her folds, stopping to attack her clit just to stop and tease again. Her juices flooded from her core, leaking between her ass cheeks, and I followed the trail with my finger, first playing in her cunt and then dropping lower to circle her tight hole.

She immediately squeezed tight but didn't say no. I even waited, and when she still didn't stop me, I pressed inside. Watching her reaction, I kept my eyes glued on her, my mouth glued to her pussy and my finger to her ass. She cringed and writhed and shook her head no, but never looked down, never said no.

"It's okay to like this. It's yours to feel what you want. And if that feeling is pleasure, then feel it, let it wash over you." She thrust her hips up, and I pressed a hard bite to her thigh, whispering my own confession against her soft skin. "I like my ass played with, too. Is that wrong?"

"No. No," she cried.

"Do you want more?"

"Yes."

"Tell me. Own what you want and tell me."

"I want to come. Please."

"How?"

"I want your mouth on me and—and your finger...inside me."

I smiled, knowing what a huge accomplishment those words were for Hanna. As a reward, I latched on to her clit and shoved my finger harder into her ass, loving her screams of pleasure. Before she could finish spasming, I moved up her body and removed one clamp at a time, sucking the tender tips, pulling another orgasm from her.

The entire time, she never let go of the headboard, and I was ready to bury myself inside this strong, wild woman begging to be set free.

Quickly wiping my hands clean with sanitizer, I tossed everything to the side and moved back to her.

"You're so beautiful. So perfect."

TEACHER

I wanted to kiss her but didn't know if the rules we started with were in play now that we were home. But I didn't have to wonder for long because she wrapped her arms around my neck and held on tight, kissing me with everything she had. "Please, fuck me, Daniel. I need you."

I need you. I need you.

The words vibrated through my body like an electrical current, raising goosebumps in its wake. They revived me and terrified me.

Becoming a wild man, I ripped open my jeans and shoved them off, hoisting Hanna up to all fours.

"No," she protested. "Not like this."

I held strong against her initial panic but didn't push her. I had thought this through and needed her to see it all before we stopped. "Look, baby," I said, turning her head to the left. The large mirror above my dresser showed her beautiful body arched. Her ass high, her breasts heavy beneath her. Me, behind her, my cock tall and proud, and desperate to be inside her.

"If you want to stop, we can. At any point. I just wanted you to see how gorgeous you were taking me."

She froze, her bright eyes scanning the scene projected back at us. I gritted my teeth, squeezed my cock to hold back, and waited.

"Daniel," she whispered. She bit her lip, and even through the reflection, I could see her eyes glazing over.

Shit. I pushed too far. "Okay, Hanna. I'm sorry. I shouldn't have—"

When I went to move, her hand flew back to hold my hip in place. "No. I want to see. I want to see what you see. I want this to obliterate any other memories."

Sometimes she said things so lightly I didn't even have time to brace myself for the hard impact of what they meant. It took all my effort to not grip her hips too tight, to relax my muscles and stroke across the firm cheek of her ass.

"If at any point you want to stop, just say so."

She nodded and held still.

Another slow stroke before I pulled back and delivered a blow to her cheek. Her mouth fell open, and she stared wide-eyed as I pulled my hand back again and hit lower this time. Five more times, and she began pushing back for more. We both groaned in pleasure when I swiped my hand between her legs, collecting all her cum. I stroked my cock and lined myself up.

Holding still, I waited for her to pull away, and when she didn't, I eased inside. I wanted to shove in hard and fast and rut against her like a wild animal, but I knew how precarious our situation was, and I wanted her to have nothing but pleasure. I held her hips and slowly eased out and back in. I continued the tortuously slow pace until she pushed back, her body begging for more.

Sliding my hand up her spine, I buried my fist in her hair and gripped, pulling her head back and held on, fucking her hard now.

"Daniel. Oh, God. Yes."

Unintelligible sounds of pleasure and begging fell from both our lips as we watched ourselves in the mirror.

"Look at you," I growled. "Look at your perfect pussy taking my fat cock. Does it feel good, Hanna? Do you like the way it stretches your tight cunt?"

"Yes. More. Please."

She was wild, her hand clawing at the mattress. One of them coming up to grip her own breast to pinch her nipple. Fuck me, that sight would be blazed in my memory forever.

Abandoning her hair, I reached around her front and found her clit and rubbed without mercy.

Both hands dropped down, and her eyes slammed shut, her

mouth opening over a loud scream. I had to hold tight to her body, so she didn't squeeze my cock out when her pussy spasmed so hard. I rode each tight clench, wringing every last cry from her lips. Just as she came down from her pleasure, my orgasm hit. My balls pulled tight, and I fucked hard inside her, pushing as deep as I could go, spilling everything I had inside her wet heat.

"Fuck, Hanna. Fuck."

By the time I came back to earth, our bodies stuck together with sweat, and I somehow managed to not collapse on top of her.

I kissed down her back, slowly easing out of her body, just to want to push back in. I never wanted to leave.

She fell forward as soon as I stepped back, and I grabbed a washcloth to clean her up.

"I'm wasted," she laughed, exhaustion mumbling her words. "Give me thirty minutes, and I'll head out. I promise."

God, I didn't want her to go. The idea alone had my insides revolting. "Don't go. Stay with me tonight."

The words were out before I could think if it was a good idea or not. I was beyond thought. My body craved her, and I wasn't ready for her to leave.

She rolled her head to the side and watched me with glazed emeralds, her lips tipping up. "Yeah?"

"Yeah." I smiled too, reaching to pull her over into my arms. "I've missed sleeping next to you these last few nights."

"Me too," she said over a yawn.

I somehow managed to close my mouth after that. Somehow holding back what I really wanted to say.

I never want you without me.

24

HANNA

"Good morning."

If I thought Daniel's voice was sexy, it didn't come close to comparing to his morning voice. The deep rumble stroked across my skin, waking up every inch.

I rolled over and drowned in his eyes. The sun streaming in through his window lit them up, reminding me of the ocean outside our cabana.

"Good morning," I whispered back, burrowing in his arms.

If lines had been blurred after our trip together, they were downright invisible now.

I'd stayed at his place five out of the past ten days.

It'd start as dinner with a friend. We'd sit across from each other, pretending we both weren't waiting to be in each other's arms. Pretending we weren't desperate for each other.

Sure, we made excuses for each visit. Drinks after Voyeur. Find a new thing for me to try. Exploring my boundaries. But what it really felt like was testing the boundaries of *us*, and each night pushed the edge of friends into more. Each night I fell in love with him a little more.

Every once in a while, he'd bring up talking about my past but never pushed. I think we were both hoping to avoid another argument like we'd had. One thing I always appreciated about Daniel was that he didn't treat me like breakable glass, and maybe because he didn't, I heard him more than Erik, who pushed too hard. Maybe Daniel's words sank in and made me want to open my box, face a little of what I kept hidden all the time.

"How'd you sleep?"

"After last night? Like the dead."

"Yeah, I think I heard you snore at one point."

I gasped and slapped his shoulder. "I did not."

He gripped my wrist and lifted it above my head, forming a loose shackle that I could easily escape, and rolled over me.

"It was sexy. I thought I was going to have to wake you again," he growled against my neck.

His erection prodded my thigh, and I happily opened to let him in. He bit and licked up my neck, sucked my ear, and kissed across my cheek to my mouth, slowly sliding inside me.

My eyes closed, and I basked in the fact that I could get lost in the feel of him. The way he stretched me. The way his chest brushed against my nipples. The way his hips held my thighs apart. The way his lips moved over mine.

All of it was mine to hold close and to not be shattered by a haunting memory in the dark. Daniel gave that to me, and I loved him for it. I loved him for so much more, but this had to be the best.

"So fucking good," he groaned, moving down my chest to bite at my nipples. He'd start soft, rolling his tongue along the tips, then suck, then bite and tug. He'd bite around each one, leaving marks for me to look at later. Marks that I would stare at in the mirror and stand taller because they were there. Not cower in shame and look away.

"Daniel," I whispered his name like a plea. He moved so slow, and I needed more.

"Yeah, baby." He looked up, and I knew he was messing with me. The devious glint, the slow pull out and soft push back in.

"Fuck me. Please."

One last bite to the under curve of my breast, and then his hand shifted. It no longer held my wrist but slid to link his fingers with mine, holding on tight. His other hand curled around my thigh and hoisted it high on his hip, moving deeper. His eyes stayed glued to mine, and he still moved slowly, but harder. His thrusts rough, precise with hard pushes to hit my clit.

My hand held tight to his, tethered to him, never wanting to let go. I breathed through every move inside my body, never wanting to feel anything else. I wanted to close my eyes, roll my head back, and get lost in the moment, but I couldn't. I couldn't look away. He claimed me with his cock, and he held me prisoner with his eyes, and I let him. I gladly opened the door and climbed inside, happy to throw away the key and never leave.

I love you. I love you. I love you.

The words played on the edge of my tongue, and tears burned the backs of my eyes at the force it took to hold them back. He moved faster, the pleasure becoming too much. I squirmed under him, rubbing my clit on every thrust in.

Lightning fast, he rolled over, pulling me with him and sat up, holding me close, letting me control the rhythm.

This position had soon become my favorite. The control and dominance of it fueled my desire and flooded my veins with more heat. Using my thighs, I rose and fell, grinding down and moving faster.

He sucked on my flesh, and I held on tight, losing all tempo and riding him hard, needing to come. Daniel gripped my hips and helped me. Sweat coated my body, and my muscles ached from pulling so tight, clenching in anticipation of the orgasm to come.

"Come on, baby. Cum on my cock. Squeeze me with that tight pussy."

Dirty talk once had me running, but now, it sent me over the edge, falling into the most blissful oblivion I'd ever known.

My world exploded all around me to the music of my own orgasm mixing with his grunts and groans.

"Fuck, yes," he ground out. "Fuck. Hanna."

When we'd both exhausted every drop of pleasure, we held tight to each other, panting, letting our sweat glue us skin-to-skin. His head pressed to my chest, where he'd occasionally gently kiss across my cleavage, paying reverence to my body. I cradled his head and dragged my nails across his scalp. When he softened, he tipped us to the side and pulled out.

I'd never tire of his cum slipping from my pussy and coating my thighs. It was as if he claimed me, and I never wanted anything more.

"It's early, but I thought we could hit the gym before you go to work."

I groaned. "Ugh. We just worked out."

He laughed and nipped at my chin. "I want to teach you something new today. And we can review what you've learned."

Once a week, we'd made time to go to the gym, where Daniel would teach me self-defense. As much as I didn't want to pry myself from this bed, I had to admit each lesson left me feeling stronger than the last.

"Come on. We can get there before classes start and have the place to ourselves."

My mind flashed to Daniel pinning me to the mat and taking me with all the mirrors around. A three-sixty of him moving inside me.

I jumped out of bed and rushed to get ready, his laughter trailing behind me.

We'd grabbed coffee and made it to the gym, which, as promised, was empty. The owner had given Daniel the keys for such occasions.

While I stretched, he removed two big pads from his bag.

"What are those?"

He slid his hands into the loops on the back. "I want to teach you how to fight. You know how to quickly disarm and get away, which is the priority, but should you need it, I want you to know how to throw a punch."

"Okay," I said slowly.

"Trust me," he laughed. "It will be good."

We reviewed the basics I'd learned over the past weeks, and each time I did them, they became easier and easier. He'd promised the more familiar I became with them, the less likely I'd forget them in a moment of panic, so I practiced all the time.

"Okay, good. So, first, let's talk about how to make a correct fist."

"Is there a wrong way to make a fist?"

"Sure is. You could end up breaking something if you close your hand wrong."

"Where did you learn all this?"

"I do kickboxing when I can."

"Sexy," I said, waggling my brows.

He winked and showed me how to make a fist. "Thumb outside over the top of your fingers." He stepped behind me and wrapped his hand over mine, and I tried to focus on what he was doing and not the delicious heat at my back. "You want your hit to focus mostly on the middle knuckles. They're in the best position to receive impact without breaking anything."

"You're not convincing me punching is the best option."

"It is if you do it right." He extended my arm and pulled the other in close. "Just like that. Keep this arm close to guard yourself."

I couldn't help it, before he pulled away, I pushed back, loving his groan.

He nipped at my neck and growled, "Don't distract me, woman."

My smile showed no regrets.

He put the big pads on and stood in front of me, holding them up in front of his face, bracing his feet wide. "Okay. Give me your best shot."

Not moving my feet, I threw my fist at the mat and barely moved his arm.

He peeked around the black leather with skepticism. "Is that all?"

I scoffed. "I just don't want to hurt you with all these muscles," I joked, flexing. In truth, I had packed on some muscles after working with Daniel, and it was nice. But not enough to actually do any damage. Especially to someone as broad and strong as him.

He smiled, and everything stopped. The sun shined through a window, and I swear, it illuminated his face like angels were going to sing any minute. His eyes creased at the corners from years of laughing, and I lost myself a little more.

I loved him so much, and it terrified me.

"Okay," he said, pulling me back to the moment. The smile slipped, and he winced, opening his mouth a few times like he didn't know what to say next. "I want...I want you to pretend I'm one of the men who attacked you."

Like a bucket of cold water, chills broke out across my skin, numbing me to the bone. "What?"

He held up the mitts and got into position. "Pretend I'm someone you hate—someone you'd have no issue punching. Someone you *want* to punch."

"Daniel," I breathed, barely hearing him through the ringing in my ears. My box cracked open, and the past crept out. It wasn't like I hadn't pictured their faces—like I hadn't pictured smashing them into nothing—less than nothing.

My bones grew too big for my body, my muscles ached with tension, vibrating with the need to release. I squeezed my eyes shut. *This* was why I didn't open my box. The memories I kept locked in the dark surrounded me, trying to swallow me whole. It was too big. I couldn't do it—couldn't face it.

"You've talked to your therapist. You've mentally handled your past, but you carry around so much hate and anger in that tiny body. Let it out. Use it to your advantage. Learn to control it, and it won't control you."

Learn to control it. I focused on his words, and braced my feet, holding one hand close and pivoted, planting my fist to the mat. The impact jolted up my arm and shook my core. The muscles pulled tighter and relaxed at the same time. I braced for more while letting it go all at once.

This was what I'd been missing. This was what barre couldn't give me. This was the release I needed.

"Come on, Hanna. Picture it. Let it out."

The faces blurred over the months. I stopped looking, praying they'd disappear from my mind. All but one.

Punch.

There'd been two men to capture Sofia and me. They'd snuck us out through the back, surprising us from behind, and the last thing I saw was Sofia's wide eyes before a pinch in my arm took me down.

Punch.

I'd woken up, handcuffed to a hotel bed. My sister's cries mixing with the slap of flesh from around the corner.

Punch. Punch.

He'd stood from the chair, a leer on his thin lips. Not even the dimples could soften the threat in his dark eyes. I'd never forget the way they looked at me as he strolled across the room, undoing his pants.

Punch. Punch. Punch.

"Good girl, Hanna. Harder."

I'd never forget his hand ripping my dress—my underwear. I'd never forget the scream tearing from my throat or the slap of his hand against my cheek. I'd never forget the way his light hair fell over his forehead when he gripped my throat and licked my face.

"I like the way you scream," he whispered, prying my legs apart and forcing himself inside.

Punch. Punch.

"Let it out, baby."

I punched again. Harder and harder, screaming now like I had then.

I'd never forget the way the cuffs had dug into my wrists, almost as painful as the pain between my legs.

My vision blurred, and I kept punching. "I hate you. I hate you. I ha-hate y-you."

I'd never forget his disgusting wink as he buckled his pants back up.

"The boss would be pissed to know I just took your sweet virginity, but I have to say, that tight pussy, bleeding all over my cock, was worth it. And what he doesn't know won't kill him, right?"

I rolled over and threw up on the pillow beside me, forced to roll back when I was done, staring up at the blood trickling down my wrist, avoiding my sister crying in the bed next to me.

Punch, punch, punch, punch, punch.

An endless loop, each hit lifting the weight in the pit of my stomach. Each blow vibrated through me and relaxed a muscle that had been tight for almost a decade. My hits became sloppy, my body trembling from the sobs I hadn't known I let out.

Before I stopped swinging, the mats dropped, and Daniel's blue eyes swam before me. I hit his chest before he could wrap both arms around me and pull me down to his lap.

I dropped my head to his shoulder and let it out, shocked that I'd managed to shove so much into that box. I'd gone to therapy. I'd accepted what had happened. I'd done my best to move on, but Daniel was right. I had so much anger, and he'd been the only one to see it. The only one to let it free.

Clinging to him, I took deep breath after deep breath, calming down a little more each time. He gently pulled my head up off his shoulder and cradled my face in his palms, brushing my hair back that clung to my damp cheeks. I could only imagine what kind of mess I looked like. But it didn't matter because Daniel looked at me like I was the only woman in the world.

"You're wrong, Hanna. You *are* strong. The strongest woman I know. You may not have wanted to survive, *but you did*. Not only are you surviving, you're thriving. You are so beautiful and strong, taking what life gave you and working with it. I'm so proud of you." His thumb brushed away the stray tears still slipping free. "Sofia would be proud of you."

In that moment, in his arms, in the safety only he could give me, nothing would stop the words from tumbling out.

"I love you."

It was as if my words froze him. Nothing moved. Nothing changed. He stiffened, and after a moment, slowly lifted wary eyes to mine. No, not wary. Scared. Daniel looked more scared than I'd ever seen him, and it was so far from the look I'd ever imagined seeing. Dread sank like the Titanic to the pit of my stomach.

Hesitance, confusion, regret, a way out. Those were all things

I'd imagined. On the best of times, I imagined my love returned. But never had I imagined he'd be scared.

Each muscle I'd just relaxed, tightened back up again, and I looked away, unable to take it anymore. "I'm sorry. Shit. I shouldn't have—"

"No. It's okay," he rushed to reassure. My heart buoyed just to sink back down when I managed to look up. Terror still marred his features, only now his mouth opened and closed like a fish out of water. "I, uh..."

The silence stretched until I couldn't take it, on the verge of screaming for him to say anything just to end it.

Voices interrupted us, drawing his eyes to the open door. People were arriving for class. The gym was opening, and we were no longer alone.

Giving us both the escape we needed, I climbed off his lap, sad that he let me go. "We should get going," I muttered, unable to look anywhere but the ground.

"Yeah," he breathed, standing to collect everything.

The room weighed heavy with everything set free inside of it. Unfortunately, with everything I let go here, I'd be carrying another weight home with me. One I didn't know what to do with.

While he packed, I ordered an Uber. The thought of sitting beside him in a small car was more than I could bear. It would be hell on both of us.

"You want to do breakfast?" he asked once we stood on the sidewalk in front of the building.

I wanted to scream, yes. I wanted so much, but while he offered breakfast, his stiff posture let me know the offer was more out of kindness than actual desire.

"It's okay. I have to get to work."

His shoulders dropped in relief, and I hated that I'd read him so accurately. "Okay. I'll drive you home."

"It's okay," I said again like a broken record. "I ordered an Uber. Our apartments are in opposite directions."

"Hanna." He said my name like a plea. For what, I didn't know. To not do this? To forgive him? To take it all back?

"It's already done," I said with a forced smile nowhere near reaching my eyes. The driver pulled up, and I opened the door.

"Hanna," he said again.

I turned back before getting in, saying the furthest thing from the truth. "It's okay, Daniel."

We both knew it wasn't, and as I drove away, I wasn't sure it ever would be.

25

DANIEL

"So, what do you think?"

I turned blinking eyes to Sabrina before looking back at the empty apartment around us. "Umm, it's nice."

"Right?" She practically vibrated with energy, but alarm bells were ringing.

"I was thinking we could put a down payment next month and move in by summer."

"What?" I breathed.

"Yeah, I already talked to the office about it."

I ran a hand through my hair. "I think you forgot to talk to me about it."

"What's there to talk about? We've been together for years. This is the next step."

"Sabrina..."

"I love you, Daniel. Don't you want us to live together? Start our future?"

The spacious apartment all of a sudden shrunk to the size of a dollhouse, compressing my body with panic. I slicked my tongue across my dry lips, trying to control my breathing. Sabrina was my best friend. I cared about her, but I—I what? What did I want from this? Why couldn't I just be honest with myself? With her?

She deserved it. She deserved the chance to be with someone who could love her. I cared about her...but if I loved her, shouldn't I be jumping at the chance to live with my girlfriend?

"Can we talk outside?"

Honest. I had to be honest with her. She was my friend. She would want what's best for me too.

The fresh air and sunshine didn't help. She looked up with her brilliant green eyes, and I felt like I was choking. As much as I wanted to be honest with her, I needed to be careful. Sabrina was...fragile.

"Sabrina, I—I don't know if I'm ready to move in together."

"Why not? Don't you love me? I know you don't say it, but you don't need to for me to know it."

"I—I care about you so much."

Her smile dimmed as realization sank in, but just as quickly, it came back more forced than ever. "Then next year. We can do the dorms for another year."

"I don't think a year will help."

"Why not? Daniel, I love you. I—" The smile dropped completely, and she gripped my sweaty palms in hers. "I can't do this without you. You have to love me."

"I care about you so much. You're my best friend."

"Then I'll love you enough for both of us. Daniel, you promised you wouldn't leave me."

"I'm not leaving you."

"You are," she shouted. "You're abandoning me because I'm not good enough. God, I'll never be good enough. Why bother? Why bother with anything? I'm a waste of air."

She tried to jerk away, but I gripped her face in my palms and made her look at me. "You are good enough. You are good enough to be loved."

"Just not by you?" she sneered.

Her eyes hardened, and I braced myself. Sabrina went through the full gamut of emotions when we fought—which had been more and more frequently since we started college. I tried to avoid it, but this felt like a freight train I couldn't stop.

"I'm good enough to be fucked by you though. Is that all it was?"

"You know it's not."

"Well, maybe until you get your shit together, I'll find someone else to fuck. How do you like that? If I'm not good enough to love, then you can't fuck me either."

"Dammit, Sabrina, don't do this."

"Do what? Act crazy? That's what Kent thinks I am, so why not act like it?"

Fuck. Things were spiraling out of my grasp, no matter how hard I tried to hold on and control it.

"This isn't about Kent."

"What do you think, Daniel? Do you think I'm crazy? Is that why you won't love me?"

"Sabrina..."

"You're always going on and on about how I need help. How I should talk to someone, but why bother. I have you. Or I did have you."

"You don't need me. They have student services you can talk to. I've looked it up to help."

"I don't want to talk to anyone," she screamed. "I want you to love me like I love you."

"Sabrina, I—I'm so sorry. I care about you so—"

"Shut up, Daniel. Take me home." And just like that, the fight seeped out of her. Her shoulders dropped as she swiped at her cheeks.

"Please, don't do th—"

"Please."

The drive was eerily silent, and I wanted to say a million things, but instead said none. I thought about lying and saying I loved her, but where did that leave us in a year? She needed help. She needed someone who really did love her.

When we got back to campus, I walked her to her dorm building, but she wouldn't let me come up.

"Just know I'll always love you."

And she walked away before I could say anything else.

I DOWNED the rest of my drink, staring at the blank screen of the TV. The only light came from the single lamp on the end table. I'd been too lazy to turn on more than that. I'd come home from work and sat on the couch, only moving to get more to drink.

That'd been my nights since Hanna had dropped her bomb on me.

I love you.

I love you.

Her sweet confession played on repeat and created so many emotions, I didn't even know where to start. The most prominent that roared through me, washing almost all the others out? Fear.

The last girl who loved me killed herself. And ever since Hanna's admission, Sabrina's memory haunted me like it foreshadowed a future with Hanna. I'd seen the hurt in her eyes when I hadn't said it back. The green had been achingly familiar, and I froze, terrified of repeating the past.

"Fuck," I shouted, fisting my hair.

I'd texted Hanna every day, trying to get her to talk to me. I needed to know she was okay. I needed to know loving me hadn't damaged her permanently. She rarely responded, but when she did, it was always an excuse to not see me.

My patience was running thin, and each night I sat on the couch fortified that I needed to talk to her.

TEACHER

I'd gone into this with Hanna because I wanted to help her, but now all I could think about was how I'd made it worse.

I always made it worse. I always tried to help, and I always made it worse.

I needed to talk to her.

I needed to end this.

I don't want to end this.

It didn't matter. Hanna deserved someone who didn't freeze when someone told him they loved him. Hanna deserved someone who didn't second guess his feelings.

Hanna deserved better.

She deserved better than a coward too scared to love.

Hanna

Daniel: Drinks tonight? We can meet wherever.

I STARED down at the phone, wanting to send a *hell yes* back, but like every other time he'd messaged, I settled for a lame excuse.

Me: I can't. I have to work late tonight and an early meeting.

Usually, he left it at that, opting to try again the next day, but not this time.

Daniel: Hanna...
Daniel: We need to talk. About what happened.

We sure as shit did *not* need to talk about what happened. I saw everything written all over his face, and it'd been painful enough. I wasn't ready to hear it from the lips I loved so much. I was too scared to lose him, but I couldn't go back to being just friends. I opened pandora's box, and now it couldn't be closed.

Me: Sure. Just not tonight. :)

The smiley face at the end wasn't fooling anyone, but it didn't stop me from trying to pretend all was just fabulous on my end.

"You okay?" Erik asked from his spot in one of the chairs around the table.

Shit, we ended the meeting a couple of minutes ago, and everyone piled out except Ian and Erik. Keeping up the pretense I was fabulous with them too, I waved his concern away and smiled. "Yeah. Just zoned out."

"You've been working too late this week and coming in too early," he scolded softly, dark brows lowered over green eyes just like mine.

"And how would you know?" I snapped. Between Daniel, and the emotional release from the week, my ability to bury my irritation was down.

"It's my office, of course I know when people come and go." I cocked a brow, knowing he made a point to check on me specifically. "Also, Jared has been working on a special project and staying late. He's seen your light on when he leaves."

I froze for a moment, letting the real meaning of Jared working late sink in. He worked for Bergamo and Brandt as an analyst...on paper. And did do that job. He just also surfed the dark web, hunting down anyone who advertised slavery. He and Erik had a system to find traffickers and take them down, rescuing any people they found and rehabilitating them at Haven. My chest squeezed that they were close to finding someone else.

Each time, I hoped it'd be the last, that maybe we got them all, but that was a joke, and each time, I remembered monsters still lurked out there.

"Tattletale," I grumbled.

"I'll let you know if we bring anyone to Haven," he assured, knowing I liked to help. We had doctors of all kinds at Haven, but I liked to help them get settled if I could; buy things they needed. All behind the scenes work, too scared to put myself out there.

Daniel's words about taking control before it controlled me crept through my mind, and I shoved them down. I didn't want to think about that or him right now. Even though it was all I thought about.

"What's really going on, Little Brandt?" Ian asked, plopping in the seat next to me.

"Nothing." I tried laughing it off, but they both knew me too well.

"Does this have to do with Daniel?"

"What? No." This time my laugh reached too high of a pitch with a scoff in between.

"What happened?" Erik asked.

I swallowed, calming my nerves, and going for a calmer, more believable tone. "Nothing. We're just friends."

"Does he know that."

"Yeah. He most definitely does."

"What does that mean?" Ian asked.

Taking a deep breath, I decided to give them the truth—at least part of it. "I want more, and he...most likely doesn't."

"Most likely?" Erik asked, leaning his palms on the table and glowering like this was some kind of interrogation.

"We haven't talked about it."

"Is there something that happened that would need to be talked about?" he practically growled.

I pursed my lips and considered just laying it out there,

letting him know we fucked like bunnies, just to make him regret pushing me like he has a right to. "Nothing you need to worry about."

"Maaaaaybe we don't want to know, Erik," Ian suggested lightly.

Erik's lip curled up, and he rolled his eyes, pushing away from the table. "If he hurts you," he said, turning back, finger pointed. "I'll kill him."

"Aye-aye, captain," I mocked his deep voice and saluted.

Ian laughed behind me and ruffled my hair like he had since we were kids. Done with the questioning and older brother glares, I made my excuses and got the hell out of there, heading back to my office.

Flopping back in my chair, I heaved a sigh and dared to look at my phone.

Daniel: You're avoiding me.
Daniel: If you won't come to me...

What the hell did that mean?

I didn't have time to consider it before someone knocked on my door. Clicking the phone off, I shoved it to the side. "Come in."

And in walked the person I was just trying to avoid.

"Daniel." Tingles washed over me when I caught his blue eyes, made all the brighter by the dark circles underneath.

"I decided to be a little proactive and come to you. This way, you can't avoid me anymore."

"Oh..." I looked away, shuffling papers and buying time to come up with a valid excuse out of this. My office was spacious, but the threat of facing him turning me away had the walls closing in. "I, um, I have meetings so I really can—"

"No, you don't. I ran into Ian in the hall and asked."

Shit.

"Come on, Hanna. Don't try to put me in a box like everything else."

My gaze snapped up at that. "I'm not shoving you anywhere."

He sighed, running a hand through his hair before almost closing the door.

"Leave it open, please."

I needed as much air in here as I could get and having the door open would prevent me from flinging myself in his arms, begging him to love me, like I so desperately wanted to.

His jaw clenched, but he nodded and sat in one of the seats across from my desk. "I didn't mean for it to come out like that. But you have been avoiding me."

"Gee, I wonder why," I deadpanned.

"Hanna..."

Just my name and fire burned up my throat, stinging my eyes. I didn't want to cry. I didn't want to hear him tell me I pushed too far and now he was done with me. I couldn't handle it. I also couldn't handle him asking if we could forget the words and go back to friends.

"I really don't want to do this, Daniel."

He watched me like I was a wild animal ready to bolt—he watched me like he was tiptoeing around my feelings. Like I was made of glass. Moisture built in my eyes, and I hated it. I hated that after everything, he saw me like everyone else did.

"Listen, we've been through a lot. What we've accomplished together in helping you, it brings two people close. We knew that going in, and that was why we set up the rules. I made a mistake in breaking them on our trip and continuing to break them once we got back."

"It wasn't a mistake."

He swallowed hard and dropped his gaze. "I told you I don't

do love, Hanna. And maybe you thought what happened between us was more because you grew to lean on me."

"Don't belittle my feelings. Don't make it sound like I've created this...transference."

"Isn't it, though?"

He wouldn't meet my eyes, and his question pierced my chest. The first tear fell, and I swiped it away. I'd have rather had him come in and tell me he didn't feel the same over this.

"I care about you, Hanna. But I told you, I don't do love. I can't, and I'm not someone to lean on. I wanted to help, but I'm not the man who can make it all better."

"I'm not asking you to make it better, Daniel. I'm asking you to be honest."

"I am," he snapped, his eyes flashing back to mine. "Do you think this is easy? Do you think I want to hurt you? After everything you've been through, what you're still going through."

"Is that what this is about? I'm too damaged for you?"

"No, dammit." This time both hands dragged through his hair. "Hanna, I—I don't think I can..."

"What? Be with the girl who's damaged goods? The girl you think needs to talk about her feelings so she can get better? News flash, Daniel. I did all that."

"Yet, you still carry all this around."

"I'm allowed to," I practically growled.

"If you would just talk to someone."

"I tried to talk to you. *You* were helping me. Am I too much?"

He paled at my outburst and blinked a few times like he was lost until he shook his head, brushing off whatever had caused him to freeze. "No. I—I care about you."

"Gee. Thanks."

Daniel squeezed his eyes shut in frustration. "Dammit, Sabrina—"

The name barely left his mouth before he cut off all words, his eyes flying open wide.

Ringing pierced my ears, and everything blurred on the edges as my chances at happiness crashed and burned at my feet.

His mouth flopped open like a fish as he searched for an excuse. But none of it mattered.

He'd called me Sabrina.

He'd called me by another woman's name.

The only woman he'd ever loved.

What the fuck did that mean? Was I some cheap replacement? Was I a fill in for him to pretend? So many questions bombarded me from left and right, and all I could squeeze out of my depressed lungs was, "What?"

"Hanna. Shit." He held his hands out, pleading. "It was a mistake. I'm sorry. I didn't mean—"

"Shut up," I snapped, unwilling to hear anymore. Every doubt bombarded me. The way he looked scared when I told him I loved him hit me hard in the chest. The way he let me walk away after confessing how much he meant to me, bubbled up, breaking free.

"Is that what this was? A way to relive the time you spent with your precious Sabrina? Did you want to save me like you wished you could have saved her? Did you replay your favorite moments with me in her place? Did you fuck me and think of her?" My voice cracked on the last question.

"Dammit, Hanna. No." He dragged his hands through his hair and tugged before letting them fall to his sides. "It wasn't like that. I'm upset and not thinking. I don't know what the hell I was thinking. I'm so sorry."

His blue eyes pleaded with me to understand, but I couldn't. All I could hear was her name. All I could think was that he used me to replace her. That all he ever wanted was her and never me.

"Well, maybe you should go think somewhere else. Not around me."

"Hanna, please."

"Get out," I breathed, unable to shout like I wanted to.

The room froze, and I held my breath, waiting for him to make his move. Part of me wanted him to come across the desk, pull me into his arms, and demand I hear him. To tell me it was always me and that I had it all wrong.

But that didn't happen. A moment passed before he growled and walked out, slamming the door behind him.

The loud bang reverberated through my bones and shook the last bit of strength from my body.

I sunk into my seat and dropped my head to my hands, letting the tears finally break free.

Would I ever not be the stupid sister who made stupid mistakes. Was I doomed to fall into the wrong hands each time?

I trusted Daniel. I found comfort with him.

If I couldn't trust my feelings on who to be safe with, then was I doomed to be alone forever? Was all of this for nothing? All of the learning how to flirt, to touch, to kiss, to make love?

I broke all over again, terrified of never feeling the safety in someone's arms.

No, not someone's arms. Daniel's arms.

I didn't want anyone but him.

And it killed me that he hadn't wanted anyone but *her*.

26

DANIEL

"Bowling?" Jackson asked, face scrunched in confusion. "Really?"

I held my hands up. "Don't blame me. This is all Kent."

I knew I was. I wanted to stay home and wallow in my misery, and he wouldn't leave me be. He never left me be. I both hated and loved him for it.

"That's big talk for a man carrying his own bowling shoes and ball in the bag," Kent deadpanned, pointing to my bag.

"The shoes they give never fit," I grumbled.

Truth was, Kent and I loved bowling. We'd even joined a bowling league for the past ten years.

Jackson shook his head and passed a pair of shoes to his husband, Jake. "You guys are nerds."

"Nerds who own a sexy club," Jake added.

"It's all about balance," Kent joked.

We snagged a pitcher of beer and headed to our lane.

"Why are we doing this again?" Jackson asked, once his shoes were on.

Kent leaned back in the plastic chair, his ankle crossed over his knee, and took a long pull from his beer, eyeing me the whole time. When he finally pulled his drink away, I already knew I was going to want to punch him. "This guy has been pissy all week, so I figured drinking and chucking a ball down to crush pins may cheer him up."

"I'm not pissy." I was beyond pissy.

"If you pout any more, you're going to give that baby crying over there a run for its money."

I didn't even bother responding. Instead, I held up my middle finger and decided I'd try even harder to crush his ass. Maybe it would give me something to take my mind off of how badly I'd screwed up.

On my first turn, I got a strike. When Kent only knocked down eight, I couldn't even find it in me to gloat.

This trend continued for the first game, adding a lot of trash talking. However, by the time we reached the second game, Kent and I had teamed up to make fun of Jackson, who had thrown more gutter balls than I thought possible. Even that didn't take my mind off of how much I was hurting. I needed to get out of here. Maybe if I drank enough, I'd at least be numb.

"Are you trying?" I asked.

"Yes," he growled. "I'm sorry I spent my life getting laid and not being a nerd in a bowling alley on the weekends."

"Do you want us to get the bumpers," Kent joked.

When Jake laughed, Jackson turned to him with an incredulous stare.

He held up his hands in surrender but couldn't wipe the smile from his face. "Note to self, don't let Jackson teach our kids bowling."

"Kids?" I asked.

Jake and Jackson had been together for a few years now. Married for one and the picture-perfect couple for marital bliss. I'd known Jackson since he was a twenty-year-old kid performing at Voyeur. Over the years, he'd become like a son to me, or at least a nephew. He'd struggled, and I'd wanted to help as much as I could. I cared for him like I cared for Olivia. I didn't have any kids, but that didn't mean I didn't have people I loved and cared for.

The thought of Jake and Jackson with kids made me feel like a proud father, seeing how far he'd come. But I couldn't ignore the pang it created, that echoed through my chest like a whisper that told me something was missing with me.

"Yeah," Jake said, rubbing the back of his neck. "We've looked into the process of adopting. Just looked."

"I tried to ask Carina to be our surrogate, but Ian shot us down pretty quick," Jackson said.

"You didn't?" Kent laughed.

"He sure did," Jake muttered before taking another drink.

"Holy shit. You've got balls, Jackson," Kent said, wiping his eyes.

"Big ones," he returned with a wink.

Jake rolled his eyes but laughed before turning to me. "Hey, D. How was your trip with Hanna?"

"Good," I answered on autopilot. Despite the shitshow of the last couple of weeks, I smiled, remembering how happy we'd been that week.

I love you.

A wave of adrenaline washed over me like it had the first time.

"Good god. Look at that smile," Kent said.

Kent had been harassing me all week about my sour mood, and I knew bowling and beer was supposed to loosen me up so I'd finally talk to him, but with three sets of eyes on me, the last thing I wanted to do was talk.

"We're just friends." The denial unnaturally rolled off my tongue, but I didn't know what else to say.

"Bullshit," Kent shouted. "I know you, and that's a load of bullshit."

Get out.

It actually wasn't a load of bullshit. I wasn't sure we were anything but a mistake right then. The hurt that had colored her tone when she told me to leave was one I'd never forget.

I dragged my hand through my hair and tugged at the strands. "It's...complicated."

"Daniel is in a complicated relationship," Jackson said incredulously. "I never thought I'd see the day."

"And with Hanna. That's Erik's little sister, right?" Jake asked.

Jackson whistled. "I don't know him well, but he looks like a scary motherfucker."

"So, are you dating?" Jake asked.

"Or just fucking? Because you don't even fuck women more than a few times," Jackson added.

"How serious are things?"

"How long has it been going on?"

"Does she know you care about her?"

"Oh my god, did you talk about feelings with her?"

"Does she care about you?"

"Does Erik know?"

"Does Ian know? He's like a surrogate big brother."

They volleyed questions back and forth, and I did my best to field them, but each one added more and more weight to my chest.

Through it all, Kent remained silent, studying my every reaction. When Kent stopped joking, things were serious. The way he watched me let me know maybe I wasn't hiding my growing anxiety as well as I hoped.

The interrogation continued for another thirty minutes until they finally gave up and headed home. The sigh of relief was short-lived because as soon as my ball was back in my bag, Kent laid a hand on my shoulder.

"You okay?"

"Yeah." I knew he was waiting for me to meet his eyes, but I couldn't. Then I'd be forced to acknowledge the lie. "I'm going to head home. Thanks for bowling."

I bolted before he could stop me. Instead of another night staring at the blank TV, I headed to Voyeur.

"Hey, Daniel," a soft voice cooed behind me. I barely turned my head to watch her perch on the stool next to me, but I saw the black hair and recognized the husky tone. Cassandra. We'd hooked up a few times on and off if we were at Voyeur at the same time, but I'd been pretty absent over the last months, hiding away in my office, thinking of Hanna. "You look like you could use some company."

My body wanted to curl into itself, not at all able to think about touching anyone other than Hanna. Not that Hanna would ever let me touch her again. Maybe I should take Cassandra up on her offer. Go ahead and move on to one-night-stands and nothingness.

"No," Kent's deep voice answered for me, leaving no room for argument. I cringed, knowing my relief at avoiding him at the bowling alley had all been false hope. I should have known he'd come for me.

Cassandra shrugged and left, only to be replaced by Kent. He made himself comfortable on the stool and signaled for a drink. I groaned, knowing my feeling bad for myself in silence was coming to a screeching halt.

He was kind enough to at least wait until he had a drink

before laying into me. "What has you looking like a sad fucking sap?"

"Fuck off," I grumbled. I wanted to talk even less now than I had earlier.

"Calm down, pissy panties."

"Fuck. Off," I repeated.

"Okay," he said like he was talking to a child. "I'll finish my drink while you calm down and tell me what happened."

My head dropped between my shoulders with a heavy exhale. Unable to look up and meet his dark gaze I knew was currently penetrating the side of my skull, I muttered toward the bar top. "She told me she loved me."

One second. Two. Three. Four.

"And?"

And? Fucking and?

What the hell did he mean, *and*?

My head shot up, and I glared. He was supposed to know me better than anyone. He knew I didn't do love, and yet, here he sat, asking me *and*. "And, I fucking froze."

The confusion marring his face slowly softened in understanding, and I hated it because under the understanding was concern, worry, and maybe even pity. The pity had me pulling my shoulders back and clenching my jaw.

"D..."

"Don't fucking look at me like that, Alexander. Don't fucking pity me like I'm some poor baby that needs to be handled with kid gloves."

"I'm not pitying you, asshole. I'm trying to understand how I missed something from twenty years ago has such a tight hold on you still."

"The last person that said they loved me killed herself. It's not exactly something you let go of. It stays with you like a mark you can't ever get rid of. It had a big enough impact that I never wanted to be in the same position again."

"Hanna isn't Sabrina," he said softly.

She wasn't, but I was still me, and there lay the biggest crux of it all. I looked away, unable to admit what really haunted me, instead staring at my thumbs sliding up and down the condensation of my glass. "What if it's not the girl. What if it's me? Sabrina killed herself because I couldn't love her back. Not the way she needed. I cared for her, but it wasn't enough. What if I'm not enough, and that's the final straw for them?"

"Shut the fuck up," Kent growled, leaning in close. "Sabrina killed herself because she had mental health issues she refused to get help for."

"Maybe if I could have at least said it. She'd have stuck around long enough for me to help her. Maybe I could have eventually loved her and helped her."

"No. Love doesn't fix sickness. It can't cure cancer, so how do you expect it to heal a mind?"

I didn't have an answer. I couldn't.

"God, is this what you've carried around? I knew you blamed yourself, but shit, D."

"Of course, I blamed myself. *She* blamed me. She wrote a fucking note making sure I knew it."

"Daniel, I don't know if you're trying to remember her as some perfect person or remember your relationship as something great because you're trying to preserve her memory or what, but you're wrong. She was toxic. I didn't know her before college, but whenever I saw her with you, she took and took from you. She'd scream at you all the time and demand you drop everything for her, and when you didn't, she always acted out to make sure you came running. She put it on you because it was easier to blame you when she didn't want to look at herself. You tried to get her help, and she didn't want it. You did everything you could, but this wasn't some angel of a woman who adored you that you couldn't love back. She tore you down so you would stay with her because you took care of her when she didn't want to take care of herself. It wasn't your fault that you didn't love her. Hell, I know more than anyone, you can't choose who you love and that it's *okay*."

I wouldn't admit it out loud, but Kent was right. Hearing him retell the past, let other memories flood in. I remembered the times I'd begged her to talk to someone because I saw her crumbling, and I hadn't known how to hold her together. I remembered caring for her and holding on as tight as I could, but the further we got from high school the harder she thrashed through life and left me with cuts and bruises, the less she wanted to stand on her own and clung to me, wanting me to fall with her.

She hadn't been the same girl I'd met in high school, and I knew a lot of it had nothing to do with me. But she'd left a note letting everyone who read it know that she couldn't go on without me and that weighed on me—it skewed my vision. You didn't remember the worst of the dead. You remembered the good times—the best of them. Apparently, I'd slapped on rose-colored glasses of my relationship with Sabrina, of the girl I used to know, and I'd let her down. She'd been perfect in my eyes, and I'd let her down.

We'd been happy, and I'd lost it, and I never wanted to feel that pain again, so I shut it off.

"Is this why you don't date?"

"I date," I muttered.

"Once or twice. Mostly just for sex. If someone wanted more, you moved on."

"It's not like you dated."

"I didn't date because I didn't want to be tied down until Olivia." I cringed at the reminder he was with my niece. "But you were always different—more settled. I wanted to travel and explore. Food, women, experiences, everything, and I couldn't do that with a partner. But you, you liked staying put. You like stability. I was shocked I somehow became the first of us to settle down."

"It's not like that. I didn't want to settle down either," I tried to defend, but he gave me a look to let me know he didn't believe me.

"You're scared."

"I'm not fucking scared."

"Okay," he said, sarcasm dripping from the simple word.

"Fuck you."

Kent laughed, knowing there was no heat behind my words. "It's okay, man," he said, slapping my back. "Sabrina fucked you up. It's traumatizing, and I get it. But Hanna isn't Sabrina. Not even close."

I finished the last of my beer and spun the empty glass a few times. Hanna most definitely wasn't Sabrina. Hanna was strong. She faced more demons than anyone I knew. Somehow, I'd lost sight of that. I'd seen her struggling the littlest bit, and my past reared its head. The panic Sabrina left me with latched on to my present, and I reacted. I reacted wrong. I pushed more than I should have. I reacted to her as if she wasn't the woman I'd come to know as strong and independent. I'd forgotten that she took control of her life and could stand tall all on her own.

She didn't need me, but somehow, she still wanted me to be the man to stand by her side. I just didn't know if I could be that man.

I'd already proven I couldn't.

"It doesn't matter. I already fucked up."

Kent's booming laugh pulled the attention of more than a few people, not that he cared. By the time he pulled himself together, everyone had stopped staring except me, trying to figure out what the hell was so funny.

"Of course, you fucked up."

"Wow, Kent. Thanks for that pep talk," I deadpanned.

"We all fuck it up. Ask Olivia."

"I'd rather not."

"Listen, Daniel. You're going to fuck up, and it's okay. If she loves you, and you don't fuck it up beyond repair, she'll forgive you the small stuff. We all get a learning curve."

"I called her Sabrina."

Amber liquid sprayed out of Kent's mouth onto the bar, where he bent over in a coughing fit. "Fuck, Daniel," he gasped, directing wide eyes my way.

"Yup."

"That's a little bit more than fucking up. Calling her by your ex's name—especially your only ex from twenty years ago—that's bad, man."

"Fucking yup." I downed my drink and signaled for another.

"What are you going to do?"

"Well, right now, the plan is to drink until I forget how much I hate myself." The bartender sat my drink down, and I latched on, lifting in a salute to Kent before downing it.

"Yeah? How's that working out for you?" he deadpanned.

"Not great."

"So, what are you going to do to get her back?"

"Did you miss the part about fucking up beyond repair?"

Kent winced as if imagining the whole scenario all over again. Rubbing a hand down his face, he wiped it away and pulled his shoulders back like he was about to do battle royale with me. Fuck, I hated when he got all self-righteous. Mainly because all I wanted to do was drink until I passed out, and he was about to ruin that for me.

"She loves you." I scoffed, and he continued like he didn't hear it. "Do you love her?"

Panic gripped my chest like a familiar friend. "I don't know."

"Yes, you do," he assured without missing a beat. "Hell, I know the answer, and it's not even me."

I remembered Hanna the first night at Voyeur—not the way I found her crying in the hallway, but the way she laughed on my couch. I remembered the first time she let me touch her and her fascination. I remembered all her math puns and the sense of humor that only popped out when she was comfortable. I remembered the pride stretching her face when she took me to the mats the first time in self-defense. I remembered the way she held my hand and screamed off a mountain with me. I remembered how brave she was when she asked me to make love to her. I remembered her waking up in my bed. I remembered her crying in my arms and still finding the bravery to tell me she loved me.

Kent was right...it was obvious.

"Yeah, I do. I love her."

"Then go tell her."

"It's not that simple, Kent," I growled.

"Actually, it is."

I kind of wanted to punch the smile off his face, like he just discovered the answer to world peace. Maybe a fight with Kent would help.

His smile softened as he watched me. "It really is that easy to tell someone you love them if you want them to know. You just say it."

I dug my hands through my hair again and tugged the strands. Kent and I were always there for each other, but these last few years, life had us talking about our feelings more and more. It didn't make it any easier.

Through a clenched jaw, I admitted what worried me the most. "What if she doesn't believe me? What if she doesn't want to hear it, or it's too late, and she doesn't care?"

His bark of laughter was not the comfort I was expecting. "What are you, twenty? You're a grown man, Daniel. We don't hide behind lack of conversation. We're getting older, we don't have time to wait around for conversations to just happen or for luck to keep throwing us opportunities and hoping for the best. You have to act. Buck up and at least give her the opportunity to decide that. Grovel like the baby you're acting like."

"You're really sucking at pep-talks tonight."

He shrugged.

"Now I'm going to ask you again…Do you love her? Love her enough to chance her kicking you in the balls and telling you to fuck off? Love her enough to let her kick you in the balls even if she does accept your sorry ass so she can feel better?"

I didn't even have to think. "Yeah. I love her. So fucking much."

"Good," another voice said behind me. I turned to find Ian and Erik glaring, arms across their chests, legs braced like they were hitmen there to finish me off.

Erik leaned closer. "Now go fucking fix her before we kick your ass, right here, in your own club."

"Hold on, boys," Kent stepped in. "I agree, he's a dumbass—"

"Thanks, friend."

"—but let's all calm down."

"I'll calm down when I see Hanna smiling again," Erik growled.

The thought of Hanna not smiling pierced my chest, an ache blooming like blood spreading across a shirt. I hated that I'd hurt her. I hated that I hadn't just told her I loved her when she said it to me.

"All right, boys," Kent said. "Let's take this somewhere less crowded so we can talk."

We got up, and Kent led us to one of the sitting areas tucked away in the corner.

I sunk into the leather chair, digging my fingers into my eyes. "She won't talk to me."

"Have you tried?" Erik asked.

"Not since she kicked me out of the office."

He lunged to the edge of his seat and bared his teeth. "Then get off your lazy ass and do something."

"What do you want me to do?" I asked, tossing my arms out in frustration.

"Fucking apologize."

"I did, dammit."

"No. You need to apologize when emotions aren't high, so she at least knows you tried, and then you need to apologize again when she's calmed down," Erik explained.

"And then a few million times after that, too," Kent added.

"The point is, if you love her, then you don't give up on one try," Erik deadpanned before getting serious. "You make her listen, and after she hears you—really hears you, then you can make your decision on what to do next. But most of the time, they just want to be reassured you want them, that they are important enough to fight for. Show her she's important enough to fight for. Unless she isn't, then I'll be happy to beat the shit out of you," he added.

"Of course, she is."

"Then why are you here drinking?"

"Because he's scared," Kent taunted.

My legs flexed, getting ready to jump across the space and pummel my best friend, but Erik's hand on my shoulder, pinned me down.

"Listen, if you push too hard, I'll kill you. But if you don't try at all, I'll have to kill you still."

Resting my elbows on my knees, I held my head in my hands. "Jesus," I breathed. Why was this so hard? I was almost forty, and here I sat with three men almost as emotionally stunted as I was, giving me advice on how to win a girl back. I'd never had to work for a woman, they always flocked to me.

But Hanna wasn't just any other woman. She was special. She radiated confidence, strength, and beauty, and women like that didn't flock to anyone. I needed to shove any insecurities aside and talk to her.

"How is she?" I asked softly.

"She's running," Erik said.

My face screwed up. "Hanna hates running."

"Exactly. She doesn't leave her office much, and she runs in the morning like she's trying to make herself feel as bad physically as she does emotionally."

Another sharp pierce, and my lungs constricted. I fought the urge to get up and go to her right then. I wanted to comfort her and make the pain go away. I just hoped she'd let me.

But hope wasn't a strategy, and if I wanted to win her back, I needed a strategy.

I slowly lifted my head to Erik, who lounged back like he didn't have a care in the world. It was going to sting to ask him for help, but my pride could join my insecurities in a dark pit. Preparing for him to gloat, I took a deep breath and sat tall.

"I need your help."

"It's a good thing I have an idea. But I may want to kick you in the balls before I tell you."

"Whatever it takes."

27

HANNA

"Are you sure?" Erik asked for the thousandth time.

I looked through the glass of the French doors at the small group of women on the other side, huddled on the couches surrounding the single chair saved for me. The pressure in my chest eased a fraction when I noticed only a few showed up. We had thirteen women housed at Haven right now, and my confidence waned when I imagined each set of eyes glued to me. I could handle the five in there.

I think.

"Yeah, I'm sure."

Erik brushed my shoulder and turned me to face him. "You don't have to do this. You do plenty for this place as it is."

I gave him the most reassuring smile I could muster past the nerves. "I know, but I want to. I want to use what happened to me for good. I want to control it. And I'm not only doing it for them. Maybe I need it, too."

Just like Daniel had suggested.

Sabrina. Sabrina. Sabrina.

Each time I thought of him, her name trailed behind it like a haunting echo I couldn't escape. Each time I thought of her name, I wanted to scream, rage—I wanted to crumble.

I'd been reduced to replaying every moment we spent together and analyzing the way he looked at me, the things he said to me, the things he did to me. Was he picturing her the whole time? Had he seen me in the past few months at all? I hated it. One small slip and everything came crashing apart. It was like taking the most bottom right piece of the Jenga game first. Of course, it was going to fall.

I overthought every single second, slowly going insane. The thoughts would keep me from sleeping, and I'd lie in bed at four in the morning, staring at the ceiling, starting from beginning to end all over again.

I'd gotten so frustrated one morning, I ran. Ran like I could outrun the thoughts running rampant over my heart. Self-doubt crept in, and I ran from that too. I hated running.

I still hated it, but I'd learned to use it. I popped my earbuds in and listened to music, drowning out the world, and processing it all. When processing became too much, I went back to the music and the thud of my feet on the pavement—the sharp knives in my lungs.

Anything was better than the worst-case scenario. Anything was better than him imagining her instead of me from the beginning.

Each morning I convinced myself a little more, that it really was an accident—a slip of the tongue in the heat of the moment. How many times had I called Ian by Erik's name, and vice versa? Everyone did it. It could be explained away so easily.

Except, I couldn't let it go that easily. What if it hadn't been an excuse? What if I gave in and believed him, only to find out later I was wrong? It wasn't like he'd admit it if it was true. Who did that? Who admitted they'd done something so terrible without being cornered? No one.

That doubt had kept me from calling him—from seeking him out for an explanation. Because I knew how much I wanted to believe him, and he wouldn't even have to try before I begged for him to hold me again.

"Are you ready?" Erik asked, bringing me out of my thoughts.

I shook out my arms, rolling my head around my neck, and breathed as deep as my lungs could expand. One thing Daniel had given me that he couldn't take away was the confidence that I could own my past. Not just accept it but own it. And I fully intended to.

"Yeah."

"I'll be right outside if you need me."

He squeezed my hand and rounded the corner to a smaller seating area. He hadn't wanted to be in the room to hear everything, and I didn't want him to know all that had happened either. It would only weigh on him more than it already did. He also stayed away from the women as much as possible to help them feel comfortable in their readjustment.

I closed the doors behind me and smiled at the women as I made my way to the empty seat. Some smiled back. Some didn't. Some looked healthy and almost at the end of their stay in Haven while others looked battered and on the brink of destruction at any moment.

"Hi, guys. I'm Hanna Brandt. My brother and I started Haven together."

"You help run the charity thing," one of the girls says. She had been one to share her story at the gala, and I envied her bravery, talking about her survival in front of hundreds to bring awareness.

"Yeah. I, uh, I'm also the catalyst for Haven. Me and my sister, Sofia." A few met my eyes while others stared at their fidgeting hands, and I struggled to swallow past the lump in my throat. "She died when we were taken as teens."

At that confession, everyone's eyes snapped to mine, and I struggled to meet theirs. I took off my bracelets, setting them on the coffee table and laid my hands on my knees, not hiding the faint pink scars.

"I was shackled to a bed for almost the entire four months. And I fought like hell to break free for the first couple of weeks," I said, explaining the marks. "Four months we survived—if you can call it that—until Sofia didn't. I was rescued the next day." Wetness leaked unbidden down my cheek, and I swiped it away.

"How?" one of them asked.

"Drug overdose."

"Why are you telling us this?" another asked.

I laughed, not one-hundred percent sure I had a good answer. "Because I think I forgot how important it is to talk about it. Because sometimes it's good to share with people who get it. Sometimes it's good to feel not so alone. Because sometimes it feels good to know that you *can*. Even nine years later. Of course, we have top therapists and doctors here. But they don't know for sure when they say you'll make it through this. They will do their best and believe in you every step of the way, but even then, it's a hope. They don't understand the doubt, hurt, and anger because they didn't feel it. They don't understand the hope that lingers that maybe you won't have to make it through this," I whispered.

Some eyes dropped away, and I knew it was true. I'd hit that point a million times, hoping that if it just all ended, I wouldn't have to feel the pain and shame anymore. Not everyone got that.

"They don't understand that you did everything right. You didn't leave a drink unattended. You never went anywhere alone. And yet, somehow, it still happened. They don't understand the fear of waking back up in the hell we escaped."

A few head nods encouraged me to keep going. "I guess I'm here because I found myself needing to talk about it. Because I realized that even though I handled it and accepted the past, shame and anger still had a tight hold of me. I think I just needed to be around people who really understood.

"I wanted to share with you that this place was founded by someone who does understand. Coming here at first feels great. You're free—physically. But mentally, the battle has just begun. When I first talked about my captivity, I didn't know how to explain to my therapist that there were days when men wouldn't come to my bed, and I'd cry, almost wanting them to. Because if they came, then they still needed me. If they came, then I wasn't trash that needed to be taken out. If they came, I was still useful and got another day with my sister.

"There were also days when I hoped that they would just come in and kill me. Probably more of those than the others. But Sofia always bitched at me to never say that again." I wiped my eyes and laughed. "She was the strong one. The brave one. The positive one. She was the one that should have lived. Even nine years later, no one can convince me that fate made the wrong choice."

"I made a friend," one of the girls interjected. "She was my brave one. And she died. How—How do you handle it? How do you live with yourself knowing you lived when you didn't even want to?" she asked, tears clogging her throat, choking the question off.

"You just do. I wish I had a better answer. A step-by-step guide to getting through it, but I don't. You just hang in there and go to therapy and live each day and each hour or even each minute. You live it enough for them. You live a life they'd be proud of. You embrace the feeling of guilt and regret. You absorb it and feel every painful ache. And slowly, you dissolve it with each step you take forward. It's been almost ten years, and mine still lives within me, but it's minuscule compared to what it was."

Motion at the glass doors caught my eyes, and I looked up and froze. Blond hair, ice-blue eyes made even brighter by the light blue shirt tucked into black jeans. His head dipped with a small smile, hitting me right in my heart. When had he got here? How much had he heard?

Not that it mattered, it was Daniel. He knew everything and never treated me differently. He never treated me as a fragile thing on the brink of collapse. He pushed me and demanded I be strong for myself in ways I hadn't known I needed to be.

"Eventually, there comes a moment—or a person— that helps you want to be more," I said, looking right at him. "We cover our darkest parts and hide it under a pretty blanket we worked so hard to make with therapy and time. We pretend it's not there until we're ready to face it. And I can tell you that one day you will be able to face it—even if it's only bits and pieces at a time."

Tears clouded my vision of Daniel. He'd been my moment— my person that had helped me face the darkest parts and beat them. He'd been the person to remind me that I could have done it all along.

"I guess I wanted to talk to you for a few reasons. One, because I think I needed to. I'm not brave like you guys are who talk every year. But I want to be. I want to be able to share my story and not have the shame of it hanging over me because there's nothing to be ashamed of. We survived." Sniffles greeted my impassioned words, and I believed them more than I ever had before. Daniel had been right. I *was* strong. I had survived even when I hadn't wanted to, and that's the hardest survival of them all. "Also, I wanted to let you know that I'm here. You are not alone. You are not surrounded by people who want to help you, but don't understand you. You. Are. Not. Alone."

More tears slipped down my face, and I didn't bother to wipe them away. They fell too fast to stop them.

"We don't have anyone," one of them said.

"You have each other. You have Haven. And if at any point that doesn't feel good enough, you have me. I'm slowly crawling my way through life, but I can feel the sun on my face the closer I get to the light at the end of the tunnel. I promise you, it's there. And if you need me to crawl back through that tunnel to hold your hand through the dark, I will. I'll go back every time because whether you wanted to survive or not, you did." I held out my hands to either side of me and waited for two hesitant palms to slide against mine. "You were strong, and you survived the worst. You will survive this too," I said, squeezing hard.

"Thank you," one of the women said. I ached looking at her sunken eyes and bruised cheek.

I looked to each of them, meeting their eyes with as much fire as I could muster through my tears. "Thank you for being here. For giving Haven a chance, for giving life a chance." Looking over their heads, I met Daniel's eyes. "Thank you for listening to me and helping me."

After we all mopped up our eyes, a few nods, smiles, and even a few hugs were exchanged. I told them to head to the kitchen where I brought a cake because sometimes every day needed to be celebrated. Before they'd turned to leave, Daniel had left. Once they cleared the door, I expected him to come back. I straightened magazines and almost tripped over the rug because I couldn't keep my eyes from the door.

Had I imagined him the whole time? Had he not really been there? Had I needed him so much in that moment, that I'd conjured him, and now he was gone?

God, I needed him. No, I didn't *need* him. If anyone taught me that, it was him.

I *wanted* him.

I wanted his arms and his love and his comfort.

I wanted to believe him.

I just wish he was there to convince me. To tell me it was all a mistake. I'd listen. I'd believe him if he'd at least try.

But he was gone, and I fell to the couch, defeated. My

muscles ached from the week I'd put it through. I wanted his warmth by my side, and instead, I was alone.

More tears burned the backs of my eyes as my chest squeezed too tight, and I buried my head in my hands, too tired to hold it up. I'd thought he'd come for me, to fight for me. But he hadn't.

He was gone.

"Is this seat taken?"

28

HANNA

THE LIGHT SHINED through the window, illuminating his eyes, bright like the sky, softened with a smile.

"You're here," I breathed.

"Where else would I be?"

It'd been a week, but it might as well have been a year for how much I missed his voice. It washed over me, easing the muscles that had tightened with each second I thought he'd left me.

"I—" I swallowed past the lump working its way up my throat. Between the confession and seeing him, my emotions were on edge. "I don't know. I just...I guess I thought you left."

He moved around the edge of the couch and finally sat next to me, so close his leg pressed to mine.

"No, I'm right here, Hanna. Always here."

I fought the urge to close what little space stretched between us and sink into his arms. But then I remembered why I hadn't seen him, and the joy tainted with the hurt that had been lingering since the last time I'd seen him.

Sabrina.

That, and he hadn't reached out to even try to convince me I was wrong. Maybe he didn't want to.

"You haven't been all week," I said, sitting tall and inching back.

He dragged a hand through his hair and winced. "Because I'm a dumbass. I convinced myself I couldn't fix this and that I wasn't good enough." He bent his head, waiting for me to meet his gaze. It pleaded with me to listen—to understand. "Hanna, I have no clue what I'm doing."

I huffed a laugh. "I don't want to shock you, but neither do I."

Daniel's hand crept closer, giving me plenty of time to pull away. But if I was being honest with myself, I didn't want to. No matter the outcome. So, when his rough calluses scraped across the soft top of my hand, I turned to link our fingers.

"What are you doing here, Daniel?" I whispered, scared to break the moment. "How did you know?"

"How? Erik. Why?" He used his free hand to tip my chin up. "Because I wasn't going to miss you being the bravest woman I've ever met."

Tears glazed my eyes, and I shook my head, swallowing them back down. "I'm not."

"You are," he said fiercely. "Hanna...I'm sorry. I—"

"I just need to know," I cut him off. "Was it real? Any of it? Did you see *me* at all?"

His hand abandoned mine, and I almost cried out at the loss, but before I could, both hands framed my face. "You are *all* I see. Jesus, you're all I've seen since we met. You steal my attention whenever you walk into a room."

"Then, why?" I pleaded. "Why did you say her name? Why did you call me that if I'm all you see?"

His jaw clenched, and his eyes bounced between mine, tinged with panic that maybe he *couldn't* fix this.

"Because I was scared. So fucking scared. The last woman

who loved me left her mark, and I just got swept up in the old feelings that had swallowed me as a teen. It pulled me back, and I felt like history was repeating itself. I was terrified of what you loving me meant for you. What if I couldn't be enough? What if I hurt you too much and I—I don't know. Because I know you're a strong woman. I know you don't need me, and you'd be fine without me. I know that. But fear doesn't care what you know. And before I knew it, I was pushing you away, and I'm so sorry."

I reached up to grip his wrists, just to touch him. "Daniel, you did help me. You taught me how to face the things I'd been hiding from. You pushed me in a way that I needed. You made me strong."

"You were always strong."

"Then you helped me see it."

His tongue slicked across his lips, and I physically ached holding back from kissing him.

His forehead dropped to mine. "Maybe I offered to help as a way to make up for past mistakes. Maybe if I helped you, it would absolve me of my past. Maybe that was how it started. But at no point did I not see you. At no point did I see you as her. I wanted to help you, Hanna. Only you."

"Daniel," I breathed, a tear finally breaking free. Unable to hold back any more, I tipped my head and met his lips with mine. They tasted like mint and Daniel. He tasted like home. His tongue slicked across my lips, and I opened, letting him in. With each moan and desperate hold, I let him back into my heart, my decision made.

I believed him, and I wanted him. I loved him.

He slowed the kiss and pulled back but didn't remove his forehead. "I want to give you something. Something I've never given anyone before."

"You've given me enough."

"I can never give you enough."

He pulled back but still stroked my cheeks with his thumbs. His nostrils flared over his heavy breathing, and his eyes flicked between mine. I rubbed my hands up and down his arms, trying to soothe nerves so clearly marring his face.

"Daniel..."

One more deep breath. "I love you, Hanna. I've never said that to another woman before."

Heat and tingles flooded through my chest, stretching to places I never knew existed. His words lit a fire that burned up my throat, and I clung to him, desperate to replay those words on repeat forever.

"What about—"

"Never. Only you. I love you. And I hope you'll give me a chance to earn your lo—"

This time when I kissed him, I didn't hold back. I pulled his body to mine, needing to be as close to him as possible. His hands sunk to my waist, and he tugged me onto his lap. Without hesitation, I straddled him and held him to me, not letting him pull away.

I bit at his full lips I'd missed so much and pulled away just long enough to whisper, "I love you too."

As if he hadn't already been holding me tight, he groaned and gripped me harder. I forgot where we were. It didn't matter. I had the man I loved in my arms. I had the man that had reminded me I was still alive under me. I had the man who'd asked me to be strong in my life. I had his love. It didn't matter where we were as long as I had that.

A throat clearing behind us had me jerking away to find Erik glaring like he was trying to set Daniel on fire.

"Shit," Daniel breathed. "Sorry."

I giggled and glared back at Erik. "Cockblocker."

He cringed, and I laughed some more. "Seriously, Hanna. I don't need to know that."

I stood, tugging Daniel with me and walked past Erik, a devious smirk his only warning. "I guess you also don't need to know I'm about to let him do all kinds of dirty things to me."

"Hanna fucking Brandt," he growled.

"Payback for all the times I caught you and Alex," I called over my shoulder.

I laughed because it was so trivial, to taunt my brother with the fact that I was having sex, to make him uncomfortable with it. It hadn't been too long ago that I'd been forced to watch him and Alex all over each other, and I'd been sure I'd never have that. Yet here I was, getting all that and more.

"Take me home, Daniel."

"Okay, but let's move quickly before your brother kills me."

We managed to make it out of the parking lot of Haven and all the way to his apartment building...but we never made it out of the car.

Daniel parked and demanded I give him a first of my own. So, we moved to the back, and I learned what all the fuss was about fucking in the back seat.

I couldn't wait for our life of him teaching me all the firsts I had to give.

EPILOGUE

DANIEL

"How are you hanging in there?"

"It's...interesting and..." I shuddered. "I don't know. I try not to think about it too much."

Pulling my eyes away from Olivia mooning over Kent, I instead focused my gaze on Hanna.

"She's a beautiful bride."

"She really is, and as long as he keeps taking care of her, then he can live."

She looked over to the happy couple dancing in the middle of the floor, Olivia's fitted dress trailing behind her when Kent spun her in his arms. "I don't think you have to worry about that."

"I have better things to worry about," I whispered in her ear.

"Oh, yeah?" She smiled, not looking my way.

I nibbled my way down her neck. "Yeah."

"Like what?"

"Like what kind of panties you're wearing under this dress."

"That's easy," she said, finally turning, her lips inches from mine. "None."

A growl worked its way up my throat, and I struggled to keep from tossing her over my shoulder and carrying her out. "Fuck, Hanna."

"Calm down, Neanderthal. We still have dancing."

"What about a quickie, and then we can come back for dancing?"

She laughed and slapped my shoulder, but didn't say no. Just as I was about to grab her hand and make good on it, the song ended, and the DJ came through the speakers.

"All right, party people. Let's get the wedding party out here to join the lucky bride and groom."

"Come on, lover boy." Hanna stood, tugging me behind her.

The slow violins of "At Last" by Etta James flowed through the speakers as I pulled Hanna in my arms, gripping her small waist. Her hands slid up my neck and into my hair. To our left is wereOaklyn and Callum. Across is wereCarina and Ian. Sitting at a table to our right is wereAlex and Erik, and Jake and Jackson.

Olivia and Kent's families and business partners watch on with shining eyes, and I can't help but look at my niece and best friend, beyond happy they found each other. Even if it did gross me out.

But it mattered less with the beautiful woman in my arms.

Love hit you when you least expected it, no matter how hard you fought it.

I was just a lucky enough bastard to find a woman who fought harder than my fears.

"This is another first for me," I confessed.

"Oh, yeah?"

"Yup. I've never been to a wedding with a date. Too serious."

"Well, I'm glad you're here with me," she said, smiling, her emerald eyes shining under her dark lashes. She was exquisite in her champagne-colored dress. The soft silk brushed against my thighs, and my fingers played at the open back of the dress, her skin hot against my fingers.

"I love you," I whispered against her lips.

"I love you, too."

"I can't wait to get you home tonight."

"Maybe this time we can make it through the boxes and make it to the bed."

"I'm not worried. I plan on having you in every inch of our apartment."

Our apartment. Hearing it never got old.

We moved in last week. It'd been a quick move since it was still in my building, just a bigger apartment. And she'd been moving her stuff into my old apartment slowly over the last six months.

"Promises, promises." She laughed, brushing her hips against my own.

"You're playing with fire."

"It's okay. I like it hot. You want to know a secret?" she taunted.

"I don't know. That smile is a little scary."

She scraped her teeth along the stubble coating my jaw. "We're staying here until the very last song, and I plan on torturing you the entire time."

"Fuck me, Hanna. That's not fair."

"Neither is the way you made me come five times last night before fucking me. That was torture."

"You loved it."

"I did. And you'll love this."

Another growl, but I was determined to break her down. If she thought she could torture me, she had no idea who she was playing with. I'd make her eat her words. Preferably as she was eating my cock in the bathroom. Or the coat closet. Or a dark corner. I wasn't picky.

The song ended, and the other couples filled the dance floor.

She made good on her promise and stroked my cock at any

chance she could. I was just about to drag her away when I saw Erik drop to one knee.

"Oh, my god," Hanna gasped, stopping to watch.

Alex's hand moved to her mouth, and I couldn't hear the words, but tears slipped down her cheeks, and she was nodding even before Erik got the box open.

Cheers erupted, and Hanna clung to my arm, her own tears sliding down her cheeks. I wiped them away and licked them from my finger. They stood, and Erik snatched her up and vanished from the room.

"Lucky bastard," I grumbled as Hanna tugged me back in her arms.

She looked up at me with zero remorse, stepping close and sliding her hips back and forth. "Do you want to get married?"

She dropped her gaze to my neck after asking the question, and I tugged her chin back up. "I do to you," I said before kissing her softly. "But, let's not steal any more thunder tonight."

She bit her lip and stepped back.

"I'm ready to go home now."

"It's about fucking time."

Similar to every time we pushed our needs to the last minute, we never made it home. Instead, I fucked her in a shadowed corner, promising her forever.

ACKNOWLEDGMENTS

My family: Thank you for always understanding and supportive. Thank you for the cuddles after a hard day and laughs when all I want to do is rip my hair out. I couldn't do this without you being the foundation holding me up. I love you.

Karla. Dream Team, baby.

Serena. We all know I couldn't do this without you. Thank you for supporting me, staying on top of me, and basically running this whole thing. You've changed my career for the better and allow me to get all the words down and help me make them as sexy as possible.

Najla Qamber. The best damn cover designer there ever was. Thank you for all your talent. Thank you for always hearing my vision and turning into perfection.

Linda. Thank you for holding my hand and petting my hair when I'm on the verge of crawling in a hole. I couldn't do this without you or your enthusiasm. I appreciate everything you do and can't wait to drink wine together some day.

Kelly. Thank you for being an amazing editor. Thank you

for being an even better friend! You give me the confidence to publish a book I know is the best it could be because of you.

Julia. Thank you for always being able to beta read. You ask the hard questions and offer such amazing suggestions. Thank you for helping me make the story better than I could've imagined.

Review team. You ladies are wonderful, fun, kind, and beyond supportive. Thank you for every share, every review, and everything in between.

Lovers. You guys are my safe place. You guys give me the best book recommendations and make me laugh. You're more than I could ever ask for. I can't tell you how many times I've scrolled through your comments and have been brought to tears. Thank you for being such an awesome group.

Bloggers. To every single one from personal pages to the bookstagrammers. You all work so hard and take beautiful pictures and write such amazingly kind words in reviews. I don't have enough words to let you know how much you all mean to me. I couldn't do this without you.

Readers. You guys rock my socks off. Thank you for taking a chance on my words. Thank you for taking the time to read something I've created. You're the best.

ABOUT THE AUTHOR

Fiona Cole is a military wife and a stay at home mom with degrees in biology and chemistry. As much as she loved science, she decided to postpone her career to stay at home with her two little girls, and immersed herself in the world of books until finally deciding to write her own.

Fiona loves hearing from her readers, so be sure to follow her on social media.

Email: authorfionacole@gmail.com
Newsletter
Reader Group: Fiona Cole's Lovers

www.authorfionacole.com

ALSO BY FIONA COLE

ALL BOOKS ARE FREE IN KINDLE UNLIMITED

The King's Bar Series

Where You Can Find Me

Deny Me

Imagine Me

Shame Me Not Series

Shame

Make It to the Altar (Shame Me Not 1.5)

The Voyeur Series

Voyeur

Lovers (Cards of Love)

Surrender (A Lovers Novella)

Savior

Another

Watch With Me (A Free Liar Prequel)

Liar

Teacher

Printed in Great Britain
by Amazon